ISBN: 978-1481826723
ASIN: B00ARQHYXI

Tau Ceti

An Ell Donsaii story #6

Laurence E Dahners

Author's Note

This book is the xxx in the series, the "Ell Donsaii stories."

Though this book *can* "stand alone" it'll be *much* easier to understand if read as part of the series including

"Quicker (an Ell Donsaii story)"
"Smarter (an Ell Donsaii story #2)"
"Lieutenant (an Ell Donsaii story #3)"
"Rocket (an Ell Donsaii story #4)" and
"Comet! (an Ell Donsaii story #5)"

I've minimized the repetition of explanations that would be redundant to the earlier books in order to provide a better reading experience for those of you who are reading the series.

Other Books and Series by Laurence E Dahners

Series

The Hyllis Family series
The Vaz series
The Bonesetter series
The Blindspot series
The Proton Field series

Single books (not in series)

The Transmuter's Daughter
Six Bits
Shy Kids Can Make Friends Too

For the most up to date information go to

Laury.Dahners.com/stories.html

Table of Contents

Preprologue

Ell's father, Allan Donsaii, was an unusually gifted quarterback. Startlingly strong, and a phenomenally accurate passer, during his college career he finished two full seasons without any interceptions and two games with 100 percent completions. Unfortunately, he wasn't big enough to be drafted by the pros.

Extraordinarily quick, Ell's mother, Kristen Taylor captained her college soccer team and rarely played a game without a steal.

Allan and Kristen dated more and more seriously through college, marrying at the end of their senior year. Their friends teased them that they'd only married in order to start their own sports dynasty.

Their daughter Ell got Kristen's quickness, magnified by Allan's surprising strength and highly accurate coordination.

She also has a new mutation that affects the myelin sheaths of her nerves. This mutation produces nerve transmission speeds nearly double those of normal neurons. With faster nerve impulse transmission, she has far quicker reflexes. Yet her new type of myelin sheath is also thinner, allowing more axons, and therefore more neurons, to be packed into the same sized skull. These two factors result in a brain with more neurons, though it isn't larger, and a faster processing speed, akin to a computer with a smaller, faster CPU architecture.

Most importantly, under the influence of adrenalin in a fight or flight situation, her nerves transmit even more rapidly than their normally remarkable speed.

Much more rapidly...

Prologue

Author's note

"He, she, his, hers, him, and her" are not misspelled, this is part of the story.

I believe you would rather discover the reason for yourself, so I won't give it away here. But if you do want to know ahead of time, here it is:

The odd pronouns in the Teecees' sections of this book are an attempt to deal with the fact that the Teecees each function as both sexes.

Dex rose onto hies toes, stretching hies neck to peer over the edge of the rocks near the border of the little meadow. Hies wings quivered involuntarily as hie resisted their effort to lift hies eyes a little higher. A wing beat would quickly give away hies location.

Yes! Syrdian stood in the meadow, just on the other side of the rocks, sunning himrself. Dex admired Syrdian's pose; tall, neck stretched high, rare and gorgeous silvery yellow wings canted to the sunlight. Syrdian's pose seemed relaxed, meditative, and peaceful.

It seemed to Dex that he'd admired Syrdian hies entire life. He watched Syrdian from afar, with intense… hope and… longing. Dex fantasized that someday, something would change. Something that might make

Dex a plausible mate for Syrdian.

Beautiful, graceful Syrdian. In Dex's mind, by far the most desirable member of the Yetany tribe.

Syrdian, whose rank in the tribe stood so high above Dex's that Dex's aspirations to win Syrdian's love seemed laughable.

But a young dalin could dream, couldn't hie?

The sounds of a strong wing beat came from Dex's back-up-right and Dex dropped down from tiptoe and turned to cant hies own wings to the sun. Whoever was back there would surely see himr, but hopefully wouldn't recognize that Dex had been on tiptoe peering at Syrdian. Rather, Dex hoped they'd believe Dex and Syrdian just happened both to be sunning on opposite sides of the odd little group of rocks in the meadow, completely unaware of one another.

Looking back-up-right, Dex recognized Qes' distinctive wing strokes even with the low quality vision of hies back-eyes. Spying Syrdian, Qes stopped flapping and began gliding a smooth curve down to himr, back wings pumping gently to provide a little thrust. Dex's hearts sank. Handsome Qes nearly matched Syrdian's desirability and hies parents ranked high in the tribe. While the tribe would laugh at Dex's aspirations, no one doubted Qes's suitability for a mating with Syrdian. Qes and Syrdian had been spending more and more time with one another recently. And doing it to approving glances from the elders.

Worse, Qes might suspect Dex's infatuation and thus recognize the reason Dex happened to be sunning himrself across the rocks from Syrdian. Qes was *just* the type to make fun of Dex at the tribe's fire tonight. Dex's wings sagged as hie contemplated the situation.

"Qes!" Dex heard Syrdian sing out joyfully just

before Qes landed. Whatever else they might be saying, Dex couldn't hear as they spoke quietly. "Sweet nothings" Dex supposed as hie hunched down in hies misery. Dex peered again and saw them clasping one another, wrapping wings and necks around one another and, hie suspected, at least pseudo-mating. Qes must not've noticed Dex. Surely they wouldn't be doing that if they thought there might be witnesses?

Dex's hearts leapt out of hies chest into hies neck. Could they be *actually* mating? Could one of them be carrying a child soon? If so, Dex's ridiculous hope of someday mating Syrdian… would truly be hopeless.

Suddenly a huge shadow flashed over! Dex panicked that a talor was stooping on himr. Hie slammed hies body down into the underhang at the bottom of the rock beside himr, rolling onto hies wings to face up with hies big hind claws up and free. Without conscious thought on hies part, hies knives appeared in hies hands. But there was no talor there, the shadow had flashed past Dex and on toward the meadow.

Syrdian! Dex thought desperately.

Dex rolled back out in a terror, scrambling to hies feet, then kicking frantically into the air, catching wind with a violent front wingstroke that launched himr over the rocks, hind wings pumping.

Horrified dread clutched Dex's hearts. An enormous talor stood over the hapless Syrdian, one enormous hindclaw pinning Syrdian's right wing to the ground. Pinned thus, Syrdian couldn't even turn over to fight for hies life. Qes beat wings away down the meadow, fleeing the tragedy, skimming rapidly just above the meadow's surface and vanishing into the trees.

Wondering at hies own insanity, Dex beat higher,

then tilted over to glide silently toward the back of the talor.

It was lifting another hindclaw onto Syrdian's wing and reaching forward with its enormous beak.

Dex slammed into the talor's back, sinking hindclaws into the great muscles at the base of the wings and slamming hies knives downward into the base of its neck.

With a tremendous screech the talor rose up, turning its long neck and questing beak back toward Dex.

The knives were too short! Dex had hoped to penetrate the brain at the base of the talor's neck, but too much muscle protected it! Hie ripped the knives up and out, flaying muscle on the way, but doing too little to stop the talor. A wing beat and a step forward with hies hindclaws and Dex sunk hies blades into the neck itself, twisting and ripping.

The ravening beak approached from hies front-low-left and Dex leaned to the right, avoiding the snapping maw. The beak swung back around front to try from the other side. Dex beat wings again, stepping slightly higher on the talor's shoulders and reached around, crossing knife hands in front of the talor's neck, sinking the knives in and ripping back out again with all hies might.

Blood from the talor's neck arteries squirted over Dex's hands. It coughed.

The beak approached from the front-low-right and Dex leaned away again.

But the talor rolled its entire body to the right, threatening to crush Dex beneath itself.

A few swift wing beats lifted Dex off the talor and back-up-left. In despair hie realized that hie'd lost hies protected position behind the talor. Now hie'd be facing the talor's beak and the crushing impacts of its wing wrists if it attacked him again.

Dex fluttered back-right and away, hoping to draw the talor away from the lifeless appearing Syrdian.

The talor rolled all the way over and back to its feet but to Dex's astonishment began coughing almost continuously. *It* backed away from *him*. Blood poured down the front of the talor's neck and evidently into the in-breathing orifice at the base of its neck. Sprays of blood indicated that the blood was what was causing its now paroxysmal coughing.

Dex turned to Syrdian who lay sprawled, unmoving, still in the position the talor had pinned himr before. Three huge tears rent Syrdian's right wing and, with dismay Dex realized hie couldn't hear Syrdian's breath moving. With an agonized moan Dex leaned an earhole down next to Syrdian to listen more carefully. Yes! Breath did hiss into Syrdian's intake and out hies vent. Low volumes but, still, Syrdian was alive!

Suddenly remembering the talor, Dex brought hies head up to check the threat level. The talor was actually *farther* away, sagging, wings and neck drooping, its breathing labored. It didn't appear to be a danger.

Dex crouched by Syrdian to study the holes torn in those gorgeous silver yellow wings. Small wounds in wings often repaired themselves, but these were huge. They might heal a little if Syrdian lived, but Syrdian would never fly again. Dex tugged the edges of the biggest tear together. The edges easily reapproximated, especially with the wing relaxed. But they wouldn't *stay* together. Dex felt hies wings tremble. "Syrdian..." hie gasped.

Dex picked up hies knives from where hie'd dropped them in the dirt and wiped them. The left one slipped back into its sheath. The right one caught and wouldn't go back into its place. Dex looked down and saw that the opening in the knife's sheath had been crumpled shut in hies fight with the talor. Hie put a claw into the sheath and pulled the opening back apart, sliding the knife in.

Dex stared at the stitching that hie'd used to form the folded piece of leather into a sheath for hies knife.

The stitching that held the sheath to hies harness.

The stitching that held the harness together.

The fine stitching that Dex was known for, trading hies leather work for goods from others. That's how hie'd obtained these fine flint knives. Hies eyes drifted back to the rips in Syrdian's wings. *Could stitching repair a wing?* Dex wondered. Best done now while Syrdian lay unconscious, puncturing the holes for the stitches would be very painful if Syrdian were awake.

Dex's hand fumbled in hies pouch, pulling out the stick hie kept wrapped in fiberlin. Fiberlin, so useful for binding flint blades to handles and for setting snares.

And for leather work.

Dex took hies more finely pointed left knife and made a tiny puncture in Syrdian's wing next to one of the large tears. Syrdian didn't respond so hie made a puncture across from it and fed a bit of fine fiberlin through it with a claw, tying it just tightly enough to press the gap shut there. Hie tilted hies head and examined it. It might not last, but it seemed better than leaving the beautiful Syrdian with huge rents in those lovely wings.

Crouching down, Dex made tiny punctures all along the edges of each of the wounds. Then came the interminable passing of fiberlin through the holes, pushing it through with the tip of a claw and then pulling the stitches just tight enough to close the hole without causing a ragged overlap. When Dex got to the end, he went back and loosened some loops where they were too tight and further tightened others. Syrdian began to moan and move slightly. This both raised Dex's spirits and made the suturing more difficult. At last Dex tied the last fiberlin at the end of the third hole and leaned back to examine hies work. There were small gaps at two locations. Thoughtfully Dex pulled out hies knife and made a puncture in preparation to putting a supplemental suture across the first of the two little gaps. Syrdian's eyes flew open and hies wing ripped out of Dex's grasp.

Eyes wide Syrdian pushed himrself to hies feet, "What! What happened? Dex, what're *you* doing here?"

"You were attacked by a talor."

"Get out! Why am I still alive? Ow!" Syrdian said, pulling hies wing around to inspect it, "What happened to my wing? What are these little strings?" Hie reached a finger to pluck at the wound, "Ow!"

Dex ducked hies head, "I, uh, attacked the talor and it backed off."

Seemingly not hearing Dex, Syrdian suddenly looked panicked, "No! Qes was here. Where is hie?! Did the talor kill Qes?" Syrdian's wide eyes focused on Dex.

"Qes escaped."

"Where is hie?" Syrdian looked frantically about.

"Qes flew front-down-left into the trees there," Dex said, pointing with a wingtip.

"Qes wouldn't leave me!" Syrdian turned to look suspiciously at Dex, "Where's this talor you chased away?" Hies eyes narrowed, "Did *you* do this to me?!"

Dex looked around, the talor was nowhere to be seen. Hie stepped closer to Syrdian, "No! No, I would never do anything to you! I... I..." Dex couldn't bring himrself to say, "love you."

Syrdian backed away in the direction Dex had indicated Qes had gone, "Stay away! Leave me alone!"

Wings sagging in despair Dex watched Syrdian shuffle through the meadow grasses toward the woods Qes had disappeared into. Syrdian flicked hies wings once but the right one appeared to seize in place with a quiver, holding a stationary position while Syrdian's head turned to look at it, then it slowly folded behind hies back. *It must hurt pretty bad,* Dex thought.

Syrdian resumed walking but then suddenly stopped, looking front-low-right.

Dex could see nothing. Hie rose to hies tiptoes, still seeing nothing. He beat a few strokes up into the air.

Syrdian was staring at the talor, slumped into the grass, a large puddle of blood soaking into the ground around it. Dex nosed over and coasted a glide down to the talor, landing just short.

Syrdian had taken a few steps closer and said, "There *was* a talor."

Dex dipped hies head in agreement.

Chapter One

Raleigh, NC—Velos' "Concert at the End of the World," a recording made when Velos played a concert at D5R on March 1st has, almost overnight, become the biggest music video sensation in the world. Played against a backdrop of thousands of shooting stars from the broken comet and featuring an astonishing dance by Ell Donsaii, it's attracted over one billion viewers. Velos' leader Gordon Speight spoke of his gratitude to Donsaii for...

President Flood turned to his Chief of Staff, "We need to give that Donsaii girl some kind of award. What's the highest award we can give a civilian?"

"The highest is the Presidential Medal of Freedom. She already has one."

"What? What did she get it for?"

"Uh, she was instrumental in stopping the invasion of Taiwan by the PRC. The whole thing was pretty hush-hush so her award wasn't publicized."

Flood's eyes widened, "What awards hasn't she won? I know she's got the Medal of Honor and the Nobel!"

The Chief of Staff raised an eyebrow. "Yeah. Well, she hasn't gotten any *little* awards. Seems kind of silly to give her those after she's won the big ones doesn't it?"

Flood leaned back in his chair and sighed, "What can

we do? We need to recognize her somehow for what she did to stop that comet."

"We could give her another Medal of Freedom; this one publicly." The man shrugged, it didn't seem like much after what she'd done...

***

Professor Norris felt embarrassed as he looked out over his class on Planetary Science.

Bracing his shoulders, he began, "I'd like to begin class today by apologizing for my absence from this class last week. Like many of you, I got caught up in the worldwide hysteria over the impending impact of Comet Hearth-Daster. I, like many others in the University community, could not conceive that there would be any means available to deflect the comet. Therefore, I also concluded that the end of our world as we know it was at hand..."

Norris found a frog in his throat and with a shaking voice said, "I hope someday I can express my gratitude to the fine people at NASA who launched the nuclear weapons that deflected the major fragments and to the people here at D5R who deflected the smaller fragments..."

He cleared his throat, "That said, we have some course work to catch up on, so, let us begin..."

When Norris finished his lecture and had offered some make up discussions for his missed lectures—which were, of course, also available on video—he turned to find Belle Donovan standing behind him again. The pretty platinum blond girl's grades were destroying the curve in the class this semester just like she had during the first semester. This, despite her missing large numbers of the classes during the run up to the comet's expected impact. She'd missed a lot of classes even before the comet problem became widely known, and thus before his own absences. He smiled, "Yes, Ms. Donovan?"

She looked seriously at him, "I'm wondering what types of precautions we might want to take before landing on an extraterrestrial planet? You know, to prevent contamination of that planet with materials and organisms from Earth... and vice versa."

Taken aback by the question Norris said, "I don't think we really need to worry about that issue Ms. Donovan. We've almost certainly already contaminated Mars with Earth organisms from some of the many robotic missions sent there. Probably even more so with the mission sent there recently by D5R because the transit time of that little rocket was short enough that it seems quite plausible that microorganisms on their little rocket could have survived the trip. However, aside from Mars, there seems little reason to believe that Earth organisms would have any chance of survival on the other planets in the solar system. Those planets have very inimical environments. And, anything that could survive on the other planets seems unlikely to thrive on Earth."

"But what about planets in other solar systems? Ones that were more Earthlike than the ones in our solar system?"

Norris snorted, "That would be a different matter wouldn't it? But there's no point worrying about it in any real sense. There's no way we can reach them, they're light years away. If you haven't yet considered just *how far away* the nearest stars are, you should."

"Well, but hypothetically?"

Norris sighed at her persistence. "'Hypothetically,' we *shouldn't* worry about it. Ain't gonna happen. If it did, we should sterilize everything we send there and shouldn't let anything from there return to us here."

"Not even if we sterilize everything that comes back?"

"How would we know that what came back would be killed by the sterilization methods *we* use? Organisms from this hypothetical planet might not be susceptible to the same sterilization techniques that work on Earth organisms."

She frowned, "How would we figure out whether or not they were susceptible?"

"*Ms.* Donovan! I don't have time to waste on such ridiculous hypotheticals. If we were actually about to make contact, I'd be willing to spend time considering them."

"Are there any scientists in the triangle who *are* interested in these types of questions?"

Exasperated he said, "You know, you're like my wife's yappy little dog when it's sunk its teeth into a rag! Just won't let go even though someone's picked you up and you're dangling from it." He sighed, "In short, the answer is no. No one else in the area is interested in other planetary systems. It's my field of research and I'm as much of an expert as you're going to find, but I'm not interested in hypotheticals that have no conceivable application."

"OK," she said, beginning to turn away. Then she turned back, "At the beginning of class you said you'd like to meet the people from D5R. Would you like me to arrange for you to be introduced to some of them? I have a friend that works there."

Norris' eyes snapped back to hers, "Ell Donsaii?"

Donovan looked panicked for a moment, then said, "You could probably meet her. Would you like a tour of D5R?"

"Absolutely!"

"Tomorrow?"

"You seem pretty sure you can work this out? Are you sure Ms. Donsaii'll be there tomorrow?"

"Yes sir. Would nine O'clock be OK? Or do you have a class then?"

***

"What happened to the talor?" Syrdian asked.

"I attacked it while it was attacking you."

"You *didn't*! No one attacks a talor! No one's ever killed a talor."

Dex lifted hies wings in a shrug, amazed himrself, but not knowing how to refute Syrdian's argument.

"And, *if* someone were to kill a talor, it certainly wouldn't be you."

Dex lifted wings in another shrug.

"Qes," Syrdian called out, resuming hies trek to the woods. Over hies shoulder Syrdian said. "What are these threads on my wing?"

A couple of wing beats moved Dex closer and hie began walking parallel, but just behind-right to Syrdian. "The talor stood on your right wing and its hind claws ripped your wing membrane."

"What!" Syrdian stopped and unfurled the right wing to look at it again. "It's just scratched! It isn't ripped!"

"It *was* ripped. I sewed it back together with fiberlin, the same way I do my leatherwork."

Syrdian's eyes flashed wide with panic and focused on the largest rip. Hie moaned. A quiver flashed through hies wings and hie sank to the ground. For a moment Dex thought Syrdian would lose consciousness again, not unreasonable on the thought of never flying again.

Then Qes called from the forest verge, "Syrdian! Is that you?"

Syrdian's eyes lit and hie rose back up, "Qes! I'm right here!"

"Where's the talor?" Qes said leaning out and peering about.

Dex could not help but admire Qes. Tall, handsome Qes with the golden yellow wings. Not as beautiful as Syrdian, but close. However, the Qes that Dex knew always talked and acted as if hie were bold. Hie didn't appear bold now, standing between the boles of two trees, darting hies head this way and that as hie looked for the talor.

"The talor's dead!" Syrdian said beginning to run toward Qes.

"Dead?" Qes said, "What happened to it?" Rather than move out from the trees to meet Syrdian, Qes waited where hie stood.

Syrdian reached Qes and threw arms and wings around himr.

***

Wilson Daster walked to Donsaii's office with some trepidation. Now that his eponymous comet had been disposed of, he'd developed a—he hoped irrational—fear that he'd soon be let go as superfluous. Donsaii'd claimed that they needed someone with his forensic accounting skills, but he couldn't imagine what for? D5R had divided itself into three organizations, none of which were very large. Apparently they were all funded by a venture capital organization of some type and, Daster thought, that VC group must have some accounting firm checking up on things?

So, now that his comet was dealt with, there didn't really seem like there should be a need for someone with his talents in an organization like this. He worried she was calling him in to let him know he was no longer needed. "Yes, Ms. Donsaii?" he said stopping outside her door.

Ell raised her eyebrows, "'Ms. Donsaii?' I thought you were going to call me Ell?"

Wilson ducked his head, surprised again to be so intimidated by someone much younger than he was. "Uh, sorry, Ell. You asked to see me?"

She grinned, "Yeah, come on in and close the door, please?"

Daster's heart sank. He stepped in and closed the door that rumor claimed was always open. Probably closed when she was giving bad news, he guessed. He sat and raised his eyebrows attentively.

"I want to tell you some stuff that no one here knows, not even my good friends. I need you to reassure me of your complete discretion. These things need to stay just between you and me. Is that OK?"

He nodded, spirits rising. This didn't sound like the prelude to a firing, though he had no idea what it might preface? On the other hand, he wondered, why would she tell *him* secrets?

"I want to warn you that I consider your agreement, as recorded by our AIs, to be an enforceable contract?" She raised her eyebrows questioningly.

"Yes Ma'am. I agree."

"OK, I'd like you to pop the chip out of your AI (Artificial Intelligence) headband so the only recording of our conversation going forward will be on my AI. Mine's a lot more secure than yours."

Raising his eyebrows, Daster pulled off his AI and popped the PGR chip out of the back. Laying them on the desk he looked up at Ell expectantly.

"OK, first thing for you to understand before you start investigating our finances is that the 'investors' who're supporting D5R and the companies split from D5R are essentially myself and the employees of D5R. Those employees, like yourself, all have shares accruing from their employment."

"Wait! Where's all the money coming from? What you're describing is a snake eating its own tail. You can't finance an organization like this from the paychecks paid to the employees!"

"I have a lot of money." Ell said quietly.

"From endorsements?" Daster said, thinking to himself, They're spending millions, endorsements can't possibly pay for that!

"From the PGR chips."

Daster's eyes dropped to the chip he'd just pulled out of his AI headband. "I know they're based on your paper, but..."

"I patented the chip technology too."

Daster's eyebrows went up again, "So you're getting royalties?"

She nodded.

"And *you're* the majority shareholder in D5R and subsidiaries?"

She shrugged, "98% owner at present."

Daster stared at her while he tried to process this. Could she possibly be telling the truth? *Of course she is, I've seen what she did with the comet. There probably isn't anything she can't do if she puts her mind to it.* After a moment he said brilliantly, "Uh, OK."

"I'm telling you this so you'll understand you're actually working for me, not some nebulous board. I want you to examine *all* the financial arrangements and expenditures, etcetera, for D5R and its sub-companies. I even want you to examine my personal finances and the outcomes of my charitable donations. Because I believe in incentives, you get 10% of any misappropriated monies that're recovered."

Daster sank back in his chair. "Just how much money are the PGR chips paying you?"

"You're going to be seeing all of those figures yourself pretty soon so I'd just as one would tell you. It's a minimum of 2.1 billion dollars a year."

My God, no wonder she can afford to finance D5R!

***

Bridget met Professor Norris at D5R's entry. "Hello, Dr. Norris. You're here for a tour and to meet with Ms. Donsaii?"

"Yes please, I would greatly appreciate that. Will Ms. Donovan be with us?"

Bridget tried not to go cross eyed over Norris' reference to Ell's alter ego. Ell had set her down last night and explained her "Belle Donovan" persona, asking her to play the part of Belle's "friend" that worked at D5R. As such she'd take him on a tour and introduce him to Ell as "Ell." Brightly, she said, "Nope, Belle doesn't work here, though she does know Ms. Donsaii. I'm a friend of Belle's though and I do work here. She asked me to take you around, then introduce you to Ms. Donsaii, if that's OK?"

"Sure."

Figuring he wouldn't be interested, Bridget didn't take him on a tour of the admin offices. Instead she took him directly to the big research room. As they entered, she said, "This first area's where the Portal Tech research group's working at present. They've moved most of the actual manufacturing of ports to a separate facility, but they still do research and design processes here."

"Portal Tech?"

"Yes, it's an offshoot of D5R that does the actual manufacturing of the ports. The ports are then leased to other companies for use. Portal Tech's got an exclusive license to manufacture and lease ports, though President Teller's commission negotiated for anyone to be able to use ports." She tilted her head, "Well, not criminals." She resumed, "Teller's commission also extended the patent on the port so that the introduction of ports could be slowed to diminish the economic upheavals that'll result as the ports come into widespread use."

Norris narrowed his eyes. "Can you explain that? What kind of upheavals?"

Norris wound up sitting down, shaking his head as Bridget explained how ports would someday replace pipes and wires and tankers, etcetera. He'd heard how ports supplied the space station and flew little rockets, but he'd failed to consider all the more mundane things they could do. Bridget took him to a central area of the big room where a group of men were cursing at a machine that intermittently clanged. She said, "This is the current home base for ET Resources. They're mining an asteroid, though it doesn't sound like they're having a very good day today."

Norris looked at the screen the men were swearing at. Everything was lit in the sharply demarcated fashion that one expected of a picture from space since there wasn't any air to diffuse the light. One window appeared to be looking out over a field of rubble that had an empty conveyor belt running out over it. The belt was moving slowly out away from the field of view. Another view seemed to show the underside of the belt running back in to converge on paired belts. Rocks were stuck to the underside of the belt as if it were magnetic but when they hit the paired belts at the near end the rocks were scraped off by a plate and pinched between the paired belts. "What's going wrong?" he asked.

"Well, it's surprisingly hard to move material like the broken rock you're seeing, from one place to another in a weightless, airless environment. They need to feed it into a crusher to make it small enough to port back here to D5R. It won't fall in because of the microgravity and it can't be blown or sucked in without any air. If you try to move it too violently, the microgravity lets it just bounce away. Those magnetic belts pick it up, but then won't let it go. The crusher jams all the time. They're making an electromagnetic belt system now. The idea being that then they can pick up rocks with magnets on one belt, then transfer it to another by just switching the power from one set of magnets to the other. While they're waiting for the new system they keep working with what they have out there, trying to get a feel for the kinds of problems that're going to crop up next."

Norris watched in fascination for a while, then he and Bridget moved on down to the end of the room. Two young women and two men were clustered around a screen chattering excitedly. His eyes initially focused on the tall young man who appeared to be the oldest of the group. Suddenly he realized that one of the two young women was Donsaii. *My God, she's just a kid! Even younger looking than she appears to be in photos and vids.*

Bridget said, "Ms. Donsaii, this is Dr. Norris... The professor my friend Belle Donovan was hoping you'd meet with?"

Ell rose and shook his hand. "Hi Dr. Norris. This is Emma Kenner, Roger Emmerit and Manuel Garcia. We pretty much make up the Quantum Research part of D5R. Wilson Daster here works with us part time and we consult with a lot of other experts. Some from the University... like yourself."

A frisson of excitement went through Norris at the thought there might be some reason *they* would want to work with him. Maybe he could piggyback some of his own research onto their rockets as they sent them around the solar system?

Donsaii turned to the others, "You guys keep working on that while I talk to Dr. Norris, OK?"

They all nodded and turned back to the screen as Ell led Norris over to one side and sat down at the corner of one of the big tables, motioning him to the other side of the corner.

Norris sat down across the corner from Donsaii. He realized Bridget'd disappeared. He'd only expected to get to shake Donsaii's hand and express his appreciation, not actually sit down and talk! It was hard to take his eyes off of Donsaii though. "Ms. Donsaii," he began, "I'm here, for the most part because I mentioned in my class that Ms. Donovan attends, just how much I wanted to personally express my gratitude for the role you and D5R played in stopping the comet. I'm sure I, as well as countless others, owe you our lives."

She grinned at him. "Well thanks. Though, I feel a little guilty accepting your gratitude for doing something so self-interested as saving the planet I live on."

Norris chuckled, "I see your point. Still, that doesn't mean that I'm not grateful that you saved my life along with your own. You may know that Ms. Donovan attends my Planetary Science class?"

Donsaii grinned again, "Yep."

"That's my area of research too. So you may understand how I'd love to piggyback some of my own research onto some of your missions around the solar system? For instance, just a few samples of that asteroid you're mining would be a huge boon to my studies!"

"Well, now you're relieving some of my guilt."

Norris tilted his head questioningly.

"You see we desperately need some solar system expertise, and I actually had Belle out looking for someone who could be that expert. She suggested you."

"Oh." Norris' spirits lifted at the thought that they wanted the very help he wanted to give.

"We could give you some asteroid fragments today.

But, I think we have something a lot more interesting to offer you than some of those."

"You do?"

"Yes, but we'd want you to sign a confidentiality agreement first."

Norris frowned. "Confidentiality? About what?"

"Well now, I can't exactly tell you what it's about until you sign."

"I think that would violate my academic freedom. I'd want to be able to publish my findings…"

"Oh, and we think you should. But we'd want to be able to delay publication for up to two years if we believed something should be kept confidential for a while. And we'd want any methods you learned from us to be kept confidential for five years. I've sent you a Non-Disclosure Agreement you can read on your HUD (Heads Up Display). If you don't feel comfortable with its restrictions, we'll have to look elsewhere for an expert. Read through it at your leisure either here or back in your office. If you can agree to it we'll get started."

Norris glanced up at his HUD and saw the text of an agreement displayed. He didn't want to leave without learning what this was all about, so he said, "Let me look at it here. Maybe I can agree to it now and we can get started."

"OK, I'll be with the team. You can just come over there and get me when you're done." Donsaii got up and walked back over to the other people from the Quantum Research team.

Initially Norris' eyes tracked her graceful walk back over to her team. Reluctantly, he turned them up to his HUD.

***

Dex dispiritedly watched Qes and Syrdian holding one another for a moment. Somehow hie'd thought that hies attack on the talor and the saving of Syrdian's life might compensate for hies low status.

Might even improve hies low status in the tribe?

While hie'd sutured Syrdian's wings hie'd imagined Syrdian looking at himr in a new light.

Or at least noticing himr.

Well, hie laughed bitterly, *Syrdian had actually spoken to himr*. something that hadn't happened in recent memory. Hie shook hies head at hies own naiveté. Wings drooping, hie turned back to the talor, wondering if the meat would be any good.

Dex hacked a couple of big chunks of meat out of the talor's thigh. About as much as hie thought hie could carry back to the tribe. Hie looked up and saw Syrdian and Qes at the forest verge, Syrdian's wings spread. Qes started inspecting the right one. Then Syrdian beat hies wings gently a couple of strokes. They drooped quivering down onto hies back. As Dex watched, Qes leaned close, reached for hies knife and brought it to Syrdian's wing.

Dex's hearts sank, what was Qes going to do?

Qes' wings rose in alarm and hie cried out. A beat of hies wings backed himr away from Syrdian. Then crying, "Dyatso!" Qes beat into the sky and up away from the meadow.

"Dyatso!" Dex thought in horror. "Dyatso" was a term meaning "walking dead." Doubly horrifying because it encompassed not only the inability to fly, but also the approach of death that inevitably followed the

loss flight. *How could hie say "dyatso" to Syrdian?! It might be true, but how... how could hie* say *it? The Syrdian that hie* says *hie loves?*

Syrdian collapsed to the ground as Qes flew away. Dropping the meat hie'd cut free from the talor, Dex flew to Syrdian with a few powerful strokes, dropping to Syrdian's side. Hie looked in horror at Syrdian's wing where a few of Dex's fiberlin sutures had been cut. They'd pulled out, allowing the largest rip to pull open about a third of its length. Evidently traumatized by the realization that hies wing truly *was* ripped, Syrdian had fainted again. With a sigh and a shrug of hies wings Dex crouched, pulling out hies roll of fine fiberlin.

Dex was tying the last knot in hies re-repair job when Syrdian's eyes opened again. Syrdian lifted hies head anxiously, "Qes?" Seeing Dex, Syrdian said, "Where's Qes?"

Dex shrugged hies wings, "Gone."

Syrdian relaxed. "Hie must have gone for help from the tribe."

Wide eyed, Dex wanted to shake Syrdian. Hie thought, *Didn't you hear himr call you "dyatso" as hie left you here alone, other than for me?* Dex's eyes narrowed. If Syrdian really couldn't fly with the holes in hies wings sutured shut hie probably was dyatso. The heat of summer would be upon them soon. The start of the big migration south had been planned for tomorrow. Life in this region during the heat of summer would quickly become impossible.

Dex sometimes wondered if it might be possible to live in this area if you moved higher up on the mountain. Everyone knew it was cooler as you got higher. It'd be harder to fly because the air was thinner, but it could be done with effort.

However, getting higher on the mountain without flying? That seemed impossible. Syrdian would have to walk through a lot of forest if hie couldn't fly. Despite the fact that Qes had hidden from the talor in the forest, the forest was far from safe. There were a lot of large wingless predators in the shadows.

Thinking of that, Dex looked over at the verge to make sure one of those large forest predators wasn't presently sizing them up from just inside the trees. Hie didn't see any large infrared objects, only the expected smaller animals. He puffed his lips, tasting the air, "Syrdian? We should move farther from the verge," hie said. "Who knows what might be lurking there."

Syrdian's head rose, turning violently to allow himr to study the verge himrself, "Why? Do you see something?"

"No, but by the time we see it, it might be too late."

Syrdian got to hies feet and said, "OK, let's move." Hie looked at hies wing, "Hey, the hole's gone!"

"I tied back the sutures that Qes cut."

Syrdian looked at Dex, then at hies wing, then back at Dex, "You really did sew my wing up like you do your leatherwork?"

Dex nodded, turning to walk back to the talor. Flying back when Syrdian couldn't seemed rude.

When they reached the talor, Syrdian said, "Look at all that meat! I'm hungry!"

Dex said, "Shall we cook some?"

"Do you know how?"

Dex shrugged, "Sure. Not like they do it at the cave, but well enough to eat."

"OK," Syrdian said, crouching and looking expectantly at Dex.

***

Qes stared disconsolately into the distance, thinking, *How could this have happened to me?* This morning hie'd been on top of the world, highly ranked in the tribe, nearly mated to the beautiful Syrdian. Syrdian, likely the highest ranked among the tribe's youth. They'd been pseudo mating for days now and this morning Qes had suggested that they sneak away to their favorite meadow to do it again.

Now, with the beautiful Syrdian mutilated, Qes would have to find another potential mate. A difficult task now that many of the higher ranked youth were already committed to others.

Briefly Qes wondered if there was any way that Syrdian could survive. A shiver ran over hies wings, *Obviously not.* Even if Syrdian somehow made it back to the cave through the forest, the migration would be tomorrow and there would be no way for Syrdian to fly south, nor to survive the summer heat if hie stayed here. And... if Syrdian somehow survived... Qes didn't *want* to be mated to a mutilated, low status, Syrdian. *Hie'd* loved the beautiful *highly ranked* Syrdian.

Qes dreaded hies return to the cave. When Syrdian didn't return, dalins would start asking Qes if hie'd seen himr. Especially Syrdian's parents. Qes would have to deny seeing Syrdian or they'd want himr to lead them to the meadow. Hie shrugged hies wings, *Crueler really, to take them to Syrdian and have them find their child with a mutilated wing.* Then they'd all have to come to grips with Syrdian's eventual death.

No, it'd be better and kinder not to tell them what'd

happened. Let them think Syrdian had died immediately at the hands of a talor... or something else. Better by far than seeing himr alive and having to leave himr to hies death anyway. Qes wouldn't even have to admit to being with Syrdian when it happened.

Hie shouldn't return until nearly dark to eliminate the chance that they'd go out searching and find Syrdian by some unlucky chance. A flightless Syrdian couldn't possibly survive the night. That would spare hies parents the pain of finding Syrdian mutilated, begging for help they couldn't give.

Chapter Two

Norris walked over to where Donsaii still sat with the others staring at a screen. “I agree except for clause 2.6 where I would want to limit that to one year as well.”

Donsaii’s eyes narrowed a moment, then she smiled, “OK. My AI’s recording this as a binding contract, do you agree?”

Norris shrugged, “Sure.”

“Great, look at this with us.”

Donsaii turned the screen they were looking at a little toward him and he saw an image of Earth from space. Although… he tilted his head curiously… The cloud cover was really heavy… Could it be Venus? No he saw a swath of blue in a break in the clouds. Norris narrowed his eyes and said, “That’s more clouds than I’ve ever seen…” He looked at the four of them and found them all grinning widely. He looked back at the screen, “What is this?”

In a hushed voice, Kenner said, “That’s the third planet of Tau Ceti.”

Norris stared at her, then at Donsaii, then back at the screen. “There’s no telescope big enough to…” The skin prickled on his scalp, “How?”

Emmerit said, “The girls here sent a rocket out there with a camera.”

“Oh Jeez,” Norris put a hand down on the table and leaned on it, taking an almost gasping breath. “Really? How?” He looked at the screen again, “Is that *blue* showing through the clouds?”

"Yeah, oxygen, nitrogen, CO_2 atmosphere," Emmerit whispered almost reverently. "We're *assuming* the blue's water. Initially, when the planet looked white from far away we thought it must be an ice world. It's pretty far out at the outer edge of the habitable zone where the temperature should be right for liquid water. We assumed it'd be mostly frozen." He looked back at the screen, "There's more CO_2 than Earth and quite a bit of methane. They may be boosting the greenhouse effect."

"My God! There must be some kind of life to produce the oxygen. What's it look like?"

Donsaii shrugged. "We don't know. We haven't sent anything down into the atmosphere yet. There's a huge green area in the southern hemisphere though; we're thinking maybe some kind of supercontinent like the original Pangaea here on Earth? Maybe the green means something like chlorophyll?"

Norris' eyes widened even further, "Really?"

"Yeah, so that's what we've been working on. We're trying to design a vehicle that won't contaminate TC3 with our organisms and vice versa. Then we can go down and have a look."

"TC3?"

"Short for Tau Ceti Three. We don't have a name for it yet. Here, look at this."

The screen filled with a diagram of a rocket. Donsaii said, "We can send data back through PGR chips, so that avoids any transfer of organisms to us. As long as we sterilize the rocket before we put it through the port to TC3 we should protect them. However, normally we have ports sending LOX and LNG to the main rocket motor and just plain compressed gas through ports to act as attitude jets.

"Presently, our plan's to use steam for the attitude jets, since that should be sterile. At first we were thinking that the cold would kill organisms in the LOX and LNG that we use for our main rocket propellants. However, we've since learned that cryogenic temperatures are actually used to *preserve* bacteria. We've also been counting on the fact that microbes should be killed in the rocket's flame, but we've gotten worried about the little puffs of gas that leak out right before ignition. We've been thinking about putting something toxic in the first puffs so it'll be sterile until the flame starts, but then we'd be squirting toxic stuff into the atmosphere there... And the mechanics of putting something toxic in the initial puffs are problematic." She frowned.

Norris said, "How about using ethanol. Bacteria are killed in alcohols."

Emmerit frowned, "That'd be good, but we'd still have bacteria in the liquid oxygen."

"Use hydrogen peroxide as your oxidizer, bacteria die in that too."

"So both propellants are bactericidal, but not horribly toxic?" Donsaii mused "And they burn to water and CO_2?"

Norris said, "Well, they're both pretty toxic at high concentrations."

Ell shrugged "No toxic exhaust at least. Great idea!" she smiled broadly at him, "Already glad to have you aboard." She looked around at her little group, "Remember, we can't use port supplied fuel cells to power the stuff on board the rocket either. We don't want to leak bacteria through those ports either. I'm figuring that we have to keep the fuel cell here and send sterilized wire through a hot interface into tiny ports in the rocket. The wires can supply the power for the camera, PGR chips and ports. Maybe we should start supplying power through wires to all our ports, even here on Earth?"

Though Norris didn't really understand the issue, eyebrows rose over that idea. They went back to discussing how to assemble a sterile rocket. Or a sterilizable rocket anyway. Then they started talking about what instruments to put on the first rocket that'd descend to the surface of TC3? Norris suggested instruments to measure gravity, atmospheric composition and an instrument to detect DNA.

"DNA? Surely alien life will use a different molecule for encoding genetic data?"

Norris shrugged, "DNA in bacterial spores or viral capsids could have spread all around the universe on stellar winds and through explosions of supernovae. Such DNA could then re-evolve life on each new world." He raised his eyebrows, "We have no idea if this theory is true, but now we can begin to find out."

~~~

Eventually, his world view sorely shaken, Norris left D5R with video of TC3 and a number of samples of asteroid 2019 UB40.

As Ell walked Norris out, Emma smiled up at Roger. "I thought you explained things very nicely to Norris."

"You did?" Roger said, trying to remember what he might've explained well. "Thanks." He looked momentarily at Emma. She'd done something interesting with her hair. It looked like a curly tangle, but he suspected a purposeful tousle. Anyway it looked good. "Hey, you know it's a lot of fun working with you.
~~~

Too bad you weren't in Johnson's lab with us back at NCSU."

Emma wrinkled her nose at him, "Nope, I never could've worked with that bastard." She tilted her head. "It might've been OK if *you'd* been assigned to the Sponchesi lab..."

Roger grinned at her, "Nah, I never get the easy way out." He gave her a wink.

***

Dex thought Syrdian was nothing like the wonderful, competent dalin hie'd always pictured when admiring himr from afar. Hie seemed to be waiting for Dex to do everything. To be fair Syrdian was injured, but it was only hies wing. The selfless and wonderful Syrdian Dex'd always imagined would have pitched in to help with hies perfectly functional hands. Dex examined the verge for infrared, then beat into the air and flew close to it puffing to take the scent of the air there. It smelled safe. Hie landed by a downed tree and quickly picked up some deadwood, one branch of which had a cluster of dead leaves. A few beats took himr back to Syrdian and the talor. Hie cleared the grass from an area and shredded some of the dry leaves. Hie pulled out hies flint and striker and struck a few sparks to start the shredded leaves burning. Dex laid a few dry sticks on the leaves, then a couple of larger branches. Once the fire was burning hie flew back to cut some straight green sticks. Soon hie had some pieces of talor speared on a stick and suspended over the fire. During the entire time Syrdian watched with interest as if hie'd never seen anything cooked in hies life. *Hasn't hie ever even watched while the food's prepared back at the cave?* Dex wondered. *Why isn't hie helping?! Is it just that hie doesn't want to sully himrself by helping a low status dalin like me?*

When Dex took the meat off the fire and cut off pieces for Syrdian and himrself, hie could see that hie'd had it too close to the fire. The outside was a little burned while the inside was just past warm. Dex wished hie had some salt to season the meat, but it was quite a flight to the nearest lick Dex knew of.

Syrdian bit into one of hies pieces. "It's tough!" hie exclaimed.

Dex shrugged hies wings, "Predators usually are."

Syrdian laid hies piece of talor down, "I'll just wait for them to bring something better."

Dex's eyes widened. Syrdian still didn't seem to have any idea how serious hies situation was. "Uh..." Dex began but found hie couldn't continue. *What would I say? "Your lover Qes has given you up for dead and probably told the tribe you were killed?" I don't actually* know *that that's true.* Unable to bring himrself to tell Syrdian, hie said nothing after the "Uh." Hie resumed eating hies talor.

Syrdian said, "What?" and then when Dex didn't respond said, "I can't believe you're still eating that."

"I think we're going to be hungry," Dex said darkly.

Syrdian frowned, "Why? Surely when they come, they'll bring food."

Dex shrugged hies wings and turned to contemplate nightfall. A lot of ground based predators roamed the nights. Would a fire keep them away? Would the scent of talor deter them or would the scent of death bring them? "Syrdian?"

Syrdian'd been looking up the mountain in the direction of the cave, as if wondering where hies rescuers were. Hie turned to Dex, "Yes?"

"I don't think we should stay here near the talor. Scavengers are going to show up sooner or later. You don't want to be between a brek and its dinner."

Syrdian looked surprised, probably because breks were too slow moving to be threats to a dalin like himrself. But that assumed the dalin could fly. On the ground, breks were pretty fierce. Syrdian's look became shadowed as hie realized that hie actually could become a tasty morsel for a brek. "OK, where do you think we should move?"

"Over between some of the rocks over there," Dex pointed a wing. "Not exactly a cave, but as good as we can get here. I'll fly over and look for a good place, you carry over a brand from the fire?"

Syrdian shrugged hies wings, "OK." Hie picked up a reasonable brand from the fire and turned to go.

Dex picked up several of the sticks he'd brought earlier, "Can you take some wood too? I don't want to make a lot of trips."

Looking irritated, Syrdian stopped and went back for more. "Why do we want a fire over there? We aren't cooking anymore."

"Fires keep away predators," Dex said, beating into the air. Hie flew above the rocks where they stuck up to form their little ridge near one side of the meadow. Three of them closed off a small area and hie landed there, waving a wing at Syrdian. Hie cleared a small area at the front edge of the closed off area and laid the wood hie'd brought there. Then hie beat into the air and back across the meadow to the dead wood at the verge. Once again hie checked visually and puffed hies mouth, sucking air over the olfactory patches on hies lips to smell for predators. Fairly confident there weren't any predators, hie landed and loaded up with more wood.

Dex made another trip, but when hie returned with the load of wood found that Syrdian had piled Dex's entire first load on the fire. The flames had risen so high that Syrdian'd had to leave the rock enclosure. "You put it *all* on the fire? Why!"

"Why did you get so much wood?" Syrdian asked indignantly.

"So we'd have some for later!" Dex said exasperatedly.

"Later?! Why?"

"Syrdian! What if no one from the tribe comes?! If we're here all night, we'll need fire to keep predators away for deks! I won't be able to go get more wood in the dark."

"Why wouldn't they come?" Syrdian asked in an astonished tone.

"Qes..." Dex said disdainfully, then paused, unable to think how to remind Syrdian what Qes had said.

"Qes what?" Syrdian snapped indignantly.

"Qes called you dyatso!" Dex said in frustration. "Hie hasn't gone for help, you're *dead* to himr."

"Hie wouldn't!"

"Hie did. You heard himr, you just won't admit it to yourself."

"Wouldn't!" Syrdian turned to look off over the trees in the direction of the cave. Waiting, presumably, for some dalins to wing into view, thus proving Dex wrong.

"I'm going to go get more wood." Dex said

disgustedly, "*Don't* put any more on the fire."

Dex made six trips to the verge and back and built up quite a pile of wood. Syrdian simply sat and stared sullenly up the mountain. Dex made another trip to the talor and brought back meat. This time hie had to chase away some dlak that were scavenging the carcass. As hie sat, cutting the meat into strips and hanging it near the fire to dry, hie wondered why hie was staying with Syrdian. Yes, Syrdian was beautiful and yes Dex had longed for Syrdian for… forever. But now that hie'd actually spent time with Syrdian hie found himr annoying and… shallow. And, worst of all, incompetent to take care of himrself! Dex felt like hie was staying out of sympathy now, not out of hies previously misguided sense of love.

Just before the sun went down Dex flew back to the verge and cut four straight shafts about hies height. After dark hie trimmed and peeled them, then sharpened a point onto one end of each of them. He carefully fire-hardened their points. Such pointed staves were supposed to be useful for fending off predators though Dex'd never used one himrself. Hie laid a stave on each side of the fire and then leaned the others against the big rock at the back of the small enclosure. He crouched down back there himrself. Partly because it was too warm by the fire and also because hie worried about something dropping down from above. Hie tried to reassure himrself that the big flying predators like talors didn't fly at night. Besides, they were afraid of fire, weren't they?

***

Deltain looked up from the harness he'd been working on. The sun had set. Hie stood and walked over to the edge of the flat ledge that provided a work area in front of the great cave. Deltain looked out into the dimming sky. *Where's Dex? Hie'd promised not to stay out close to dark like this!* Worry fought with irritation in Deltain's hearts.

Dex was at a difficult age. A young adult, angry with the low position in the tribe's hierarchy that Genex left himr. Shifting from the compliance of youth to the defiance of young adulthood.

Dex knew how Deltain worried when hie didn't get home well before dark, yet hie frequently pushed it close! Deltain's wings rippled in frustration. Would Dex behave this way if it weren't for hies low status? Hie wondered if Dex might be less rebellious if hies status rose, something Deltain hoped might happen as Dex's ability to produce fine leatherwork became more and more apparent.

Distantly Deltain realized that several other parents were standing on the ledge looking out into the dimming light, perhaps frustrated with the same issues?

A dalin appeared against the sunset sky, winging its way toward the cave. Deltain's hearts lifted, Dex? Hies hearts sank as the dalin approached and Deltain recognized the handsome Qes, an age mate of Dex, but very high status. Qes landed beside hies parents and clasped them. Then Qes glanced at the other parents waiting on the ledge. Deltain recognized the parents of Syrdian, Qes' romantic interest. Qes spoke quietly to hies own parents while repeatedly glancing over at Syrdian's parents.

Syrdian's parents approached Qes. Deltain heard

them ask, "… seen Syrdian?"

Qes waved hies head in negation and the parents, wings drooping, returned to their vigil, looking out over the enormous valley below.

As Qes and hies parents moved back into the cave Deltain approached. "Did you maybe see Dex out there today?" hie asked.

Qes glanced at Deltain, appearing startled to be asked, then again waved hies head in negation.

Deltain returned to hies vigil at the front of the cave, thinking how unlikely it would have been that Dex and Qes would've encountered one another. Hie searched hies memories, trying to remember if Dex had told himr where hie was going when hie left that morning.

***

Allan, Ell's AI (Artificial Intelligence) said, "You have a call from Kant Fladwami PhD, President Flood's science advisor."

Ell stood up from the table where she and Roger had been looking at some of the components for the next TC3 rocket, "I'll be back in a sec Rog'." To her AI she said, "Put him on. Yes, Dr. Fladwami?"

"Hello, Ms. Donsaii. Chip Horton, my predecessor here in the Presidential Science Advisor's office suggested I get to know you. Something about, not knowing what you were doing' being a frequent source of embarrassment."

Ell laughed, "I don't think that's really true, Doctor."

"Nonetheless I thought I'd check in to see if you had any new technology that was about to turn our entire economy upside down?"

"No sir."

"Nothing exciting happening at D5R anymore?"

"Well, exciting things are happening, but they shouldn't impact the economy."

Fladwami chuckled "Are you telling me I don't have a need to know?"

Ell laughed again, liking Fladwami already. "I guess you could say that, Doctor."

"OK, the President also asked me to find out why nothing seems to be happening with putting your ports into action out there in the real world. Our understanding from Horton was that you were going to try to slow down the release of that tech somewhat so there wouldn't be such severe economic upheavals. But we're surprised that we don't seem to be hearing *anything* about it so far?"

"Uh, yes sir. Outgoing Transportation Secretary Bayless was vehemently opposed to the release of that tech, so the Pipeline and Hazardous Materials Safety Administration has been refusing us licenses except for space portals so far. We've been hoping that the new Secretary will get them to loosen up a little. We've made all the applications as required and no one's told us have anything wrong with the applications. Nothing that we've been directed to fix anyway. But they' haven't been approved, they just tell us approval's pending."

"Really?"

"Yes sir."

"Well that's just the kind of government interference with private enterprise that President Flood campaigned on. I'll bring that to the Secretary's attention for you."

"Thank you, sir."

"You'll let me know if anything else world changing is about to pop out of your labs?"

"Yes sir. I may be calling sometime to tell you about something that won't change the economy, but's still scientifically important?"

Fladwami raised his eyebrows. He wondered what that could be. "You do that... Next item on my agenda, the President has asked me to invite you to the White House for a personal meeting next week. Would you be able to come up?"

"I'm in the reserves and he's my Commander in Chief. Of course I can come. Is there something in particular on the agenda I should prepare for?"

"No preparation needed. Would Thursday evening, dinner at the White House, 6:30 PM be satisfactory?"

"Yes sir. Just show up?"

"Well," he laughed, "Wear something nice, the dinners tend to be formal."

"Yes sir."

~~~

Disconnected, Fladwami leaned back in his chair. It was hard to reconcile the respectful young voice on the other end of that call with what Horton—and he had to agree—had called 'the greatest scientific mind in of the century.' Well, Horton, had said 'of all time,' but Fladwami wasn't sure about that yet. He shrugged, *But that might well be true too...*

***

Ell turned to go back to her Quantum Research
~~~

group but found Wilson Daster standing between her and the rest of the group. She raised her eyebrows.

He said, "I'm afraid I have some bad news."

Ell closed her eyes. "You've found someone diddling the books?" she sighed.

"Yeah."

She laughed hollowly, "Well, I guess this isn't as bad as when you called to tell me a comet was going to wipe out everyone on the planet?"

"Not quite that bad, no."

***

Dex woke in the night to find the fire burned out. Hie heard snarling and snapping from the direction of the talor's carcass. When hie got up, Syrdian's voice came out of the stygian darkness, "Where are you going?"

"To restart the fire." The residual of the fire was easy to see in infrared. Dex got up and felt around for the firewood. A meteor's fireball streaked over, starkly lighting the area for a moment. With the wood and the fire's relative locations fixed in hies mind, hie quickly found several sticks and stirred through the fire until the motion activated a few coals. The sticks caught and Dex moved some more wood close by. Hie looked out into the darkness and saw the eyes of some nocturnal creature looking back at himr. Hie shivered and lay down, closer to the fire this time. After all, he'd have to add wood frequently.

***

"OK," Ell said, looking around. "The test ports still functioned after we sterilized them with chlorine dioxide. So each of us need to look over the plans again to be sure there are no cavities inside the TC3 rocket that are closed off, we want the gas to be able to get into every area. Dr. Norris, your ethanol-peroxide rocket engines are working fine. I'm confident that we've protected TC3 from Earth microorganisms. I'm still worried about backflow from TC3 to Earth, especially through the attitude jets we usually just blow compressed air through. Firing and killing ethanol-peroxide rockets doesn't happen fast enough to give us the fine attitude control we're used to."

Roger said, "I've been worrying about that too, and I have a suggestion that I think's doable with port tech?"

They all turned to him. "You put a long pipe out in space through a port. I'm talking hundreds of meters. It has a port at one end we pump compressed air into from down here. At the other end you put a series of ports that go to the attitude jets. Then we wrap the Earth end of the pipe with heating elements so we can keep the 20 meters closest to Earth at about 500^{0}C. That's far, far beyond the temperature any Earth spores can survive. Presumably it'd sterilize any TC3 organisms too. So air flows in one end, gets heat sterilized in that first 20 meters, then flows down to the cold end of the pipe where it cools back down. Anything back-flowing through the port at the TC3 end would have to pass through the hot end before it could get back here to Earth. You put the pipe into a decaying orbit around the sun so that, after we're done with it, if it *were* contaminated with something bad, no one could retrieve it and accidentally encounter any TC3 microorganisms."

Roger said, "We could black the hot end and mirror the cold end so that the sun would help us keep one end hot and leave the other end cool. I'd also suggest we make it so we can heat 40 meters when we're expecting to use the jets and only 10 meters between jet uses. Then we can be sure nothing from this end might move through the hot section so fast it doesn't get killed."

They added to the list of instruments they wanted on the rocket and finally included one of Ben Stavos' mechanical arms and a port behind a glass window that they could shine light through at night, or use to fire lasers through, ablating materials for spectroscopic analysis. That port was a double port with the intermediate section in the "space pipe" and filled with toxic gas.

Wilson Daster suggested that every port to the TC3 rocket have an intermediary on the space pipe, if possible in the hot end.

Eventually, happy with the design, they broke up to order materials and design the machining of parts.

Ell reluctantly headed back to the offices. Wilson caught up to her, "Do you want me to be the bad guy? I've done it before and I don't know her like you do."

Ell looked at him, sorely tempted. "No. I actually don't want people to know what your secondary task is. Don't want them trying to work around you. And, believe it or not, I may not fire her."

Daster's eyebrows went up. "You're kidding, she's been *stealing* from you!"

"She's a great employee, otherwise." Ell shrugged, "A really great employee. I think she deserves a second chance."

"Okaaay." Daster shrugged, "You're the boss."

~~~

Ell knocked on Sheila's doorframe and Sheila looked up saying brightly, "Come on in Bosslady."

Ell entered her office, closed the door and sat down. Then she just stared at Sheila.

A minute passed while the blood drained from Sheila's face, then she crumpled, "I'm so sorry," she gasped. "*So* sorry. I'll be packed up in a minute."

Ell said, "What do *you* think I should do?"

"You should call the police. I'm hoping against hope that you'll settle for just firing me... I don't know what's wrong with me. I love working here. You're paying me more than anyone else ever would. My shares..." She blinked rapidly, then grabbed for a Kleenex.

Intently focused on Sheila Ell said, "I'll bet this isn't the first time?"

Sheila blew her nose, "First time I've gotten caught."

"So if we fired you, you'd probably just wind up preying on your next employer."

"I hope not. Course, I probably," she choked a little. "I probably wouldn't be able to get another job."

"Sheila, you've been a great employee. Probably one of the most important people we've had in making all of D5R work. I don't want to ruin your life. I don't want to send you out there to prey on someone else. So I'm going to offer you a chance to stay here..."

Sheila's eyes widened and she stared at Ell.

"But, I suspect you have a personality disorder that compels you to steal like this. Will you seek treatment?"

Sheila nodded spastically, gulping.

"And you have to be aware we've got systems in place to catch you if you do it again?"
~~~

Sheila nodded again.

"And you need to return everything you stole, plus 10%?"

"I will! Thank you," she whispered

Ell nodded and got up. "I thought of you as a friend, and I still do. I hope you don't make me regret this."

"No Ma'am!"

~~~

When Ell got back to her office, Roger was waiting for her, "Hey, who shot *your* dog?"

"Bein' the boss shot my dog. Sometimes you have to make decisions that seem like they're no win.' Do you have another problem for me?"

Roger grinned, "Nope, I've got an opportunity."

Ell closed her eyes momentarily, then opened them. "Power generation?"

Roger narrowed his eyes, "Yesss... What are *you* meaning by power generation?"

"Your black pipes in close solar orbit. You want to squirt water in one end and harvest steam out the other end using ports, yes?"

"Yeah! Did you have the same idea?"

"Kinda. There are issues though. You know that there is a velocity limitation to how fast stuff can pass through a port right?"

Roger smacked his forehead, "Damn! And the steam would be going too fast when it exited the pipe. Right?"

"Right. Unless we have a really large diameter port for it to flow back through at a lower velocity, but then it'll *take* a lot of power just to energize the port."

Brow furrowing, Roger tilted his head back to stare up at the ceiling. "Wait! We could use a heat transfer fluid, like Therminol." He brought his eyes back down to
~~~

look at Ell.

"Heat transfer fluid?"

"Yeah, a fluid that wouldn't boil at the temps we're shooting for, say 340-degrees Centigrade. Therminol's just one brand. We pump it through our black pipe in near solar orbit and then back here to Earth. The transfer fluid doesn't boil at those temps so it doesn't expand into steam and there's no increase in velocity. Once it comes back here hot, we run the transfer fluid through a pipe in a water tank. The water boils into steam and powers our electric generator." He sat back up and lifted a finger, frowning, then smiling, "Then, instead of just exhausting the steam into the atmosphere and heating the Earth, we cool it against a second heat transfer fluid loop that we've cooled by running it through a pipe way out in *deep* space. That pipe radiates the heat away. We condense our steam, don't heat the planet and save ourselves the cost of buying more water!"

"Roger, that's brilliant!"

"Oh! And... we don't just sell steam for power generation; we can use it for heat! And we can use the deep space pipes for air conditioning! Holy cripes! Talk about energy conservation! My God, this could solve a *lot* of problems!"

Ell jumped up and gave him a hug. "Way to go Rog'!" She held him back out at arm's length. "Way to go," she whispered, her eyes getting a little misty as she looked up at Roger. Roger, her handsome, smart, "friendly boy." The boy she loved but couldn't seem to *love*. The boy she wanted Emma to have, but didn't want to let go of, especially when he was having a moment of brilliance like this.

Roger, not recognizing the tumultuous thoughts

pouring through Ell's mind, waggled his eyebrows, "Want to spin a company off D5R with me? We'll be rich!"

Ell looked wistfully at him another moment, then let go and sat down. "Yes, you will. I'd rather keep doing research instead of trying to be a commercial success. But I'll wish you the best of luck and help you get started."

Roger looked like he'd been poleaxed, "No! I want to do it *with* you Ell!" He quirked the corner of his mouth, "I want us to be rich together. If this is an invention, it's partly yours."

She looked wistfully at him then said, "I'd rather license my share to someone else so I can keep doing research."

Roger brightened, "OK, who?"

"ET Resources for one, this is right up their alley."

"OK! Let's go talk to them."

"First let's get you some patent protection. And, you should build a working model."

Chapter Three

Morning found Dex huddled next to the fire with Syrdian crowded next to himr. Dex's thoughts stumbled, remembering hies old fantasies about sleeping next to Syrdian. Hie thought about trying to snuggle even closer to Syrdian to "ward off the cold" but, fearing rejection, instead hie got up to put wood on the fire.

~~~

A little later Syrdian tore into the pieces of talor hie'd rejected the evening before. Hies eyes widened, "This tastes better today."

"You're hungrier today."

"No, really, I think something happened to it to make it better."

Dex shrugged hies wings in doubt and started taking the strips of dried meat off hies green withe frame over the fire and stuffing them in hies carry harness. When hies harness was full hie passed some to Syrdian.

Syrdian frowned without taking it, "I don't think I'm going to want to eat any of that. I'm pretty sure it'll be too tough to be any good."

Dex stared at Syrdian disgustedly for a moment, then turned and thundered into the air, turning to head back to the cave. Hie couldn't believe that hie'd ever found Syrdian desirable! Hie certainly wasn't going to stay, at considerable risk to himrself, to help someone so incapable of recognizing hies dire situation or
~~~

undertaking any efforts to try to save himrself. Dex assuaged hies guilt at leaving by thinking that hie could just turn this problem over to Syrdian's parents. A niggling doubt told himr that Syrdian's parents couldn't save himr either. Dex had some crazy ideas about how to do it, but hie doubted that anyone else would even consider them.

So, essentially hie was leaving Syrdian to hies death. Even if Syrdian couldn't, or wouldn't, recognize that.

As Dex rose over the verge and out over the forest a fireball popped through the clouds above, moving slower than any meteor Dex'd ever seen. It dropped down, appearing to be sinking toward the meadow Dex'd just lifted from. Dex would've sworn that the fireball was, as bizarre as that seemed, moving slower and slower as it dropped toward the meadow.

Dex banked back toward the meadow. To hies utter astonishment the fireball came to a halt, just above the grass of the meadow. The flames shooting out of the bottom of it started a fire in the grass; good thing the grass was really green so it couldn't start a big fire. The meteorite gradually sank to the ground, then stopped. The fire went out, but the grass still smoldered.

Dex curved around to circle it, beating gently with hind wings only. It seemed to be a long slender object, mostly silver in color. It had little legs sticking out of the sides near the bottom that were keeping it upright! *It looks nothing like the meteorites I've seen before!*

Meteorites were considered powerful omens, sometimes for good, sometimes for evil. Dex found them fascinating. However, every meteorite Dex had ever seen—ones that others had found after they came down *and* one that Dex had seen crash into the ground himrself—were black and lumpy.

Actually, they were hot right after they landed and bright infrared. Then, astonishingly, they quickly got so cold they gathered frost. When they landed, they landed hard, usually making a hole in the ground. They frequently started fires like this one had, but eventually became irregular lumpy black things. No one had ever described anything like what Dex had just witnessed! A silvery narrow meteorite, shaped like a short, thick stick, which came down slowly, and landed gently!

With legs!

Dex banked around it, spiraling down to land about 6 paces away. The very bottom part of it was bright infrared. Hie crouched down to watch it for a while.

***

Norris walked into D5R, resisting the impulse to trot. He'd taught his 11 AM class and arranged for a grad student to teach his afternoon class. Donsaii and the others had probably already started the rocket's descent to TC3, but he hoped he wasn't going to miss the touchdown. The rocket they'd designed to be sterile had been put through the Tau Ceti port and flown to the planet, arriving during the night last night. The landing site they'd chosen based on glimpses through the clouds was on the side of an enormous mountain and it'd be just past sunrise there about now. He tilted his head curiously, *Tau Ceti rise?*

He strode into the big room down near the end where Donsaii and the others did most of their work, but no one was there! He looked around, hoping no one thought he looked frantic, though that's the way he felt.

One of the machinists walked by and he said, "Hey, any idea where the Quantum Research folks are today?"

The guy frowned, "Yeah, they're all down in the little conference room. Not sure why." He pointed and Norris turned to head down there in a disappointed mood. *Has something gone wrong? Are they just having a post mortem?* He knocked on the door and tried the knob. *It's locked?*

Emma opened the door a crack, "Dr. Norris! Come on in! You're just in time; we should be coming out of the clouds any time now." She spoke quietly as if she didn't want to disturb anyone.

He frowned, "Why are you in here?" Donsaii, Emmerit, Garcia, Daster and Kenner were the only people in there. He'd kind of expected a lot of people and a party atmosphere.

"Um, we decided we didn't want people to accidentally get a look at the screens. So far, if folks walk by and see TC3 on the screens, they just think they're seeing a cloudy Earth or Venus or something. But today, we hope we'll be seeing things on the screen that anyone would recognize came from somewhere else. We don't want anyone getting freaked out."

Norris tilted his head in puzzlement, wondering what they thought people might "get freaked out" about, but then excitement took over and he turned his eyes to look at the screens himself. At present all six screens showed unremitting pale gray. "I assume everything's gray because we're still in the clouds?"

"Yep," Donsaii said. She pointed to the screens which were arranged in a row of four with a large one in the middle. There was a lone screen above and another below the row. She pointed to the top one, "View looking up," she pointed to the bottom one, "down." She swept across the middle row, "four cameras pointing each direction."

Norris had already noticed a reddish orange glow on one side of the bottom image, presumably exhaust from the rocket slowing the descent. Suddenly the gray cleared away to show brilliant green everywhere. Immediately the middle row also cleared, showing green across the bottom of their images and grey on top. A little cheer burst out.

"OK, where do we land?" Donsaii asked.

Roger said, "I think the darker areas are something like trees. Probably dangerous landing in them. We should shoot for one of the lighter areas, they look like clearings."

Norris said, "Look at that spot in the left screen, it's light and it looks like it has some kind of rocks sticking up on one side." His eyebrows rose as he realized that everywhere else was unremitting green. "It'd be good to land near those rocks since it looks like we can't see any other rocks. After all, we set up the laser in this rocket so it could do spectro on some rocks and that's the *only* likely site I see."

Ell spoke to Allan and the meadow Norris had chosen slowly rose to meet their rocket while they all stared in awe at their first view of this new world. The meadow was a ragged oval and had the odd row of rocks or boulders strung partway across it, somewhat nearer to the northern side. Emma said, "Look! On the right screen! Over by the rocks, it looks like smoke!"

Sure enough, there did seem to be some tendrils of smoke rising from just in front of the boulders. Norris wondered what in the world could cause that. If it were volcanic you'd think there'd be some lava or something.

The rocks were rounded as if they'd been exposed for a long time. They didn't look like lava. Well, didn't look like Earth lava anyway.

Emmerit said, "Holy jeez, the atmosphere is dense! We're registering 695 kPa! That's about seven times the density of Earth's atmosphere! Oh, and it's 36% oxygen!" He paused, then, "Ah, crap we couldn't really live there; it'd be like deep sea diving. We'd get oxygen toxicity and nitrogen narcosis."

Ell laughed, "Roger, I can't believe you were hoping to go build a house on the first extra-solar planet we visited!"

He put a hand to his chest, "Hey, a young man can dream can't he?"

Norris wondered how Roger thought he'd get there through a four-inch port. *Or can they make bigger ports and just haven't told me—or the rest of the world—about it?*

The view rocked a little and settled at a slight cant. Donsaii said, "We're down." Norris noticed the very bottom screen showed something that looked, for all the world, like a blade of grass! As he watched, it curled and blackened.

A loud pop sounded and Manuel stood up suddenly. Champagne was foaming out of a bottle he held over the cooler he'd pulled it out of. He set the bottle down and passed out some plastic champagne flutes.

While Norris held his flute waiting for some of the champagne, he kept staring in wonder at the screens. The meadow was surrounded by what appeared to be a rainforest. Very tall, though very slender tree boles were visible through the forest verge, shooting up to a high canopy with darkness underneath. "Whoa! Look at that huge... bird?" Everyone else's head snapped back to the screens. He wasn't seeing feathers. Maybe it was more like a bat?

Emma said, "The wings look *way* too small, how can it fly?"

Donsaii mused, "Really dense air should help. High oxygen means its metabolism can run really hot. But that would just help it launch and fly fast. What's the gravity Allan?"

Allan, Ell's AI answered the question in all of their earphones, "0.27G."

Ell said, "Low gravity would make it easier to fly too." Looking past the large flier she realized there were lots of small fliers flitting around the meadow on small wings, moving so fast they were hard to see.

Emma said, "Wait a minute, if the gravity is so low, why's the atmosphere so dense?"

Norris said, "Gravity doesn't necessarily correlate with atmospheric density. Venus has about the same gravity as Earth, but the atmosphere is *90* times denser. Remember that Tau Ceti has that huge ring of cometary debris. If this planet's been getting pelted with a lot of comets, they may well have brought a lot of ice and frozen gas that'd result in more water and atmosphere..."

Norris sipped his champagne as he watched the flyer circling the rocket. He had the impression it was big, though he couldn't really tell how far away it was. To his surprise it seemed to be flying by gliding on some front wings while beating its tail, like a dolphin pushes itself through the water. It spiraled in closer, then landed nearby on long slender birdlike lower limbs like. In fact, its legs even seemed to have forward and backward pointing toes with claws like a bird's feet.

They all stared in awe. It had upper limbs too, with... with... claws. They were also something like bird's feet, but looked very flexible... more like hands...

It wore a harness that looked like it was made of leather straps.

***

Syrdian startled Dex by appearing back-up-right in Dex's back-eyes and whispering, "What is it?"

Dex looked guiltily back-up-right at Syrdian, whom hie'd completely forgotten about. Hie shrugged hies wings and said, "I don't know. Some strange kind of meteorite, I guess."

After a long pause Syrdian asked quietly, "Where were you going? Before... you know... before the meteorite landed?"

Dex thought about lying. Trying to sugar coat it somehow. But hie was sick of Syrdian's attitude. Hie shrugged hies wings again and said, "I was leaving. You don't seem to want—or appreciate—my help." Hie heard a gasp of indrawn breath back-up-right. Dex rose and took a step closer to the meteorite, then crouched to watch some more. It didn't seem to be doing anything.

Syrdian whispered, "I'm sorry."

Dex shrugged hies wings, still intent on the meteorite.

"I... I know I've... been rude. And I haven't even thanked you for what you've done for me. I've been scared that I... *am* dyatso. But I guess I'll be able to fly with the leatherwork you did on my wing... once it stops hurting so bad?" Syrdian paused, and when Dex said nothing, Syrdian finished in a near whisper, "Thank you Dex."

Dex looked back-up-right at Syrdian. "You're welcome. But I'm not thinking that the leatherwork will be forever. I'm just hoping your wing will heal if the gap is held shut. Like wings can heal little rips."

"Really?" Syrdian said, raising hies right wing and looking at the stitching again. "I've never heard of anyone doing that before."

"Neither have I."

"Why did you do it then?"

"Didn't seem like it could make your wing worse." Dex shrugged a wing. "And if it does work, it'll make your wing a lot better." Hie took another step closer to the meteorite. Still nothing bad had happened.

"How long will it take to heal?"

Dex looked back-up-right with widened eyes. "How would I know? I assume about four eight-days, the same as little rips."

Syrdian's eyes widened, "But the migration! It's today!"

Dex blinked, "I know."

"But how will I go?"

"I don't think you'll be able to."

Syrdian's eyes were opened wide in full panic mode now. "But the summer heat… I won't… I won't live through that." The last five words had come out in a whisper. After a pause, Syrdian continued in a juddery voice, "That's why Qes called me dyatso isn't it?" Syrdian slowly sank down until hies chest nearly touched the ground. Hie sobbed softly.

Dex sighed. "I had some ideas about that too. But I don't know if they'd work or not." Hie turned back to the meteorite. It was just sitting there. Not even crackling or hissing like the first one hie'd seen come down. Well, the first one had been partly *in* the ground. Hie thought this one looked... beautiful! Like the finest "made" object from the very finest craft person. Very symmetrical, and smooth, it seemed polished, with a number of fine glassy beads near the top. Though it still looked infrared at the very bottom, the infrared coloring had faded just above the bottom. Dex wondered if hie could touch it without being harmed.

In a choked voice Syrdian asked, "What're your ideas?"

Dex shrugged hies wings, "They probably wouldn't work."

"What *are* they?" Syrdian asked plaintively.

"Go *up* the mountain, not south. The higher you go, the cooler it is. I think a lot of the non-flyers climb up higher in the summer."

"But it's hard to fly up there!"

Dex turned to look balefully back-down-right at the crouching Syrdian.

"Oh, right," Syrdian whispered. "*I* can't fly anyway."

Dex turned back around and stepped another step closer to the meteorite. It continued to sit there, slowly getting less infrared, but otherwise seeming unchanged. Tempted to reach out and touch it, hie decided to wait a little longer in case something bad happened.

Syrdian whispered hoarsely, "I'd have to walk through the forest just to get out of this meadow!"

Dex nodded and reached out to touch the meteorite. It felt cool. Nothing happened so hie stroked a finger over it. It felt hard. And smoother than hie could believe. Smoother than a polished stone out of a stream. Smoother than the beak of a great predator. Like the feel of a recently flaked flint surface, but without the ripples. Hie gripped it and lifted it off the ground. Hies eyes widened, it was lighter than hie'd expected! Most meteorites that reached the ground were heavier than rock. Some weren't, but they were porous. This one seemed to have holes in it, but only a few. Looking at the regular spacing of its features, its smoothness, its symmetry, hie couldn't help but think that someone had *made* it. Maybe it was hollow? Could there be a tribe somewhere that could make something like this? Could one of them have dropped it out of the clouds above and even now be watching and laughing as Dex made a fool out of himrself? Hie looked balefully up at the clouds, but saw no one flying in and out of the lower layers to watch.

Syrdian fearfully asked, "Will you stay with me?"

Dex set down the meteorite and turned hies head to look back over hies shoulder, "Will you carry dried meat?" he asked drily.

"Yes, yes! Whatever you say." Syrdian said eagerly.

"OK." Dex turned back to the meteorite. "I'll stay with you." Hie wanted to take the meteorite with himr, but hie wouldn't want to have to hold it in a hand all the time. Hie tried to think how hie could attach it to hies harness. "Let's start up the mountain. You get the staves and the rest of the dried meat. I'll meet you at the verge." Dex beat up into the air carrying the meteorite in one hand.

"Wait!" Syrdian plaintively called behind himr, but Dex ignored the cry, reaching height and coasting to the verge, beating gently with hies hind wings while carefully examining the verge for large splotches of infrared.

***

In awe, Norris stared at the creature. In the screen it seemed to be staring back at him. Actually he had the impression its eyes were moving up and down and around as if it were examining the entire rocket. He assumed they were eyes anyway. Shiny, smooth and yellow with a black pupil, mounted in a pair on the head.

A head that was far too small to hold much of a brain, even though the creature's approach and harness suggested intelligence. He wondered briefly if their nervous tissue was more efficient than Earth animals, allowing intelligence with a smaller brain. The eyes seemed to be closer to the bottom of the head than the top and it looked like there might be a cleft above the eyes, as if there was a mouth located *above* the eyes. No nostrils though, only the cleft and the eyes. Covered with fine golden brown fur, or something like fur, the creature looked... pretty, graceful, and... dangerous. He thought it stood about twice as tall as the three-foot rocket.

Another creature approached from behind the one examining the rocket. It seemed to be the same type as the first one, but walking, not flying. Its coloration seemed more silvery-yellow as opposed to the golden brown of the first one.

Was it friendly? Or coming up from behind to attack? Norris saw the second one also had a harness, though its leatherwork looked much simpler than the harness on the first one.

The golden one's head turned to look at the silvery

one. When its head turned Norris was astonished to see more eyes on the back of the head. Smaller and wider set, the posterior eyes looked somehow less important than the main ones. He realized they must either be nonfunctional or have less acuity. Otherwise the golden alien wouldn't have turned its head to look at the silver one with its frontal eyes. Behind the front eyes and in front of the back-eyes were four small trumpet shaped holes, the front ones facing forward and the back ones backwards. Even though he was trying to resist the temptation to assign familiar functions that belonged on Earth organisms, he immediately thought of them as ears.

Norris glanced around at the others. They were all gawping at the screens as well.

Emma said, "Do you get the impression they're communicating with each other?"

Norris said, "Yeah, they keep looking at one another then back at the rocket."

The creature moved closer to the rocket again. Roger said, "How are they communicating? Their mouths aren't moving and they aren't making any sound."

Ell laughed, "We didn't put a microphone in the rocket. They could be speaking English for all we know."

Roger snorted, "Duh. You're right... Hmmm, we should be able to use reflections off the laser window to pick up acoustic vibrations like spies do."

"Good idea, any ideas on where we'd go to pick one up?

Emma said, "Hey, I'm the instrument lady, remember? I'll get one ordered in a minute, just let me watch a little longer."

Norris said, "Don't forget they might communicate

with something other than audio?"

Ell said, "They don't seem to be making signs. I don't see any visual changes in their surfaces, they aren't emitting light. I'm not sure what other physical methods they might communicate with? You aren't thinking telepathy, are you?"

"Radio? PGR?"

Ell chortled, "Hah! PGR—in my face! Though it's hard to imagine using PGR for organism to organism communication since it would only hook you up with one other organism."

Norris smiled at her, "Maybe they all come from a queen creature that has entangled PGR communication to each of her subsidiary units?"

Ell grinned, "Hah! In my face again. OK, I'll grant your point, but I'm betting on plain old acoustic audio received through those holes between the front and back-eyes."

Norris grinned back, "And I'm betting with you. I just don't want to anthropomorphize and miss something important."

The golden one, which had moved closer, reached out and touched the rocket, causing their view to vibrate and tilt a little. Its eyes approached, presumably for a closer inspection. It turned its head back toward the silver one a moment. Then its wings extended and with a few beats it was airborne, taking their rocket with it!

Ell snorted, "I'd just been wondering whether we'd be able to have the rocket follow this creature when it left the area. Not an issue, eh?"

The group laughed with her. Emma said, "We've got to give them names to tell them apart when we're talking about them. I'm suggesting 'Goldy' for this one and 'Silver' for the other one?"

"OK, where are they, or 'we' going?"

They all watched in fascination as Goldy, carrying their rocket and their point of view, flared in to land at the forest's verge.

***

At the verge, Dex puffed hies lips for the scent of predator while pulling a pair of hies carrying straps off hies harness.

When hie felt fairly certain it was safe, hie set the meteorite down and cut a small branch off a limb. The end of the stick fit into one of the holes in the meteorite and Dex tied it to the carrying strap, then around the shaft of the meteorite. Hie did the same thing at the other end, then tied the two straps to hies harness so that the meteorite laid along the right side of hies chest. One of the little legs at the bottom of the meteorite dug into hies abdomen. Hie tugged at the leg wondering how to keep it from irritating himr. To hies amazement all the legs suddenly retracted down against the meteorite! Hie moved around, it felt fine now.

"What are you doing with the meteorite?" Syrdian asked coming up behind-left himr.

"Taking it with me. I've always liked meteorites."

"Why?!"

Dex shrugged hies wings and pushed through the verge into the forest. Hies back-eyes showed Syrdian following. Because of the thick canopy overhead, the underbrush thinned out for lack of light in a few paces.

Dex stopped and looked around once again, checking for any large infrared objects that might be predators. Hie puffed hies lips to smell as well. It seemed clear and so hie led the way uneasily up the mountain. Hie didn't like being in a situation where hie couldn't fly to safety.

"What are we going to eat?" Syrdian asked.

Irritably Dex said, "I hope you're working on figuring that out."

"Figuring it out? How?"

"How do you think anything *ever* gets figured out? Somebody thinks about it and tries to come up with a solution. You *have* been hunting and gathering haven't you?"

"Elders have always shown me how to do things Dex" Syrdian said quietly. "I've been hunting and gathering, yes, but never without flying."

"Well it's not as bad as it could be. At least I can fly. But I might not be able to catch enough food for both of us. I can scout. I can catch some of it. But what if something happens to me?"

"Like you decide not to stay with me?" Syrdian almost whispered.

Dex stopped and turned. "No! We're *walking* through the forest. I could be attacked and killed." Hie took a deep breath, "I'm planning to stay with you Syrdian, but you know anyone else in the tribe would leave you rather than risk their own lives not migrating. They wouldn't even walk through the forest with you."

Syrdian hung hies head, "I know. I know and I'm scared. I wouldn't have stayed with you and it makes me ashamed." Hie raised hies head, "I'm grateful, I really am. I hope that someday... I can repay you... somehow."

Despite hies recent recognition of Syrdian's selfishness, Dex had to resist the urge to wrap arms and wings around the still gorgeous Syrdian. "Well for now, try being quiet so we'll have a chance of hearing predators. And keep watch for large infrared objects and puff for predator's scent."

Obediently Syrdian pursed lips to pull air into hies mouth over hies olfactory patches, turning hies head to look around.

Dex stepped out again, heading uphill and wondering how hie'd let himrself promise Syrdian that hie'd stay.

~~~

Dex soon wearied of the long walk uphill through the unending dimness of the forest. The constant flittering about of the small forest fliers irritated himr. A couple of small territorial flitters had attacked himr and one had attacked Syrdian. They couldn't do a lot of harm, but trying to bat them away frustrated himr. Hie mused about how hard it was to walk up this hill compared to the easy glide down it yesterday. Suddenly Syrdian hissed, "Dex! I smell a predator!"

Dex looked around and saw a large infrared spot to hies right. Hie strained to see something besides the ill-defined infrared blob. Reaching back hie whispered back, "Give me two of the staves."

Syrdian handed two of the staves with their fire hardened points over and held the points of the other two staves toward the animal himrself. They stood waiting and wondering. After a few minutes the infrared blob moved closer, passing near a small shaft of sunlight. Dex thought it looked like a zornic, a medium sized forest omnivore. It was bigger than hie
~~~

and Syrdian together and doubtless would eat them if it could, but maybe... Dex raised himrself to full height and spread hies wings, whispering to Syrdian, "Lift your wings, make yourself big!"

The zornic stopped, then slowly backed away.

As the zornic faded out of sight, Dex turned and began trudging up the mountain again. Syrdian whispered excitedly, "That was amazing! How did you know it'd go away if you lifted your wings?"

"I didn't. But I think it was a zornic. They never leave the forest, eating carrion and plants and occasionally killing something. But, I wondered if, always living in the forest, its regular vision might not be very good and it might mostly see infrared. And it wouldn't have seen many winged animals or know that we weren't really as big as our wings make us look. I suppose it thought it'd found an animal big enough to eat *it,* so it took off."

***

The group watched the view from the rocket's camera zoom up to the edge of the forest and stop, presumably as Goldy landed. The view wiggled a little then stabilized at a slight tilt. Goldy stepped past their viewpoint and grabbed a small branch. Pulling out a wicked looking knife it cut a stick a couple of inches long off the branch. Norris said, "Is that a flint knife?" It had a rippled surface but none of them knew for sure what a flint knife looked like. Goldy came back and wiggled the rocket a little as it worked on it, just below the camera they were watching through so they couldn't tell what was happening.

Ell said, "I think it's shoving the stick into one of the

attitude thrusters! Why in the world...?"

In a moment Goldy brought a strap into view and seemed to be working with it, this time leaning close as if wrapping the leather strap around the rocket. Again, he was working just below the view of the camera. Then Goldy crouched out of view with another piece of stick and another strap in his hands. More wiggling ensued.

Norris turned to the others, "Do you suppose he's plugging one of the lower attitude jets too, and tying the plugs in place with the leather straps? If so why?"

Manuel said, "Maybe he's..."

"Yeah?"

"Um, I'm not sure. Maybe he's attaching a carry strap?"

A moment later Goldy stood and lifted the rocket up to his chest as evidenced by one of the screens showing nothing but a close up view of a fuzzy chest. Goldy's hands could be seen working around the rocket, blocking first one then another of the cameras as they moved. The bottom camera which had shown only the ground was up in the air now, showing Goldy's birdlike feet.

Manuel said, "Maybe just using the attitude thrusters as convenient attachment points for strapping the rocket to his harness."

No one said anything because Manuel had to be correct. The screens kept wiggling back and forth. Emma said, "I'll bet she can't get it comfortable because the legs are digging into her tummy."

Ell said, "Retract the legs." A moment later the wiggling stopped.

Roger said, "She? Are you seeing sexual characteristics that I'm missing?"

Emma elbowed him, "No, but you guys are calling her a 'he' which I see no evidence of either. So I'm calling her a 'she' until we know. They might not even have sexes!"

Grinning, Roger rolled his eyes, but said nothing. Their view moved forward into the forest. The view darkened and then brightened up as the AI compensated, though some of the contrast was lost in the low-light conditions.

A long period of walking through the forest followed. Shortly it got boring. "Why are they walking instead of flying?" Roger asked.

Norris said, "Maybe there's something in the forest they want and they can't fly to it through the trees?"

"I don't know, the trunks of those trees are pretty far apart and their wings are pretty short."

Norris shrugged, "I really have no idea. Maybe their flying agility isn't up to weaving around all the trees?

As the hike settled down to walking uphill and nothing else, Emma went off to work on a laser acoustic pickup for the rocket. Ell turned to the others, "This is exciting, but it's also kind of boring. I'm thinking that at most we should have one of us watching and telling the rest of us if something interesting happens?" She looked around at the others who all nodded. "I don't mind taking the graveyard shift from midnight to 6."

Norris laughed and said, "Sad to say, I'm an early to bed, early to rise person. I'm always up at 4AM and I don't have a class until 8. It'd be easy for me to do 4-7:30."

Roger said, "Why do we have to watch in real time? Why not just record the video? Then cruise through it at high speed later looking for the interesting parts?"

"What happens if Goldy starts to take the rocket apart?

"How would we stop him?"

"Fire up the engine, fly away if necessary?"

Emma signed up for 6 to 10PM so Ell took 10PM to 4AM. Wilson, Manuel and Roger all wanted to take shifts, but Manuel worried about how to handle a shift when he might be urgently needed to make things in the machine shop. Roger had to work around meetings with Bynewicz and Mullis. "But maybe Wilson, Manuel and I could work things out between us to cover the daytime hours each day?"

Wilson said, "My other assignments can be worked whenever I'm not busy with this, so I'll take the daytime observation whenever you two can't be available. When you guys can observe I'll do my other work."

Ell said, "We need to bring someone else in on this. Our group is kinda small for something this huge?"

Norris said, "How about hiring a student? Bridget's friend Belle Donovan from my Planetary Science class is astonishingly smart. She's killing all the tests and really enthusiastic about this kind of stuff. Students are usually pretty excited to have jobs where they don't have to do much." He looked around at the group. When no one said anything, he asked, "Should I ask her? Or you could get Bridget to ask her?" He looked back and forth. Roger and Emma were grinning at Ell who looked embarrassed. Manuel looked as puzzled as Norris felt. "What?"

Ell looked down at the floor and blushed, "Sorry Dr. Norris, but I need you to keep another secret for me. I *am* 'Belle.' I wanted to take your class, but it causes a lot of problems when I go to public places like the campus as 'Ell.'" She shrugged, "So I wear a disguise."

Dumbfounded, Norris stared at Donsaii, trying to reconcile Belle's long platinum blond hair, chipmunk cheeks, acne and thick hips with the beautiful young woman in front of him. Despite her flaws Belle was cute, but compared to Ell… He'd never seen anyone who could hold a candle to Ell, stunning no matter what she wore. Why would anyone disguise themselves that way? He looked at the grinning Roger and Emma, "Are you guys kidding me?"

Emma laughed, "Nope. Believe it or not, that's really her."

Flummoxed, Norris leaned back and gave way to a guffaw.

Ell cleared her throat, "But if you have any other students you think we could trust; we'd be happy to hire them. Meantime, how about if we start designing a follow-up rocket. Like this one, but with a microphone and speaker? A swiveling camera? Maybe some other means for communication?"

The team worked on a plan for the new rocket as the aliens, or "teecees" as they'd begun calling them, clambered through the forest for hours on end. They stopped to watch for a few minutes when Goldy and Silver stopped and confronted a large wingless animal with their pointed sticks. The animal walked on four limbs. Coming off its back in a location that seemed somewhat analogous to Goldy and Silver's wings there were two large limbs that reminded Norris of a gorilla's arms. Goldy and Silver stood tall and lifted their wings. This created a little tableau for a moment, then the big animal turned and ambled away.

~~~

They worked out most of the requirements for the
~~~

new rocket, but decided to finalize the actual plan when Emma had picked some of the actual components. Satisfied, they shut down the screens in the conference room and headed home. Emma started her shift watching the aliens' progress on her HUD, but when she got home she put it up on her big screen.

***

A couple of deks later Dex and Syrdian climbed down into one of the ravines and drank all the water they could, then filled their water skins. As they climbed back onto the ridge they were following up the mountain, they came to an enormous meadow. Dex distantly remembered the fire that'd cleared this area a few summers before. The huge area had some small trees clumping up in a few areas, but the grasses and other small meadow plants were still holding their own over most of it. Hie turned to Syrdian, "I think tonight we should stay in that clump of little trees near the high end. Can you clear a spot and start a fire?"

Syrdian narrowed hies eyes, "What are *you* going to do?"

"Try to catch some food."

"Oh, OK. Yes. Thanks!"

Dex beat into the air gratefully, tired of walking. Hie lifted along the tree line and once hie had altitude, curled out in a glide over the meadow, watching carefully for prey animals or food plants. Hie saw a patch of large flat leaves that hie thought signaled tubers and almost missed the burrower sitting near them, facing the other way. With a curl of hies left main wing and a flip of hies back wings hie stooped on the burrower, reaching out at the last moment for it.

Unfortunately, the burrower saw himr coming with its weak back-eyes. It darted for its burrow. Dex banked hard and stretched out hies left hind claw, touching, but not catching it.

Landing, Dex stepped over to the burrow, pulling out hies roll of heavy fiberlin. A pace away hie found some of the burrower's scat to rub on hies hands and on the fiberlin. Hie placed a noose of fiberlin around the inside of the burrow a few inches down inside. Then hie tied it to a hooked stick hie cut off a branching stem. More fiberlin connected the hook-trigger to a sapling Dex bent over. Hie hooked the trigger stick on the rock at the edge of the burrow so the tip of the stick obstructed the hole.

When the burrower came out and bumped the stick aside, the bent sapling would snap up, pulling the noose tight. Unfortunately, the burrower might get itself free if Dex didn't get there in time. Hie'd have to listen for it.

Dex then dug a couple of disappointing tubers up from under the broadleaved plants hie'd seen.

Sighing in disappointment hie beat into the air and over to Syrdian who was clearing a spot under five small trees for a fire. Syrdian looked askance at the tubers, "From the way you stooped I thought you'd gone after an animal we could eat."

"I did." Hie shrugged hies wings, "I missed. Tubers are better than nothing."

For a moment Dex thought that Syrdian would to turn hies nose up at the tubers, instead hie said, "Do you want me to cook them?"

"That'd be great! I've set a trap. I'm going to go watch it." Hie untied the meteorite from hies harness and leaned it up against one of the trees. A couple of beats lofted himr into a glide down to the burrow. Just before hie landed hie thought better of it and after coasting past the burrow hie beat up into the air to circle high over the burrow, examining the surrounding terrain for any other possibilities. Hie saw a couple of other burrows though the burrowers themselves weren't evident. After checking the one with the snare hie coasted down to the next burrow. This one didn't have any rock to hook the trigger on so hie had to cut and drive a stake to hook the trigger on. Then, in frustration, hie realized that hie didn't have enough fiberlin to reach the closest sapling. Looking around hie saw a worn path from the burrow running beneath the sapling. Hie cut a notch for hies trigger hook near the bottom of the sapling, bent the sapling, hooked the trigger and ran the noose from there to drape over the path. Then hie beat up into the air and over to Syrdian, pleased to see a small fire burning with the tubers spitted over it.

Syrdian said, "I thought you were going to watch your trap?"

"I set another one. I'm hoping we'll be able to see and hear them go off from here. I'm really hungry, how about you?"

"Yeah, I could even eat some talor."

Dex looked sharply at Syrdian and saw himr grinning ruefully, "Me too."

Syrdian said, "I'm afraid to ask, but why don't you fly back to the cave? I think my parents would come for me. Then you wouldn't have to do this."

Dex looked off into the distance, "And what if they told me you're dyatso? What if my parent won't let me come back?"

Syrdian's hearts hammered, "But, but my parents... wouldn't..."

"Don't be too sure. You know the tribe's policy. 'If you can't fly the migration, you're dyatso. You *must* fend for yourself.'"

Wings quivering Syrdian said, "But..."

"Besides, don't you think it would be easier for them... if they think you died cleanly at the beak of a talor... than if they had to come visit you dyatso... then fly away leaving you here? They have responsibilities to your younger siblings so they couldn't stay with you even if they were willing to give their own lives for you."

After a long pause Syrdian said, "Dex, I'm embarrassed to ask, but who are your parents?"

Embarrassed Dex shrugged hies wings, "Deltain and Genex."

"Oh, I know of Deltain. Hies leatherwork is famous, that must be where you learned." Syrdian looked meaningfully at Dex's elegant harness.

Dex thought it was polite of Syrdian not to mention the embarrassing Genex. Handsome and artistic when young, Genex had gotten addicted to fermented tubers and died many seasons ago. Deltain never told Dex exactly what happened, but Genex hadn't died well. Genex's poor standing had dragged Deltain's and their child's status down and was to a large degree responsible for Dex's low rank. The low rank that meant Dex could only admire Syrdian from afar.

Dex looked up at Syrdian, "Thanks, Deltain did teach me my leatherwork. I hope someday I'll be half as good as hie is." Dex's head snapped around at a flicker and a "twoosh" sound behind himr. The motion hies back-eyes had seen was the farthest of the bent saplings snapping upright. Dex beat into the air and coasted down to it. Seeing a burrower struggling in the noose hie pulled out hies knife. A quick stab down into the brain at the base of the neck ended its struggles. Hie loosened hies noose from under the two front limbs, carefully wrapping the heavy fiberlin back on the stick from hies harness pouch.

***

Emma watched in astonishment as Goldy and Silver broke out of the trees into a clearing. She got the distinct feeling they felt much happier in the open than they'd been in the forest. With a few vigorous wing beats Goldy rose into the air, though in the side camera Emma saw Silver continuing to walk out into the middle of the clearing. Once Goldy'd achieved level flight, Emma began watching the nose camera of the rocket which faced the direction Goldy was traveling. Occasionally her gaze flickered to the camera that'd been facing forward as Goldy walked and which now faced down at the ground. Emma didn't see the cause of Goldy's swoop until the last moment when she saw the small animal diving into its burrow.

Emma sent out an email message to the group, "Check attached video, Goldy hunting from air." Shortly she sent out another email, "Check attached video, Goldy building a snare!"

Emma's eyes widened as she realized that Silver'd built a fire, then to her amusement Goldy detached the rocket from her chest and leaned it up against a small tree. One side camera showed the tree's bark, as did the nose camera. The side camera opposite the tree showed mostly sky. One camera faced up the mountain. The last camera showed a small cleared area with the fire burning on one side of the image. Some lumpy things like ugly potatoes hung over the fire on sticks. But nothing was happening in the view she had. Emma considered extending the rocket's legs and using the attitude jets to set the rocket back up and shift the cameras around to get a better view. But she knew if she frightened Goldy and Silver away it'd be a tremendous loss. Emma settled in to do some reading while waiting for something else to happen.

Quite a while passed, then a brown object landed in the cleared area in front of the fire. The camera facing the fire had a good view of it. Emma narrowed her eyes as she examined it. It wasn't in the center of the picture, but pretty close. Emma'd zoomed all the way out to try to see something interesting at the periphery of the picture. Now she zoomed in on what appeared to be a small dead animal. She was pretty sure that it was either the animal that Goldy had stooped on earlier or a similar animal. Since it had escaped into a hole in the ground Emma thought it must be a burrowing animal like a rabbit. It appeared to have eight limbs. Four smaller ones that came off one side and four larger ones that came off the other side and reached around to the same side as the small legs. Goldy stepped into the picture and pushed it with a foot so it rolled, then stepped away. Suddenly it made sense. The four smaller legs were on the bottom now. The bigger legs came off the top of the animal, reminding her of a spider's legs. The big legs were long enough to reach the ground on the bottom side as well. The big legs, like those of the large animal in the forest had big claws on them. The modified claws looked like they could also be used for something, though Emma wasn't sure what.

Goldy reappeared, pulled out its knife, crouched and began cutting up the burrower. The skin peeled off with a few quick strokes of the knife, pulling up over the head like a shirt. The skin and the head were then chopped off. Then instead of making a longitudinal slice into a body cavity like Emma'd seen her dad make on fish, Goldy cut the neck off the body. Next Goldy cut transversely through the burrower just behind the front limbs. Goldy seemed to pause to break something bony at the back and the front before cutting the rest of the way around to separate the burrower into front and back halves. Then Goldy finished cutting through the body, exposing a cavity that she quickly pulled organ and intestine looking things out of, casting most of them aside, but keeping a few solid looking chunks. The limbs were twisted and cut loose. All the pieces were spitted on a stick and hung over the fire.

Emma had her AI send another email, "Check attached video, caught a burrower, cut it up. Cooking it!"

***

Darkness had fallen by the time Dex and Syrdian tore into the burrower and tubers. It tasted great! Dex wondered if it was just because everything tasted better if you'd hunted it yourself. Or perhaps just because walking all day had left himr so hungry? Hie eyed Syrdian who looked back at himr and said, "This is really good Dex. You're a great cook!"

Deeply affected by the praise, nonetheless Dex shrugged hies wings, “I think it’s just ‘cause we’re so hungry, but thanks. The tubers are done just right too.” Hie cocked hies neck, “I’m glad we didn’t have to eat talor.”

Syrdian ducked hies head. “The dried talor wouldn’t be *that* bad.”

Dex snorted, “Yes it would! But we’ll eat it before we starve and be grateful of it.” Hie found himrself very pleased with Syrdian’s changed attitude. “We should collect some more firewood so we can keep our fire burning all night.”

Syrdian said, “I already got some while you were cooking. Would you show me how your snares work? In case… in… if…”

Dex rescued himr, “In case I need help later?”

Syrdian shrugged hies wings in embarrassment, “Yes. In case.”

~~~

During the night another twoosh sound signaled the triggering of Dex’s second snare. Sure enough when hie looked that way Dex could see the infrared shadow of a burrower struggling in the air beneath the first sapling hie’d attached a snare to. Dex started to get up, but Syrdian said, “I’ll get it.”

Dex settled back down by the fire, somewhat amazed at the turn around. Syrdian had really begun to contribute. “Bring back the fiberlin,” hie called out.

“I will.”

***
~~~

Deltain landed on the ledge back at the cave, his hearts heavy. Hies wings sagged as hie walked back to hies leatherworking area. Someone was there and hies hearts lifted momentarily before hie recognized it wasn't Dex. Still, it might be someone with news of Dex. Then hie saw it was Ercole, one of Syrdian's parents. Hie said "Hello."

Ercole drew himrself up, "Your child Dex. The other youth tell me hie watches Syrdian… a lot."

Deltain shrugged hies wings, "I wouldn't be surprised. Syrdian's very beautiful. I didn't know."

"Syrdian didn't come back yesterday or today."

"I know."

"We think that Dex might have had something to do with it."

Deltain tilted hies head curiously, "How would hie have… 'had something to do with it'?"

Ercole's eyes narrowed, "One of the children saw himr leave the cave just after Syrdian did yesterday."

"So?"

"So, where did they go?"

"*I* don't know! I just spent the day searching for Dex. Hie hasn't returned either!" Deltain tilted hies head questioningly, "You think they're together just because they left at about the same time? Why aren't you asking Qes? Qes and Syrdian have been spending a lot of time together."

"Qes never saw Syrdian yesterday."

Deltain's head lifted and pulled back, signaling some disbelief, "You got that from himr?"

"Qes wouldn't lie."

"I hope you're right."

***

Ell took over watching TC3 events from Emma at 10PM. Once night had fallen and the teecees had settled down to sleep by the fire, she just kept an occasional eye on the screen with Allan monitoring to tell her if anything happened. Meanwhile, she opened Emma's files of the breaking down of the burrower's carcass, trying to understand what each of the structures Goldy exposed might be.

The preparation of the burrower had some elements in common with a dissection, though the handling of the internal organs left a lot to be desired. Still, Ell had only a modicum of familiarity with anatomy. She'd learned a little bit about Earth's animals in her biology class. They'd dissected a frog and studied some comparative anatomy. Nonetheless, she felt lost trying to compare what little she knew to what she saw on the video. She felt surprised to see that some parts of what she saw seemed a little bit like what she knew of Earth's animals. She wondered if it could be because, like Norris had mentioned, these animals might spring from DNA? That reminded her that they hadn't yet taken their biologic sample for DNA analysis.

Ell boosted the low light function of the rocket's cameras. Some leaves of the tree the rocket had been leaned against were pretty close to it. A bright light streaked across the screen that carried the view from the camera facing up at the sky. There must be a big break in the clouds because she could see a few stars. Tilting her head, she watched both cameras that had sky on them for several minutes. During that brief period she saw several meteors streak across the sky.

She thought, *This planet is getting pelted with a lot more space junk than Earth does.*

Ell again looked at the sleeping flyers who appeared to be dead to the world. Speaking to Allan she said, "Open the door over the rocket's arm."

The field of the camera didn't show the door, but Allan said, "It's open."

Ell looked at the teecees. They hadn't moved. Still keeping an eye on the teecees, she said, "Bring the arm out." Still no reaction from the teecees, so Ell directed the arm out to grasp a leaf and bring it back, putting it in the DNA testing compartment. "How long will the DNA test reaction take?"

Allan said, "Thirty minutes."

Ell went back to looking at the burrower "dissection" as she'd begun thinking of it, watching parts in slow motion and trying to parse the structures she saw.

We really need an expert, she thought.

Chapter Four

Harald Wheat walked back to his office from teaching his class on comparative anatomy. He'd been thinking about something else and almost gone to his old office. NCSU had certainly changed since someone began donating millions of dollars a year several years ago. The biggest part of the money was being spent in Physics, but Biology had a new building and salaries were up. The department had finally obtained some equipment that Wheat'd been lobbying to get for years. Everyone's enthusiasm was up and Harald's mood had improved.

Sara, the admin for the professors in his pod in the new building, looked up and gave him a weird look, "Dr. Wheat, your appointment's waiting in your office."

Wheat grimaced; he must have forgotten an appointment. He stopped and looked up at his HUD, asking his AI for his calendar.

He saw a listing for a "Raquel Blandon." She worked for some commercial company out in the Triangle. Interested in "consulting" services. *Oh,* the appointment had just been made this morning, and he hadn't re-checked his calendar until now.

He frowned, his experience with firms that asked for "consulting" hadn't been good. They frequently assumed he'd be happy to consult for free. Even worse, some seemed to believe that, if they did pay, he'd be willing to whitewash whatever environmentally unsound project they were undertaking.

He walked over to Sara and said in a low voice, "How'd this woman get on my calendar? You do remember I don't want to talk to commercial people unless they've agreed to pay full fare for consulting?"

Sara looked at him with a twinkle in her eye. "I tried to tell her you wouldn't agree to it until I'd talked to you. She agreed to pay *double* the usual consulting fee if I got her in this morning. I told her I'd put her on, but that you might still refuse… I think you'll be sorry if you don't talk to her though." She raised an eyebrow, "Would you rather I told her to leave?"

He rolled his eyes. "No. I'll talk to her if she's actually going to pay. But I'll bet you I'll be tossing her out."

Sara's eyes twinkled, "I'll take that bet. Lunch?"

Harald tilted his head in surprise, "You're that confident? OK, you're on."

Bemused he headed on over to his office. Stepping in he saw a pretty girl in cutoffs and a t-shirt. *She looks like a student. Not like some corporate drone from out in the triangle.* "Hello Ms. Blandon," he said, sitting down and turning to face her…

Ell Donsaii!!

"Hello Dr. Wheat," Ell said, taking in his startled look. "Sorry to have scheduled this appointment under a pseudonym, but it sometimes causes problems if I make appointments under my real name."

"Uh… I suppose it could. Not a problem." He grinned, thinking to himself that Sara'd already won her lunch and he hadn't even started talking about the "consultation" yet. He winked at her, "Thanks for saving my planet!"

"Um, you're welcome. I'll relay your thanks to the folks at D5R that did the real work."

"OK, but I think no amount of real work would have solved that problem without a certain 5th dimensional theory?"

She actually blushed, "Thank you sir," she said quietly, "though it does feel like I just got lucky with that theory."

He chuckled and said, "Well, *I* feel lucky to be able to help you. What can I do?"

"We, at D5R, have need of someone with your expertise on a fairly urgent basis. We'd be happy to continue paying twice your standard consultation fee if you can look things over for us immediately?"

"Sure, though I probably owe you some free consultation for saving my planet. Tell me what this is about?"

"Um, yes sir. We'd need for you to sign a non-disclosure agreement first?"

Wheat narrowed his eyes. "OK, send it to me, but it'd have to be time limited. I won't have my academic freedom restricted."

"No problem, it should be on your AI now."

"Give me a minute to read through it? Or would you rather come back another time after I've read it? Or I could come to you out in the Triangle?"

"No sir, go ahead. I've got some work I can do on my HUD while I wait."

Wheat settled back to read, bemused to have Ell Donsaii waiting for him. And calling him sir! Even though her field was physics instead of biology, in his opinion she was the most important scientist in the world at present. And the person who'd saved his, and everyone else's life a few months back when comet Hearth-Daster came calling. He'd have been absolutely delighted and considered it a privilege to go to her office and wait on *her* convenience! He stole a glance at her, *And she's just a kid! A beautiful young woman, yes, but still, just a kid!*

Wheat looked back at his HUD. This NDA seemed pretty reasonable. It only required that he not talk about his findings for two years unless D5R agreed to earlier release. Any papers prepared regarding the findings couldn't be submitted for two years unless D5R agreed. His eyes narrowed and he cleared his throat. When Donsaii looked at him questioningly he said, "You realize that if my finding is that your company is doing something illegal or damaging to the environment or endangered species, that this agreement would not bind me against disclosure to proper governmental authorities?"

She looked surprised for a moment, then said, "Yes sir."

"Well then, I can agree to this. Do you want me to print and sign?"

"No sir, my AI has recorded your agreement. That's sufficient for us. I assume that your AI's made a copy for you?"

"Yes, and the AI record's fine by me too. However, you really should stop calling me 'sir,' Ms. Donsaii."

"Oh, I wouldn't feel right about that, Dr. Wheat."

Wheat rolled his eyes, thinking he owed her more respect than she owed him. She was the one with the Nobel Prize, after all. He shrugged, "OK, what is it you want me to do? Some strange animals on your property or something?"

Donsaii smiled enigmatically, "I'd like you to watch some video with me. Can I close your door?"

Wheat nodded and noted with some surprise that

she made the simple act of rising to shut the door remarkably graceful. Gazing at the closed door with a far away look in his eyes he tried to understand just what there was about the way she'd moved that so entranced him. He'd watched animals in motion for much of his life and her flowing movement seemed better than "catlike." He felt pretty sure it wasn't just her attractiveness, instead it was something about the way she moved, more confidently, smoothly and elegantly than anyone else. No wasted motion, simple smooth perfection. He shrugged mentally, *No wonder she won those gold medals at the Olympics.*

She interrupted his woolgathering, "Dr. Wheat?"

"Um, yes?"

"Is it OK if I put it up on your big screen?"

"Sure." He turned to face the screen as an animal was tossed to the ground in the center of the picture. At first offended at the callous treatment, then dismayed to realize it'd just been killed, then feeling the hair stand up on the back of his neck. *It has eight limbs! And that's no arthropod! Fur? How big is it? Floppy neck. No tail. This was a completely unknown animal! It didn't even fit into any known phyla! My God... and someone just killed it!* With dismay he considered the horrifying possibility that this might've been the only remaining live specimen. *The large upper arms have horny looking tips that might be adapted for fighting? Or digging? What if this species's been living underground and simply hidden from modern observation all this time? Please, please don't let this have been the only one?!* He turned to confront Donsaii but then a large clawed foot appeared and rolled it over. Could this thing be tiny? Maybe filmed with macro lenses? And the clawed foot's from some kind of bird? If so the video must have been slowed down because, in the world of the small, things happened much faster than what he was seeing on the screen.

Wheat's eyes narrowed. The animal appeared to have been rolled onto its stomach, four smaller limbs below. The larger limbs seemed to come off the upper part of the animal. The front pair of the upper limbs at present dangled down to the ground. Did they normally reach the ground and assist with locomotion? Or did they serve some other purpose and were just dangling to the ground in the flaccidity of death? Limbs on the top, i.e. wings, and limbs on the bottom, i.e. legs, was a common body plan in Insecta but this animal didn't look like it had an exoskeleton and only had four, not six, limbs on the bottom! At first he'd thought it had a flexible snout like an elephant, but the end of the snout seemed to have eyes on it? Could that be the head?

The clawed feet reappeared. Looking like bird feet except with a fuzzy covering rather than feathers. Then another pair of fuzzy skinned limbs appeared from above, holding a primitive knife! "Hah!" Wheat sat back, suddenly enlightened. "That's some *very* good CGI. You had me completely fooled for a minute or two." He frowned, "So what are you doing in the movie business?" *They're wanting me to consult on some kind of sci-fi movie? It's comforting to know that someone in the movie business is trying to get the science right!* He looked at Donsaii expectantly.

She'd paused the video and now turned to look at him quizzically, head turned to the side. Her smile began as a little quirk of the lip, then spread across her delicate features, stopping just short of when he thought she'd begin laughing. She looked positively delighted. "How about if I get you to watch the rest of this clip, then I'll show you a few others? Then we'll talk about how I got into the movie business?"

Donsaii still looked like she was suppressing a laugh. Wheat turned to the screen again, raising an eyebrow. On the screen the skin was deftly removed with a few strokes of the (flint?) knife, peeling it up like taking off a t-shirt.

The detail here's amazing! Wheat thought to himself. *For a small throw away part of the movie, one that doubtless contributes little to the main storyline, they've invested heavily in making this look right!* Wheat's respect for the filmmakers rose immensely. He'd been impressed that they wanted his scientific help, but what they'd already done showed careful attention to detail.

The knife then went back to peel the skin off of the limbs. Then it made a transverse cut through the body of the animal just behind the front limbs.

The head of the dissector dipped into the view! Wheat leaned forward in amazement. Rather than creating an inexplicably different creature, like an amateur might have, the filmmakers had put the head of the dissector on a prehensile neck as well. It also had four eyes, like the animal it was cutting up! They'd designed this animal like it was a distant relative of the one it was cutting up—like one would actually expect on an alien world with evolution doing its thing. So many filmmakers would have thought it "more interesting" to have some *completely different* types of aliens cutting each other up in their movie, no matter how unlikely it would be to find bizarrely different body plans in the same evolutionary tree. But, these two looked like they could've evolved from a common ancestor.

The alien paused to break something bony at the back and the front of the animal before cutting the rest of the way around to separate the animal into a front and back half. Then it cut the rest of the way through the body, exposing a cavity it quickly pulled organs and intestinal looking things out of. It cast most of the organs aside, but kept a few solid looking chunks. This was done so quickly that Wheat suspected the animator hadn't wanted to spend time showing each of the organs and trying to make them appear realistic. The limbs were twisted and cut loose from the body. Then all the pieces, neck, eight limbs and two body parts were spitted on a stick and hung over the fire.

Putting the spit over the fire the entire alien finally came into view. Wheat's shoulders sagged a little in disappointment. The moviemakers had decided to give wings to their alien, but in a typical moviemaker fashion had made them far too small to lift such a large animal. He tilted his head, *unless of course these are small animals seen greatly magnified. Insects fly with small wings because they're tiny.* He shrugged to himself, *but if that's the case, it's ridiculous to imagine that a tiny animal could be intelligent. Also, look at the tiny size of the head on that thing. It couldn't have enough brain in that diminutive cranium to be intelligent, even if it* was *full size.* Wheat quirked his mouth, *the fire's wrong too. Look how energetically it's burning just a little bit of wood. They must have added accelerant to it for it to burn so brightly. Or it could be a CGI fire.* He felt disappointed that they'd gotten these things wrong after doing such an amazing job with the little alien animal, *But then*, he thought, *they wouldn't need me, would they? If they could get it* all *right without my help?*

Wheat turned to Donsaii, “So you want my critique?”

Eyes twinkling, and a couple of fingers pressed to her lips, Donsaii nodded.

Following the principle of giving compliments first and making criticisms second, Wheat told her that he thought the computer algorithms they were using had produced astonishingly realistic imagery. Then he pointed out that when the animal had been first tossed into the frame it had bounced a bit too high. He went on to compliment the similar structure of the alien and its prey, but to point out that the wings on the alien were too small for flight and the head too small for intelligence. He finished up with the fire that burned to vigorously for the fuel it was consuming.

Donsaii nodded, “Can I show you some more video?”

Wheat checked his calendar, he didn’t have anything pressing and, they were paying handsomely. His department’d be pleased to have him bringing in the cash and he’d get a share of it. *Besides, it’s for Ell Donsaii.* He nodded and turned back to the screen. An image of a planet appeared on a black background. Almost entirely white with some spots of blue. Donsaii spoke to her AI and the view jumped closer several times then curled in around the planet. A few more jumps and it descended into the atmosphere, then into the clouds, then through the clouds to show splotchy green everywhere.

The detail continued to astonish Wheat as the viewpoint slowly dropped down to a landing in a meadow surrounded by an enormous rain forest. Similar to an Earth rain forest, yet without a single piece of flora he recognized. Some obviously modeled on Earth's trees, but much too tall for the diameters of their trunks. He mused, *Perhaps, if the trunks were constructed of stronger material than the cellulose of Earth's plants?* Then something flew across the image. His eyes widened, *the alien?* It crossed the field of view again, closer this time. Shortly it crossed the field one more time as if it were circling. When he would've expected it to cross again, it landed instead, the eyes in that prehensile neck looking at him. *My God, something about that gaze... somehow they've managed to make it look intelligent! It has a harness made out of leather or something. And, there's the hilt of that flint knife. The wings may be too small, but they beat like wings should, instead of with that oddly "wrong" motion of most of the CGI wings I've ever seen.* The filmmakers must've studied tiny bird's wing beating in slow motion and modeled them. Or something? He turned to Donsaii, "That's amazing! You must be dedicating supercomputer time to the CGI or somehow doing something far more sophisticated than the big studios."

He tilted his head, "But why? I thought you were into physics, not sci-fi movie making?" He carefully didn't express his disappointment that she'd use her prodigious talents for making movies instead of continuing her research, or whatever you would call turning out profoundly new technology at an unheard of rate the way she'd been doing. He supposed she had the right to do whatever she wanted with the talents God gave her, but he felt troubled nonetheless.

Donsaii seemed to struggle with her expression a moment, then her face turned serious. "Thank you for the compliments. It's gratifying that you'd believe I could make such a movie from scratch, but I really have no talent along those lines."

Wheat cocked his head, "Who then?"

She smiled, "No one."

Wheat stared at her in confusion a moment, then felt icy prickles run down his back, "Huh?" He suddenly remembered that this girl had saved the space station and stopped a comet. She was probably more accomplished and comfortable in the realm of space travel than movie making. But that couldn't be any planet in the solar system! He frowned, *Was it?*

Wheat turned to look at the screen again, still showing the intelligent appearing eyes of the... alien? "Uhhh," he said, "You're not trying to say that's a real alien?"

"Yes sir," she said quietly.

"But... but the wings are too small!"

"Ah, yes sir. The atmosphere is seven times denser and the gravity is only 0.27G."

Wheat drew back, considering, "The dense atmosphere makes the fire burn hotter too?"

"Yes sir, besides, it's 36% O_2."

"Oh." He leaned back, thinking again about his objections. Of course the animal bounced high if the gravity was low. He thought through his other nitpickings. "But the head of that—presumably smart—alien, it's too small to hold a brain big enough to be intelligent!"

"Yes sir, we have a couple of hypotheses on that?"

Wheat nodded for her to go ahead.

"One, it has a small brain in the head that has more efficient neurons than ours, so it still has the computational power to make it intelligent."

Wheat shrugged, "Seems unlikely, but I can't rule it out."

"Two, it has a large brain, located somewhere other than the head. Similar to the possibility that many of the computations carried out in *our* brains actually occurred somewhere in the spinal cord of the enormous dinosaurs with their notably small cranial cavities."

"Well yes, but in a huge dinosaur it would make more sense for the 'computations' as you call them, to occur closer to the body parts being controlled. Otherwise the messages' transit time from the brain to, for instance, the hind limb would've taken so much time as to be problematically slow. But I assume this animal isn't huge?"

"No sir, it appears to stand a little more than twice as tall as the three-foot-long rocket that's observing it."

That statement reminded Wheat that she was claiming to be observing real aliens on another world. His eyes narrowed, "Wait, that can't be a planet in our solar system! Are you claiming that one of your, admittedly amazing, little rockets already reached another star!"

"Um, yes sir. As you know, the rockets are possible because we can send fuel to them through portals connecting us to them through another dimension?"

Wheat nodded.

"We can open a port to another location that doesn't have a port mechanism at that location, though the accuracy is poor. We opened a *lot* of ports near Tau Ceti before we had one open close enough to put a rocket through. It still took *months* for the rocket to fly the rest of the way to TC3."

Wheat sagged back in his chair, "TC3?"

"Our shorthand for the third planet of Tau Ceti. The one you've been viewing."

"You haven't named it?"

"No sir. We thought it might be nice to let the public pick a name."

"You're going public?"

"*Not* anytime soon. We want to understand it better first. We desperately need *your* help with that part of it."

Wheat felt more prickles under his scalp. *She's handing me the opportunity of the* millennium *for a biologist! The first to describe the flora and fauna of an alien world!* He wondered if he was worthy. "So, do you have questions? Or do you want to let me look at all the recordings you have and prepare a report?"

"How about if you look through the... 'dissection' we've been calling it, even though it really was more in the way of a cleaning before cooking. We'd like your thoughts on the anatomy? We're looking for your comparative anatomy expertise."

Wheat chuckled, "I don't think anyone has much alien comparative anatomy expertise."

"You get to be first then!" she said brightly.

"OK, can you take me back to the start of the dissection and run it in slo-mo?"

On the screen the knife chopped the head off the floppy neck. "Hold it there. Note that the neck appears boneless? It's hard to imagine having the spinal cord in a neck without some bony protection for it."

"Might not have a spinal cord as we think of it?"

Wheat paused a moment, then shrugged, granting the possibility. "Let's run some more video." They watched the skin being peeled away for a moment, exposing a brownish layer that Wheat had thought was muscle the first time through, but now he noticed it seemed somewhat amorphous. “Earth animals keep fat under the skin. Provides insulation and padding and the increased weight of the good times is evenly distributed. That might be what we’re seeing here even though it’s brown instead of white? Do we know anything about their chemistry?”

“The plants contain DNA, according to a reagent test.”

Wheat tilted his head, “Really? Maybe panspermia’s right after all.”

“‘Panspermia’?”

“The theory that life didn’t start here, but that DNA spread throughout the universe in bacterial spores etcetera and thus forms the basis of life everywhere. It might evolve into different life forms on each world, but it always uses DNA for genetic encoding.” He shrugged. “*I’ve* always thought it was a ridiculous theory, but it wouldn’t be the first time I was wrong.”

“Oh, yeah. We’ve talked about that theory. It’s why we equipped the rocket to test for DNA.”

Wheat turned his head back to the screen, so Ell resumed the video.

Having completed the skinning, the knife made a transverse cut in the body of the animal just behind the front limbs. “Stop!” Wheat tilted his head. “Why transverse?” he mused, “For Earth animals the next incision’s longitudinal. Run it back a little.”

Ell ran it back through the skinning.

“Watch the body as he bumps it around during the skinning. It looks pretty stiff as if it has a skeleton or ribs or something all around the body cavity instead of only parts of the cavity like Earth animals. If so it'd be hard to cut longitudinally because of the completely circular ribcage. Cutting transversely between such ribs would be easier, eh?"

Ell narrowed her eyes as she watched the video again, "I see what you mean..."

"Then there's some kind of bony structures at the front and the back that are joining the two halves he's created. Something going from one rib to another. I'd be guessing a spine except you're working so hard on me to keep me from ascribing Earthlike vertebrate structure. Slow it way down, zoom in... let's watch the transection part of the video over a few times... Stop! Back up a little. There's a circular bone like a rib exposed there for a second. Oh! And a little joint visible there at the back, see he pops it loose with a claw there? And a little bone going, presumably from the rib ring above to the rib ring below? Not hollow like our spinal columns. Ho! And look, another little jointed connector bone in the front, opposite the one in the back."

Ell paused it with Goldy popping the front joint loose. "They look like they'd let the ribs twist and tilt relative to one another, thus providing some rotational and lateral bending motion?"

"Exactly!" Run some more video," Wheat said excitedly. "No! Wait. Pause it. Let's just look at the head of the dissector alien for a moment. Hmmm, it looks like there are some big forward facing eyes below the mouth and smaller backward facing eyes above and behind the mouth. Wait... *is* that the mouth? I'm realizing I haven't seen it open."

"Yeah, we have just a few seconds of Goldy, as

we've been calling it, eating in front of the camera. Definitely a mouth. Here..." Ell had Allan play the video of the few moments Goldy appeared in frame while eating the neck of the burrower after it'd been cooked.

"Ooh, black teeth! Hard to tell much about the dentition with black teeth in dim lighting. But... look at it bite right through the neck. Can't be any spinal column in the neck if Goldy can chomp through it like that! Back to the eyes." Ell jumped the video back to where it'd been. Wheat leaned forward as he stared at the eyes. "Maybe... high quality forward binocular vision for hunting and low quality backward facing eyes to warn of impending predation? And those holes look like ears. I know you're wondering if we can assume that similar appearance means similar function but notice the translucent appearance of the edge of the one eye focused on the dissection? Translucency is a pretty compelling argument for a light receiving structure. The trumpet shape of the ear holes is also a compelling argument for a structure intended to focus acoustic energy. Again notice, forward *and* backward facing earholes. I'll bet when we go back and zoom in on the animal he's cutting up, we'll find some similarities in the eyes and ears."

"Yes sir," Ell said, "the eyes of the smaller animal are more equal in size and more evenly spaced, I'm thinking to provide a nearly 360-degree warning of predators like herbivores have here on Earth." The head of the small animal popped up on the screen.

"Yep, even better with four eyes I'd think. Oh, and look, the backward facing eyes are oval and the tops extend up higher on the head. I'll bet it can see above itself pretty well. That'd be important on a world with a lot of flyers. Wait, I'm assuming a lot of flyers, but haven't seen them. Have you seen others?"

"Yes sir, we have a lot of video of Goldy and Silver walking through the forest and there are huge numbers of small flyers in amongst the trees. And if you watch carefully, when they were in the meadow, there were quite a few little flyers popping up here and there. I think there might normally be even more, but they could've been frightened away by the descent of the rocket."

"Wait, how in the world are you following Goldy and... Silver?" At Ell's nod he continued, "Following them around with a rocket? Something like that should scare primitives half to death."

Donsaii smiled at him, "Goldy picked the rocket up, strapped it to its chest, and took it along."

Wheat leaned back in his chair, flabbergasted. After a moment he waved weakly at the screen for Ell to continue.

Goldy cut the rest of the way through the body, exposing a body cavity front and back of the cut. He pulled the two halves apart and coils of material fell free. "Those tubes look like intestines of course. It's hard to imagine a body plan that doesn't follow some kind of tubular structure wherein the food is pulled through the central tube for digestion. Food needs to go inside somewhere to be exposed to enzymes, etcetera, in order to break it down for absorption. Pulling it in and pushing it back out of the same hole is less efficient than passing it through a long tube with different things being done to the food at different stages."

Donsaii nodded her understanding. She'd stopped the video to listen and he waved to start it up again. As the video resumed, Goldy reached into the front half of the body with his knife. He deftly made some cuts and pulled stuff out. Wheat quickly put his hand up to halt the video. "I'll bet that mass of soft pink stuff is for oxygen exchange. It seems kind of flimsy like our lungs." He tilted his head, "though it doesn't look as soft as mammalian lung tissue is. A little more like gill tissue I'd say. That solid chunk that came out might be a heart analogue, or liver or kidney I suppose. We have no way to even guess about solid organs." He waved to start the video again, "Same for *those* solid looking chunks." Goldy had deftly spun the knife inside the back half of the body cavity pulling out more intestine and several more solid looking structures. "Wait! Go back!" He had Ell run the video back and forth some. "Look at that! The pulmonary tissue has a tube coming off the front and *another* off the back. I'll bet that the air comes *in* through the front tube and *out* through the one in the back. That's more efficient. Going in and out the same passage like *our* lungs do, mixes old air with new. Gills obviously pass water through for fish, but birds also have a mechanism to pump air *through* their lungs instead of pulling it in and pushing it back out the same way. He's a fascinating bugger!"

"Dr. Wheat?"

"Yes?"

"You keep referring to Goldy as 'him.' Is there something you're seeing that tells you Goldy's male?"

"Hah! No, sorry, just ingrained habit. A bad one. I've seen nothing suggesting maleness and it might not even be a reasonable concept. For all I know these guys split like yeast."

***

"And so," Ell said to the group, "Dr. Wheat's everything we could've hoped for. He had great insights into the alien's anatomic structure, etcetera. Once he believed it wasn't some kind of new sci-fi movie anyway."

Everyone'd had a good laugh when Ell described Wheat's initial assumption. Then Ell resumed, "I swear, he's so excited he'd try to watch the video 24/7 all by himself if he could. In any case, he'd really love to take some shifts and get our feeds of all the bits we think are interesting. I suspect that he'll even be watching a lot of the parts we think are boring, trying to classify the flora and fauna we don't care about." She looked at Emma, "He's going to take your shift this evening so we can go to the Velos concert."

Emma did a little fist pump. The group turned to finalizing the design of the followup rocket, now that the parts Emma ordered had come in by overnight express.

***

Syrdian stirred the fire with a stick from their pile, bringing up a coal and starting the new stick on fire. Hie laid another stick on the burning one and turned to the second burrower from Dex's snares of the night before. Hie peeled off the skin. The night before hie'd only cut out the innards, leaving the skin on to keep little crawlers out of the meat. As hie skinned the burrower, Syrdian looked at Dex in the firelight, still sleeping. It seemed surprising that hie'd really never noticed Dex before yesterday. Sure hie'd known who Dex was, but never really talked to himr. Dex ranked low in the tribe but as far as Syrdian knew that might only have been because of Dex's drunken parent Genex, not any of his own doings or lack of accomplishments. In fact, now that hie was paying attention, Dex's leatherwork greatly impressed Syrdian and suggested that hies rank would rise given time.

Spitting the parts of the burrower on two slender sticks like hie'd seen Dex do, Syrdian mused that Dex had a handsome conformation. Powerful arms and elegant wings. Long graceful body and strong looking legs. And, Syrdian thought, Dex seemed very confident in hies ability to care for himrself. And, for that matter, for Syrdian too. Much more confident than most young dalin their age. Syrdian turned the spits and thought about Qes. Wouldn't Qes be surprised if hie came back at the end of the summer and found Syrdian still alive?

How had Syrdian ever thought hie loved Qes? Dex stirred. "Hello Dex." Syrdian said.

Dex used a wing to push himrself up a little. Tilting hies head hie said, "You're cooking?" Hie sounded delighted.

Syrdian felt immensely proud, "Yes, I watched you very carefully last night. I figured I'd better learn how."

~~~

They packed up, but before they resumed their hike up the mountain Dex examined several of the small saplings that were growing in the meadow. The little trees were beginning to turn the meadow back into forest. Syrdian said, "What are you looking for?"

"I had an idea in the night," hie said pulling hies heavy knife out of its scabbard and hacking off the top
~~~

of a small sapling a little shorter than hies arm. Hie hacked off some of the smaller branches and the leaves, leaving a stick that branched several times into a wide brush of sticks at the end. Hie swished it back and forth a few times. "Remember those annoying little flyers that kept attacking us yesterday?"

"Yeah?"

"This is going to be my flyer swatter."

"They're awfully fast. Do you really think you'll be able to hit one?"

Dex's wings shrugged, "I guess we'll see." Hie strapped hies meteorite to hies chest and they started up the mountain.

***

Deltain lifted off for another day of searching. Bultaken had decided to delay the migration for one more day to allow the tribe to search for Syrdian and Dex. Actually, the tenor of the tribe's talk left Dex a definite afterthought. Deltain felt certain the migration wouldn't have been delayed if *only* Dex were missing. Dalins had spent the night before packing up most of the goods that'd be left in the cave. Things that were too heavy to be carried on the long migration. The last of the packing would occur tomorrow morning. If Dex wasn't back they'd be leaving anyway.

His hearts filled with blackness, Deltain again considered staying behind when the rest of the tribe migrated. If Dex couldn't return and Deltain couldn't find himr, what was the point in migrating? What was the point in living? Syrdian's parents had Syrdian's two younger siblings, but Deltain had no one without Dex.

Maybe hie *should* stay, hie wasn't sure hie wanted to live without Dex. Despite Genex's problems, Deltain had loved Genex and Dex was Deltain's last link to himr. Dex... Deltain thought Dex had inherited Genex's artistic genius.

Hopefully without Genex's love of fermented tubers...

Pain filled Deltain's chest.

***

Ell walked up to the doors to the White House Entrance Hall. "Hello, I'm..."

The Marine sentry came to attention and said, "Ms. Donsaii, we're expecting you."

~~~

President Flood looked up as the door to the Entrance Hall opened and a young lady stepped inside. He recognized the short strawberry blond hair. As he'd requested a staffer stepped in with her and announced in a stentorian voice, "Ladies and Gentlemen, Ms. Ell Donsaii."

She stopped inside the door, startled. She covered her mouth and in the sudden silence they could all hear her say, "Oh! Am I late?"

Someone began to clap. The assembled guests joined in, building to thunderous applause.

Flood turned to former President Teller, whom he'd invited, "My God, you're right, she *is* astonishingly beautiful. I'd never have dreamed it wasn't all retouching."

Teller shook his head, "And I've never seen her in a
~~~

little black dress, so I really had no idea just how... *gorgeous* she could be."

Like everyone else in the room, Teller stared. Medium heels made her long slender legs even more lissome. The aforesaid black dress was a simple sheath dress set off with a single string of white pearls. Matching small single pearls adorned each earlobe. And that was all...

The very simplicity of the outfit, on her slender form, made the gowns of the other ladies attending seem gaudy and... somehow... tawdry.

Flood walked toward her, holding out his hand. "Ms. Donsaii."

She held out her hand, still looked horrified, "I thought it was at 6:30? How... Oh, I must be *so* late."

Flood took her hand, covering it with his other hand, "Ms. Donsaii, the guest of honor is *never* late."

"Oh my," her hand went to the base of her neck, "no one told me. I'm *so* sorry. And I can see I should have worn something... more formal."

Flood leaned closer, "I guarantee you," he whispered, "that every person in this room wishes they had once in their lives looked half as good as you do. Now, I need to introduce you to them."

Taking her hand, he led her around and began introducing her to his cabinet, the leaders of the Senate and the House, the Chief Justice, and the ambassadors from many countries. The Prime Ministers of Canada, Australia, and the UK were present in person. Wide eyed, nonetheless she met each of the guests with aplomb, and obviously knew exactly who each person was prior to the introduction, murmuring appropriate words to each.

When the President turned to his last two guests, her eyes flashed wider than before. He said, "And I believe you know..." eyes shining, Ell threw her arms around them, "your mother and grandmother."

Flood heard her hiss, "You *knew* and you didn't *tell* me!"

~~~

The news anchor said, "And now we take you to the White House where a special announcement is to be made by President Flood."

The screen faded to the White House State Dining Room, then zoomed in on President Flood at the head table as he rose to speak at a lectern. "Hello, I would now like to welcome the world to this dinner, held in honor of a most astonishing young woman."

He cleared his throat, "On March 1st of this year, our planet Earth had a date with destiny... Comet Hearth-Daster's trajectory... had very likely scheduled the end of civilization as we know it." He reached up and rubbed the corner of one eye with a forefinger, then continued huskily. "It's quite possible that most major life forms, including man, would have become extinct on that fateful day."

He looked around the room, then into the camera, "Just a few short years ago, there would have been nothing we could have done to prevent the impact of that comet. Because, that would have been prior to the advent of the astonishing young woman we honor tonight." He turned to Ell, "Please stand." The President waited while she did so and the room again burst into spontaneous applause. Ell stood blushing demurely, nonetheless drawing the eye. Flood turned back to the cameras, "Bursting into our awareness five years ago at
~~~

the summer Olympics, Ms. Ell Donsaii not only won four gold medals in the gymnastic portion of the Olympics, she single handedly stopped a terrorist attack directed at our Olympic athletes. For this, President Teller," he waved a hand at Teller in the seat to his left, "awarded this young lady the Medal of Honor, our highest military honor, for 'acts of valor, above and beyond the call of duty.'"

When the applause subsided the President continued, "Having begun her college career at the United States Air Force Academy under a special dispensation allowing her to start at the unheard of age of 15, she completed the requirements for graduation within two years, graduating at the age of 17. During her time at the Academy she wrote a paper entitled 'A Possible Mechanism for Quantum Entanglement through an Unperceived Dimension.' A paper destined to shake the world of physics to its very core. A paper for which she was awarded the Nobel Prize in physics this last December."

Flood paused again for the applause, surveying the room. He turned back to the cameras, "Within six months of entering a graduate program in physics at North Carolina State University she had worked out the principles of the quantum based PGR chips many of you have already begun incorporating into your lives." He chuckled, "Having accomplished that minor task, she dropped out, though I understand that NCSU intends to award her, not an honorary degree, but a full doctorate in physics for the work she did there, including a separate paper explaining the dual slit experiment, a conundrum which has beleaguered physicists since 1803." The room again filled with applause and the

President waited for it to die out.

"In any case, she dropped out of school, every parent's worst nightmare," he winked and turned indicating, Ell's mother Kristen Donsaii with a hand, "right, Ms. Donsaii?" he chuckled. With a grin she nodded and this time laughter, rather than applause broke out.

The President continued, "At this point, Ell Donsaii returned to active duty as a Lieutenant in the Air Force, where her country, in its wisdom, used her *prodigious* talents to fly Unmanned Aerial Vehicles or UAVs. You might think we had successfully shelved her in a location where she could no longer astound us? But, no, no, in less than one year on active duty in a minor post, Ms. Donsaii had, believe it or not, solved an enormous sociopolitical problem. The details of these events must remain confidential for now, but suffice it to say that she was awarded the Presidential Medal of Freedom, our nation's highest honor, other than the Medal of Honor, which I'll remind you," he raised a finger and made a checking-off motion, "she already had." Flood laughed with his audience.

"While on active duty as a UAV pilot, in her evenings, just to keep herself busy, the young lady did the research that confirmed the principles on which her ports are founded."

"Those ports, my friends, are what the intrepid Ms. Donsaii used to save the Space Station the next year... Those ports, are what she's provided to us, with which to explore the resources of our solar system. Those ports, are what are going to replace pipes and ships, and power lines, and tanker trucks, and... innumerable other things in this world. They... they're what *saved* us from Comet Hearth-Daster!" he said hoarsely.

Bracing himself on the podium and taking a deep breath, he continued, "Almost all of you know that the comet broke up into large fragments which were taken out by NASA using nuclear weapons provided by our military. Unfortunately, this left hundreds of smaller fragments, which, though they wouldn't have wiped us out, would have caused untold destruction and loss of life. You're aware that Ms. Donsaii's company, using her port based small rocket technology, took out those small fragments so that only two fragments reached the ground that were large enough to cause significant damage." He snorted, "We *did* lose a satellite... But, there was *no* loss of life! Even more astonishingly, she and D5R did this without even *asking* for compensation from us, the taxpayers."

"What you almost certainly don't know is that NASA could *not* have reached the comet with the nuclear weapons in time—without using rockets powered by Ms. Donsaii's ports!

"Ladies and gentlemen, every living person on this world of ours likely owes this young woman their life. If that comet had struck and you *had* survived, it would have been a mean and lonely existence.

"Therefore it is with some embarrassment that I tell you we are gathered here on this somber, yet joyful occasion, to award Ms. Donsaii a *second* Presidential Medal of Freedom, with distinction. It is our country's highest honor yet..." his voice broke, "and yet, it seems not nearly enough for... for what this young woman has," he cleared his throat and finished in a hoarse whisper, "has done for *us*."

The standing ovation lasted through the time it took the President to remove her pearls and put the ribbon of the medal around her neck. Silence fell as Flood gestured her to the microphone. Blushing again, she cleared her throat and in a voice barely louder than a whisper, said, "Thank you so much for this honor. Really... I've been *so* lucky... to have been born where I could get an education, where my dreams were not stifled, where I was lucky enough to become a part of some amazing teams. From West Carteret High School, to the Air Force, to the Olympics, to the teachers at NCSU, to the team we have at D5R, and to this country as a whole. I've been unbelievably lucky to have guessed right about how some things might work in physics. And I'm so grateful that this, *miraculous* streak of luck... allowed us to stop Hearth-Daster. I continue to believe... that I've simply been blessed... being in just the right place at just the right time." Her voice had faded to a whisper at that point. Nonetheless, she could be clearly heard in the dead silent room. Stiffening her shoulders, she stepped closer to the mike and in a trembling voice said, "Thank *you*."

As she stepped away, the room, still on its feet, built to thunderous applause once again as tears streamed down the cheeks of many in attendance.

Chapter Five

Harald Wheat settled in for his first session watching the aliens. He'd begged off his usual Friday night "date" with his wife and set himself up in his den where he had three screens. The biggest one he was dedicating to his main view. The second one displayed the view from the top camera. He'd divided the third screen into sections for the other three side cameras. A little portable screen that he'd borrowed from his son was showing the view from the bottom camera. Per his promise to Donsaii, he'd locked the door, hoping his wife wouldn't try to open it. It'd be difficult convincing her that any part of his work as a biologist deserved to be kept a secret from her.

Like Roger Emmerit had told him in the handoff, the teecees were hiking up the mountain through the forest. When Harald first opened his screens they'd dipped down to the stream for a drink. Harald's eyes flashed back and forth, trying to take it all in. All the flora seemed to have the gracile stems you might expect in low gravity. Little flyers fluttered here and there. Some flyers attacked others. Smaller ones seemed to be eating the plants and trees. None of them seemed to have feathers, reminding him of big bodied, small winged bats. Or to some degree, seeming like big soft bodied bugs.

One of the flyers dive bombed Goldy! Surely it was too small to pose a threat? Goldy ducked violently, thrashing out with the stick it'd been carrying. The stick reminded Harald of a tennis racquet, though, of course, it was slender. The ducking and swinging swayed Harald's view about in a sickening manner. Goldy missed the flyer, but made it abort its attack with a quick dart to the side. As Harald watched, the flyer buzzed up and off to the side, then pitched over for another dive. This time Goldy waited a moment then swung accurately, the branches of the stick savaging the wings of the flyer. The flyer bounced to the ground. Harald got the impression that Goldy only felt relief that the flyer wouldn't be attacking any more, but Silver darted forward. Holding the flyer down with a hind claw, Silver sank a knife into the base of its neck. The flyer quivered a moment then went flaccid. Wheat's eyes widened, could the brain be inside the body just behind the neck? There it'd be protected by what Wheat had thought were "rib like" bony rings during the "dissection." Located there, a brain would be protected from the bites of other animals, but easily taken out by a knife plunged down from above like he'd just witnessed.

***

Dex watched Syrdian with puzzlement as hie killed the flyer. "Why'd you kill it? With its wings broken it would've died anyway."

Syrdian shrugged hies wings, "Dinner," hie said, quickly cutting the flyer into front and back halves and scooping out the organs.

Dex tilted hies head curiously. Hie'd never eaten a forest flyer, but hie supposed they might should be edible. After a moment hie resumed hiking up the mountain. Syrdian fell in behind himr.

***

As the sun descended the next day, Dex and Syrdian reached the cliff below the Yetany tribe's cave. They were both tired but Syrdian had two more of the annoying flyers on hies harness. They watched the cave area for part of a dek. No fliers came or went.

The tribe had migrated.

Dex turned hies gaze to the cliff. Hie'd failed to consider that that cliff might be a problem. Hie'd flown over it hundreds of times. But now Syrdian couldn't fly. Looking up at it hie wondered if it might be possible to climb it. Dalin practically never climbed anything. Why would you climb something when you could *fly* to the top of it instead? Even if a dalin did climb onto something, a few reflexive wing beats almost always assisted the climbing.

Stilling hies wings, Dex stepped forward and sunk claws into some crevices in the cliff face. Hie pulled himrself up a bit, fighting the urge to beat hies wings a little. The limestone of the cliff face gave way, chunks falling out. The porous limestone on the surface had softened under the onslaught of the recent rainy season. It wouldn't hold himr.

"How am I going to get up the cliff?" Syrdian said, sounding dismayed.

In hies back-eyes Dex saw Syrdian staring up at the cliff in horror. Hie shrugged hies wings. "We'll think of something. Can you gather wood for a fire while I scout the cliff from the air?"

Still staring up at the cliff, Syrdian nodded. Dex beat into the air to circle up and out, then swung around to land at the top of the cliff. The cliff had been a constant feature of hies life. During the winters, the tribe lived in the cave above it, but hie'd never given it much thought. It wasn't useful and, because hie could fly over it, it wasn't a problem. Hie realized now the cliff may have hindered some of the big ground based predators from reaching the cave and that such protection had likely been a good thing. The cliff was about six body lengths high and extended as far as he could see to either side of the cave.

Hie didn't really know how far it extended without a break. Hie supposed that should be hies first mission. Perhaps Syrdian could simply walk north or south a ways and climb where there wasn't a cliff, or where there was a break in the rock face? Dex looked up toward the cave a moment, wondering if hie should fly up there, maybe it would give himr an idea?

Instead, hie beat into the air and rode the east wind rising up the mountain, sliding to the north and looking for a break in the cliffside. Though gliding easily through the rising air felt exhilarating after days of walking, Dex despaired at the unbroken wall of limestone, it'd take a long time for Syrdian to walk this far and hie still hadn't found a break. Dex turned and sailed back the other way, passing over Syrdian with a little wave and coasting along over the cliff to the south.

Once again, the cliff seemed to go on forever.

Dex eventually turned back, deciding it would be better to find a way to help Syrdian climb the wall. Walking around seemed like it'd take forever. At best walking around the cliff would be a way for Syrdian to continue climbing the mountain. But Dex would need to fly back to the cave alone and scavenge supplies so Syrdian didn't have to walk all the way back to the cave.

Dex coasted in to land next to Syrdian. It pleased himr to see Syrdian had built a respectable little fire in front of a recess in the cliff face that resembled a shallow roofless cave. When Syrdian had seemed so pathetic at first, Dex's infatuation had withered. But now, with Syrdian displaying more capability and mettle, Dex found himr very attractive once again. Syrdian had spitted the annoying flyers hie'd collected during their trek and suspended them over the flames to cook. Dex sucked a little air in over hies olfactory patches and the smell made hies mouth water. Syrdian said, "Did you find a place for me to climb up?"

"No. Then it started getting too dark to see, so I came back. I'll look again in the morning, but I wondered if you could climb up one of these trees if we cut it so it leaned up against the cliff face?"

Syrdian tilted hies head, "Climb a tree? I don't know. I've never tried." Hie shrugged, "I'll try it now." Hie walked to a nearby tree and looked up along the trunk. After a moment to gather resolve, hie reached up and sank his claws into the bark. Raising hies left foot hie sunk a set of toe claws in too. Pulling up with hies arms Syrdian surged up and pulled hies right foot up to try to sink its claws too. Suddenly the claws on the left foot ripped the bark loose. The sudden weight on hies hand claws ripped them loose too. As Syrdian fell back, hies wings ascended to beat for some lift and prevent a fall.

Behind Syrdian Dex shouted "No! Hie stepped forward, catching Syrdian beneath the wings with both arms. Hies primary intention had been to prevent Syrdian's beating hies wings and possibly tearing the sutured lacerations.

However, Dex felt a rush of emotion to find Syrdian's body against hies. Warm, firm, wonderful Syrdian. The Syrdian Dex had dreamed of holding for so many years now.

Syrdian turned hies head to look at Dex with hies fore eyes. "Thanks Dex, I'm OK now."

With a start Dex let Syrdian go. "Sorry, you scared me."

"I frightened myself too! I appreciate you catching me. I might have torn my wings! I don't think I should climb *this* type of tree though."

"You're right, let's try a couple of other kinds to see if their bark is stronger."

Dex and Syrdian walked around to several different types of trees, sinking in their claws and pulling. The bark readily ripped off every type they tried. Dex shrugged hies wings, "Oh well, I was worried about how hard it'd be to cut a tree so it'd lean against the cliff anyway. Let's eat, maybe we'll think of something during the night. If not, I'll fly the cliff again tomorrow and find a place for you to get around it, no matter how far it is."

Syrdian shrugged, "You'll think of something."

Dex glanced at Syrdian, thinking that hie had an unrealistic faith in Dex's abilities; *but* it gave himr a warm feeling.

Though, not as warm as it'd felt, holding Syrdian in hies arms.

Syrdian handed himr a couple pieces of flyer and hie took a bite. Hies eyes widened, *these flyers may be annoying, but they're really tasty!* Hie wondered about hiking into the forest with a branch in the future, just to try to swat some of them. Maybe even some of the flyers that didn't attack? Could there be a way to catch some of those too? Some kind of snare? As hie tried unsuccessfully to picture a snare that could catch a flyer, hie took some more pieces of flyer that Syrdian held out to himr. Hie couldn't imagine catching one of the small flyers, they were so agile they'd easily dodge such attempts. Hie wondered a moment about trying to put a trap on their nests, but the nests hie'd seen were high in trees, in the midst of thick branches a dalin couldn't fly into. Hie'd just learned hie couldn't climb trees very well either.

Dex and Syrdian finished eating the three small flyers that night and they talked a little while. Syrdian said, "It's getting pretty hot. I sure hope you're right about it being cooler higher up the mountain."

"I *know* it's cooler. What I'm worried about is what we'll eat up there." As they drifted off to sleep Dex wondered what they would eat in the morning.

***

Ell's car dropped her off a couple of blocks from Vic's new club in Carrboro. As the car headed off to park, Ell pulled her hoodie up over her ball cap and started down the sidewalk. She appreciated the brisk evening air since it made the hoodie seem like reasonable attire. She smiled to see a dispirited line waiting beside the ticket booth. Ell stepped up to the window and cleared her throat. The man in the booth uncrossed his arms and pointed to the "Sold Out" sign. He said, "Gotta wait in line for someone to leave." Ell leaned close to the window, "I think you're holding a ticket for me?"

He rolled his eyes, "Name?"

"Donsaii."

His eyes widened and his stool dropped forward off its hind legs. "Oh, sorry, Ms. Donsaii! We've been *hoping* you'd come!" Since she was only twenty, he issued her a red, "non-drinking," wrist band, then popped the door open.

Ell wandered in and headed to the bar for a Coke. Velos seemed to be on break. The place was packed, but the crowd wasn't as noisy as she'd have expected. Coke in hand, she looked around and wondered if the lower noise level might be due to the thick sound absorbent materials that covered the walls. The crowd seemed boisterous and people were talking just as loudly as you might expect from a vibrant throng, it just didn't echo around. Instead of struggling to understand people in the cacophony of a crowded bar scene she heard them clearly.

She leaned up against a post and watched the crowd. To her amusement the couple beside her were arguing about whether Velos sounded great because they were "an awesome band," or whether they sounded great because "the acoustics in this place are amazing." Ell just felt happy that the consensus seemed to be that "they and/or the place sounded great." She saw Emma and Joe Chan standing near the dance floor. Joe wasn't staggering, making Ell think he hadn't had anything to drink yet.

Though the stage remained empty, the guitar lick from the intro to Velos' new hit single "Alive at the End of the World" came over the PA. Ell surreptitiously looked around, surprised that they would play a recording of their hottest song at one of their live shows. The lick repeated itself, then again. A spotlight up on the stage faded on and slowly pivoted around until it pointed out over the crowd. It gradually drifted to the right wall and then down until it lit the curly red hair of someone facing the wall. Gordon slowly turned around and the spot expanded to reveal his guitar in his hands as he stroked the lick again. The crowd went wild, hooting enthusiastically. The next time Gordon played the lick, the bass came in too. Another spot came on, swung slowly around the club and focused on the bass player standing over by the left wall of the club. They cycled through the intro licks again. Then the snare began to pop on the backbeat. Another spot came up on the drummer. He'd mounted the stage while everyone was focused out front. He brought in a powerful kick drum thump on the one and the three. The lights snapped off and the music paused for a four beat. Ell felt the tension building in the crowd as a long sustained note faded in on their Hammond D3 organ. As another spot faded in on the keyboard player, he began arpeggiating the same chord that the intro guitar lick covered. A spot faded in on Gordon, now standing in the middle of the dance floor, with a mike on a stand beside him. He leaned into the mike, whispering the words of the first verse; Ell felt goosebumps at the eerie sound of the whispered verse over the Hammond. The words paused and Gordon played the guitar lick again, then the entire band came thundering in on the chorus while the crowd went even crazier than they had when Gordon first appeared in the spot.

Standing in the shadows, Ell pulled the hoodie back far enough to be sure it didn't affect her hearing. The music was loud! She felt the thump of the kick drum resonating in her chest. Gordon's traditional rough guitar sound was powerful to the point of being intimidating. Yet everything sounded so clear! Ell shook her head in amazement—she'd never heard live music sound so good.

~~~

When the song eventually faded away to enthusiastic applause Ell slowly became aware of a large presence on her right. She glanced over and saw Vic grinning at her. "Ms. Donsaii, thank you for coming—and thank you for what you did for all of us, as the President reminded us in his ceremony." He waved around the club, "What do you think?"

Ell grinned back, "They sound awesome!" She winked, "They must be really great musicians."

He grinned back, "They are, no doubt."

She raised an eyebrow, "You don't think it has anything to do with the incredible acoustics of this venue?"

He frowned and rubbed his chin as if considering, "Might have a little bit to do with it." Then he grinned proudly. "So, you like it?" He waved his arm again to encompass the bar/venue that was his pride and joy.

"Yeah! I think it's amazing. You sure do have an ear for these things. "I'm thinking my friend Belle's crazy aunt isn't going to regret her investment?"

Vic shrugged. "Opening nights can be good, yet everything can still go to crap, but *I* sure hope not... Are you gonna dance?"

Ell laughed, "I think I've done *enough* dancing at Gordon's concerts."

"No you haven't! I know Gordon's hoping you'll dance at this one. So am I. He left some space open at the right side of the stage again."
~~~

Ell said, "How 'bout just you and I dance, then you can tell Gordon I danced at his concert for him."

"I can't do any of that crazy stuff you do on the dance floor!"

"Let's just dance like everyone else. I've made a spectacle of myself plenty of other times."

Vic shrugged and moved out through the crowd toward the dance area. Ell followed, wondering if she could keep the hoodie up and try to remain unrecognized. Vic stepped out into the midst of the other dancers, almost all of whom were freestyling, and turned to face Ell. They both began moving to the music.

~~~

Vic mused that Donsaii didn't seem to be doing anything complex, just swaying to the music like he was, shuffling her feet a little and moving her arms to the beat. But, she did it so... elegantly. Not different, just better. *So* much better. Her clothing wasn't sexy, she wasn't performing any of her unbelievable athletic feats, yet he just couldn't take his eyes off her. He looked at her clothing, an ordinary hoodie with short t-shirt under and loose pants, not so different from a lot of the others in the bar.

In fact, other than her gracefully flat tummy peeking out from under her shirt, it seemed something more likely to be worn by a guy than a girl. Yet there was no doubt she was a girl. Though you couldn't see her very well with the hoodie up, you just had the feeling she looked good. Could it just be because he knew who she was?

Vic glanced around and saw most of the people nearby were watching her, both men and women. He
~~~

didn't think they'd recognized her, just that they were fascinated with her simply graceful, dance steps.

Then one of them pointed. Like a ripple around her, people began focusing on her, turning toward her and obviously recognizing her. He would have sworn Donsaii blushed even though her face was shadowed. The people around her opened up an area of the dance floor and several waved toward it, obviously hoping she'd dance one of her remarkable dances again. Instead she shook her head and backed up to the edge of the open area as if waiting for someone else to dance in it. When the song ended Vic took her back to a dark corner of the back bar and got her another Coke.

As they talked, he found she was amazingly down to Earth, he could see why Gordon was crazy about her, even though Gordon had only ever spoken a few words to her.

When Velos took their next break, Vic took her back to the band's dressing room. "Gordon, someone here to see you."

Gordon turned, "Ms. Donsaii!"

"Ell, please." Ell said quietly, almost shyly. She turned, "Hi Emma, Joe," she said, nodding to each of them.

"How are you liking the show?"

"You guys sound great!" She turned and winked at Vic. "I'm thinking that something about the acoustics must be making you sound so good?" She winked, "Couldn't be musical talent."

"Yeah," Gordon enthused, coming over to Ell, "Vic's helped us a lot with our sound on the road, but this place he's built is *amazing*. Everything sounds so clean in here. We're hoping to turn out a live album from what we're recording tonight."

Ell turned to Vic, "You aren't manning the mixing board for that?"

He grinned, "Naw, I've got the world's greatest recording engineer on the boards tonight."

Gordon waggled his eyebrows, "His dad's running the board. He knows more about recording than any two ordinary engineers."

Vic said, "I was out there trying to learn from the old man when the ticket office told me a certain VIP'd picked up her ticket. I figured I'd better get out here to look for her." He shrugged, "But now I'd better get back to the board before Dad decides I don't care."

Once Vic had excused himself Gordon turned to Ell, "Sit, sit. I've so wanted to have a chance to get to know you. First, I want to second what the President said about you..."

~~~

As Ell walked out of Vic's she felt placidly happy. The music had been great and talking to Gordon had been a lot of fun, though it'd been hard remembering not to say something that would give away the fact she also knew him as "Belle." It'd also been difficult resisting his entreaties that she dance on the stage next set. But she *had* agreed to go out to dinner with him before Velos' next concert in Raleigh...

Her AI said her car would meet her around the corner. This was because the street in front of Vic's was so busy that AI driven cars weren't allowed to stop there to pick people up. As she turned the corner onto the street where her car was to meet her she heard steps jogging up behind her. Glancing back, she recognized one of the men who'd been dancing near her when she'd been on the dance floor with Vic.
~~~

"Ms. Donsaii? Hi, I'm Gary Palot. I've admired you for... forever and wondered if I could buy you a cup of coffee?"

Ell smiled at him, "Thank you. I appreciate the offer, but I'm pretty tired and," she shrugged, "I don't even drink coffee."

His face twisted fleetingly, then the smile returned. "Dessert?"

Ell's eyes narrowed, she hadn't liked the look that momentarily appeared on his face, but she smiled anyway and shrugged, "No thanks." She stepped off the curb to walk around to the other side of her car.

"Sam said you were a bitch, but I didn't believe him."

Falling into the zone, Ell turned to look at "Gary" again. The twisted look was back, occasionally flickering toward a smile, then back toward its uglier aspect. Gary reached toward his waistband. Ell stepped toward him, dropping into the zone and wondering why her life had so much drama in it. When his hand dipped in and pulled out a pistol she stepped the rest of the way to him and twisted the gun toward him, loosening his fingers and ripping it out of his grasp. "Call 911," she said to her AI, stepping back and dropping the gun into her purse. Putting her hands up in a fending off posture she spoke slowly so he'd understand, "Back off Gary, that wasn't nice."

Grabbing his right hand in his left, Gary said, "You little witch!" Letting go of his hand he stepped forward, reaching out.

Ell just stepped out of his reach, saying, "Gary, calm down. You're in enough trouble. Don't make it worse."

A familiar sounding voice said, "Don't move, bitch..."

Ell looked to Gary's right and saw Bridget's Sam

stepping out of the alley, right elbow locked around Emma's neck. Some kind of splint was still on his right hand. The way Emma's lower body was leaning away, there was no doubt in Ell's mind his left hand had the barrel of a gun pushed into her kidney.

A spike of fear shot through Ell as she saw the panic in Emma's wide eyes. She raised her hands, empty palms out, "OK, ok, what do you want?"

"We're all going to get into your car there, Donsaii." Sam greeted as he nodded at her car. "Then we'll go for a little ride out to your house. Then we're going to have a little talk with my Bridget. You're gonna undo whatever brainwashing you've done on her so she can come home."

Ell's eyes widened, it sounded like Sam was completely out of touch with reality. He'd built an imaginary mental world in which Bridget lived with Ell because she'd been programmed to do so, rather than because she feared Sam.

Speaking calmly Ell said, "OK" and turned to get in the car. As she opened the door she quietly said, "Allan, blitz," which was her prearranged signal to her AI to contact her security team and the police and send a constant audio-video stream to them.

She pondered the common advice that you should never go anywhere with a kidnapper. You didn't want them to take you to an isolated area. However, it sounded like Sam planned to take her to her own farm house. That'd allow her security team to operate on familiar ground.

Gary got in front with Ell, while Sam and Emma got in the back. When the doors closed Ell told the car's AI, "Take us to my house." She took a couple of deep breaths and felt herself drop out of her zone.

As the car started rolling Gary reached out and pulled off Ell's AI headband, "Sorry it has to be this way," he said. He popped the PGR chip out of her headband but to her relief didn't look for a second hidden chip. When she looked at him wonderingly he shrugged and said, "If you'd just agreed to go for coffee..."

Mentally Ell rolled her eyes, but physically she just stared at him, trying not to look as disgusted as she felt.

From the back seat Sam said, "I'll bet you girls thought you'd beaten me for good." He giggled, almost hysterically, "You probably thought with my hand trashed I wouldn't be able to *do* anything to get Bridget back."

Ell turned to look at Sam, He wasn't wearing an AI. Since he was supposed to be in prison, if he did hook himself into the net, someone would be by to pick him up pretty quickly. But it was pretty hard to get along in the modern world without some kind of AI, at least to pay for things. "How'd you get out of confinement?"

Another frenetic giggle, "Psych eval. They sent me to the state hospital to see if I was crazy. It isn't too hard to escape from that place if you *aren't* crazy. Gary here was just bein' released when I got out. I got a ride with him and his family."

Ell realized that Gary's AI must be serving for both of them. She said, "Sam, do you really think Bridget loves you and wants you back?"

"Of course she does!" he said with a brittle edge.

"Will you ask her if that's the case?"

"No! I know you done somethin' to her. She didn't even come visit me in the hospital!"

"Sam..." Ell started to ask wearily.

"Shut up!"

Emma yelped as Sam jabbed the gun into her side. "Say another word and I'll put a hole in your little friend here."

They'd traveled a few blocks in silence when Gary leaned toward Ell and said in a low voice, "Kiss?"

Astonished, Ell leaned away, staring at him and giving him a sharp head shake. *Something's deeply wrong with this guy,* she thought. *It's as if he has no concept what other people are thinking or feeling! He and Sam make quite the pair.* The remainder of the ride to Ell's house passed in silence, though Ell continued thinking furiously.

~~~

When they drove up to the house the lights were out, suggesting her security team wanted darkness so their IR gear could give them an advantage. Sam insisted he get out first and that Emma follow him out the right rear door. Throwing his arm around her neck again, he walked her around to the driver's side. With the gun firmly in Emma's side, he told Ell to get out. Gary got out the other door at the same time. Ell saw a lone tear running down Emma's cheek.

Sam gestured to the house with his chin, "Take us in and we'll get Bridget."

Ell wondered what Steve and her security team were doing. She hoped they'd gotten Bridget out of the house and worried they might do something that frightened Sam while he was holding the gun to Emma's back. Ell led the little group up the steps to the porch and told the house AI to unlock the door. She had to give it a passcode since she wasn't wearing her AI. Wanting to be sure her team understood the situation
~~~

she turned to Sam, "Sam, please take the gun out of Emma's side, you're hurting her."

Sam shook his head, "You'd like that wouldn't you?"

"Are you sure you don't want give yourself up? This is only going to make things worse for you, you know?"

"Shut up and open the door!"

Ell opened the door and pushed it open, gesturing for Sam to enter first.

"D'you think I'm some kind of idiot? *You* go first."

Ell stepped into the room and then to the left just inside the door.

"Move into the middle of the room. You ain't pulling your tricks on me again."

Ell stepped into the middle of the room. Knowing that the security team could see her on their cameras, she shook her head, hoping that they would understand that she didn't want them to come in guns blazing. She had a feeling that if anything frightened Sam, Emma'd get hurt. She had the same sick feeling about any kind of hostage negotiation.

Sam pushed Emma across the threshold. "Bridg'?" he called out. "I've come for you, honey. Don't worry about these people, babe. I'll protect you from them."

Ell sighed. Sam seemed so far out of touch with reality she wondered if anything could get through to him. If not, it seemed unlikely that the situation could end without Sam getting hurt again, and possibly hurting Emma or Ell.

"Bridget?" Sam said, louder this time. He motioned at Ell with his chin, "Where're you keeping her?"

"I'm not keeping her. She lives in a bedroom on the second floor."

"Let's go."

They made their way up the open stairway, a task

made difficult by Sam's insistence on keeping his right elbow locked around Emma's neck as they ascended. Since he was barely taller than Emma and standing on the stair below her, this forced her to arch her back and bend her knees uncomfortably. The stairs gave out onto an open walkway that went around to the rooms on the second floor. Ell stepped left and waved a hand to the right, the direction of Bridget's room. Sam said, "No, you lead the way."

Ell led as directed. Once they arrived in Bridget's room they found the bed unmade with a t-shirt tossed on it.

Gary said. "Looks like she left."

Sam turned furiously, "Looks like someone took her, you mean."

Gary shrugged.

Sam turned to Ell, "Where do you have her?"

Ell shrugged, "She's a free person. She comes and goes as she wishes."

Fiercely, "Where do you have her?" Emma yelped and bowed tensely backward as Sam forced the gun into her back.

Bridget's voice came from out in the hall, "Sam?"

Sam smiled beatifically and looked toward the hall, "Bridget?" He started dragging Emma that direction, keeping her between Ell and himself. "Bridget?"

Ell held her breath, but as he was about to go through the door he suddenly stopped, turned to Ell and said, "You first."

Careful not to slump her shoulders and confirm to him just how badly she wanted to be behind him; Ell shrugged as nonchalantly as she could and stepped out onto the walkway. Once there, they heard Bridget's voice again. It obviously came from the house AI's speakers, "Sam, I'm not in the house. I don't want to go anywhere with you..."

"Bridget..." Sam said plaintively. "No! This isn't the real you! They've brainwashed you honey. Remember how much we love each other?"

"I loved you once, Sam... But then you got jealous, and mean... And controlling."

"No! Bridget, I'm different now. Besides, they've done something to your mind. Come talk to me in person... I, I can reprogram what they've done to you, honey... I promise. We'll be back like we used to be."

Bridget sobbed faintly, then said, "Sam, I... I *hated* the way we used to be."

"We'll fix it Bridg'. Don't give up on us. We can get back to the way we used to be."

"I don't want be to back that way Sam! *Listen* to me!"

"I mean before, before it all went bad, before that... night. I just loved you too much is all..." he trailed off plaintively. Ell could see tears running down his cheeks.

"Sam," Bridget said, "let Emma go, she hasn't done you any harm."

Angrily, "She, she messed us up!"

"Sam, she didn't. We were already messed up. All she did was point out just how bad our relationship was... Sam... you were a *bully*." Her voice cracked on this last.

Gary had moved up on the right side of Sam and Emma. He said, "I don't think she likes you anymore, Sam."

Convulsively Sam pulled the gun out of Emma's side and reached around her stomach to fire a shot at Gary. "SHUT UP!"

Gary danced away unhurt, "Geez man!"

"Sorry." Sam looked up at the overhead speakers Bridget's voice had been coming from. "Bridg'?"

Ell had stepped closer when the gun was out of Emma's side, but it was digging in again. Bridget's voice sadly said, "Sam, let them go."

"No! They're gonna take me to you, then you'll see, it'll all be better." He looked at Ell, "Back off! And take us to Bridget."

Ell shrugged and took a step backward, "I don't know where she is." Her eyes narrowed. When Sam brought the gun back from firing at Gary he'd dug it into Emma's side in *front* of her arm, instead of behind like he'd had it before. She looked up into Emma's eyes and stared hard at her. When she felt Emma looking back, she dropped into the zone and looked fiercely down at the gun—would Emma understand what she wanted? Emma looked down at the gun herself, then up at Ell, seeming to take forever to Ell, who was deeply into her zone.

Emma nodded minutely.

Sam said, "Take us..."

Seeing the muscles on the front of Emma's arm contracting, Ell began stepping forward, pulse throbbing slowly in her ears.

Emma's arm began moving and Ell saw the skin on the front of Emma's elbow flatten against the gun.

Ell started reaching out, seeing Sam's fingers tightening as the gun moved from the push of Emma's arm.

The gun slid forward on Emma's side.

Ell saw the trigger depressing as she reached out.

The trigger moved farther.

Ell's fingers curled around the barrel.

The gun bucked as Ell pulled outward.

In horror, Ell saw a hole appear in Emma's shirt.

Emma's stomach rippled...

Ell twisted upward, forcing the barrel up, away from Emma and over her own ducking head.

Ell dropped to her knees under the gun as she kept twisting it back out of Sam's hand.

The gun wouldn't come free because Sam's finger was caught in the trigger guard. She backed off a little on the twist, making sure the barrel wasn't pointing at anyone, grasping his wrist with her right hand and pulling the gun free.

She tossed the gun to the floor behind her.

Sam began dragging Emma toward the railing as if he were going to try to throw her over.

Ell rose back off her knees, bringing her right hand up flat to smash the flat of her palm into the middle of Sam's face, smacking into his nose and eyes.

Too hard! Ell thought regretfully as she felt the crunching sensation of Sam's nose and right cheekbone collapsing under her hand. His head flew back, then his hands flew back to catch himself as he fell backward.

Ell glanced at Gary who'd braced himself as if at attention, back and hands against the wall.

Her eyes turned back to Emma's stomach, her hand lifting Emma's t-shirt and seeing two holes in her skin, indicating the bullet went through and through. "Call 911!" she shouted.

***

Ell sat in the ER with Emma, holding her hand while

a cute young intern nervously sutured the bullet wounds. Scans had found that the bullet had grazed her abdominal muscle, but hadn't entered the abdomen itself. She'd be sore, but not permanently injured. They heard Roger's voice outside, "Emma?"

"Hey Roger. Come in, if you can stand watching me getting sutures." The curtain moved back and Roger came in, "Hey, Em', what're you doin' getting' yourself shot?!" He noticed Ell, "Hey, Ell."

With delight, but also sadness at the depth of concern in Roger's voice, Ell said, "Hey Roger, I *told* you you should go to the Velos concert."

Roger sat down and took Emma's other hand, looking into her eyes he said, "I wish I had. I heard it was Bridget's crazy ex?"

"Yeah, he escaped the psych eval unit. Hopefully they'll put him in higher security this time."

Ell said, "Rog'?"

He turned to her, "Yeah?"

"Can you take Emma home? I've got to go deal with the police some more."

"Sure!"

Ell stood and squeezed Emma's hand, winking with the eye Roger couldn't see and putting on a brave smile. She turned to Roger, "Take care of her."

After she stepped outside the curtain, Ell wiped the corner of her eye. *Buck up!* she told herself. *Emma and Roger deserve each other. You shouldn't be sad your two good friends are getting together.* As she walked out into the cool evening she snorted, *Jealous over a guy I don't even love. What kind of idiot am I?*

Chapter Six

Though it was Saturday, the team had been so excited about their alien observations that they'd agreed to meet at nine to talk about what was going on with Goldy and Silver. Wheat was so excited, since he'd never been to D5R, he'd arrived early to be sure he found his way to the right place. Donsaii looked up when he arrived. "Sorry about being a little late taking over the observations last night."

"Hey, no problem. Congratulations on your award Thursday night!"

"Thank you."

"Actually, I was so excited I hadn't even noticed you were late until you called to take over. That's even though the teecees'd gone to sleep and nothing was happening. I was using one of the screens to go back through the trek I'd already watched, trying to categorize all the plants and animals."

"Well after you signed off, I didn't have much to do because the teecees were sleeping, so I went through the parts you'd highlighted. I think you're right..."

"Right about what?" Norris asked as he came in the door.

"Dr. Norris. Hi. Let me introduce Dr. Wheat." She turned to Wheat, "I told everyone on the team about you, so they already know who you are. Dr. Norris here is from the Astronomy Department at UNC. He's an expert in solar systems. He's been great and really helped us when we were building the rockets we sent to TC3. He made sure we wouldn't contaminate their world with our microbes and vice versa."

While Ell introduced Norris, the rest of the team came in. Emma was with them! Roger accompanied her, though Emma moved gingerly.

Ell's eyes widened when she saw her, "What are you doing here? Aren't you supposed to be resting?"

"No, I'm not even taking much pain medicine, just some Aleve. It doesn't hurt much and I'm certainly not in any danger. I wasn't gonna miss hearing what's going on with Goldy and Silver!"

Roger sighed exasperatedly. He said, "I couldn't get her to listen to reason."

Manuel turned to Emma and asked, "What's wrong?"

"Nothing! I *don't* want to talk about it." She turned to Harald and smiled, "You must be Dr. Wheat?"

Ell introduced the rest of them around. "Dr. Wheat had a pretty good idea last night. Remember how we've wondered about why Goldy and Silver are walking through the forest when they have wings and can fly?"

The group nodded, then Ell waved a hand at Wheat. "Fill them in."

"Um, well, I think only Goldy can fly. As far as I've been able to see from your notes, Silver's never been off the ground. Have any of you seen Silver flying?"

They all looked at one another, shaking their heads.

"Look at this zoomed image," Wheat continued, pointing at the big screen which zoomed in to show an enlargement of Silver's wing.

"Oh," Emma said, "those look like stitches! I thought it was a tattoo or some other kind of decoration when I saw it before."

"Exactly!" Wheat said, "I think Silver's injured and Goldy's accompanying it somewhere. Now near the end of my shift watching them, they reached a cliff," he pointed to the big screen showing the cliff in the rocket's camera as Goldy flew over it. "Goldy took off and flew along it, first one way, then the other. I think Goldy was looking for a way up. So far it seems to have stymied them. Goldy made a brief attempt to climb the cliff, but it seems to be made of soft material, at least on the surface. Goldy's claw holds broke easily. Then they tried climbing trees, but the bark on the local trees tore loose when they sunk their claws into them. I had the strong impression that they'd never tried climbing anything before. Why would they? After all, normally they just fly to the top of things, rather than having to climb. If they *did* have experience climbing trees, they'd have just ripped off the loose outer bark and sunk those impressive claws into the deeper layers."

Roger said, "So they weren't able to get up the cliff?"

"No, and I think we could get a start on making friends with them due to this situation."

Ell turned to him curiously, "Really? You didn't tell me about this part."

"Yeah," Wheat said excitedly, "gesturing at the cliff on the screen. *We* know how to climb cliffs. They've never had any reason to do it, so they don't have any ideas. Isn't there any way we could show them how to do it?"

Ell raised her eyebrows and turned to the others.

"Really? Should we be interfering in their lives?" Emma asked.

Ell shrugged.

Norris said, "Hmmm, first communication with an

alien intelligence. It might be that the government has some rules or regulations about how it's supposed to be done."

"I looked that up the first day we saw Goldy and Silver," Roger said, "There've been think tank discussions and the military's worked out some protocols, but no laws have been passed restricting what we can or can't do as private citizens."

"I don't know; a lot of harm befell primitive societies here on Earth when advanced civilizations made contact with them."

Manuel looked around at the group, "Oh there's no doubt that Columbus brought some nasty diseases to the Western hemisphere and that the Europeans subjugated, enslaved, and exterminated Native Americans... but we're doing everything we can think of to keep from transmitting disease and we can hardly exploit them when we can't even get there." He shrugged, "Also, even though some of my ancestors were ill-used, I myself am very happy to be living in a modern society. It's a two-way street that has some very bad things *and* some good things on it."

Wheat said, "Personally, if some alien was watching me struggle with a difficult and life threatening problem, I'd certainly appreciate a little help. Those people who think that the lives of primitive peoples were noble and peaceful should look into how most of them actually lived. I'm not saying that primitives are bad people. I'm saying that living without modern technology would suck. Big time. In the United States today, even the poorest have access to bathrooms, sewers, immunizations, antibiotics, communications, televised entertainment, air conditioning, spices and innumerable conveniences that the *kings* of yore would have been ecstatic to have…" He grimaced, "Sorry. I'll get down off my high horse… Anyway, I think one of the best ways for us to make contact would be to help them solve a problem. We don't have to give them blueprints for how to build a steam engine and hook it up to an elevator; we could just show them how to use a vine as a rope."

Ell looked around the group, "Just knowing that Goldy's helping Silver when she's injured is making me feel pretty kindly toward these two. I don't know if they're representative of their people, but I like them and I'd like to help if I can. Does anyone have a serious objection to trying to provide simple suggestions?"

Shrugs and shakes of the head greeted her query. "But how are we going to suggest anything to them? So far we can't even hear them, much less talk to them."

Emma put her hands up, "I'll have the laser acoustic pickup working early in the week and we've got most of the parts for our second rocket. But it'll have to be assembled, sterilized, then flown from the deep space portal to TC3. And don't forget we need to put another intermediate pipe out there in a degrading solar orbit before we can *use* the new rocket."

Ell lifted her hands palms out. She said, "Hey, no one's accusing you of being slow… though we *do* wish you were faster," she grinned. "But even after we have acoustic reception and eventually transmission it'll probably take a long time to understand them and then to translate what we say into something they can comprehend. What I'm thinking is that there might be some visual means of communication? Like hieroglyphics maybe?"

Manuel pulled his screen to himself and started

marking on it the way he usually did when he was planning out how to build something.

Roger frowned, "Hieroglyphs weren't really word pictures, the pictures were kind of like our letters, representing sounds or syllables."

Ell said, "Yeah, but maybe we could make word pictures work for us?"

"Couldn't we just send them a drawing of someone climbing a cliff using a rope?" Wheat said, "Or not someone, it'd need to be a Teecee. We'd need an artist."

"Wait a minute, it's all very well to talk about showing them pictures, but there aren't any vid screens on the rocket either you know?"

Ell lifted her eyebrows, "But there is a window we can shine a laser through."

Manuel said, "How about this?" He slid the screen that he'd been drawing on out onto the table and people's eyes widened.

***

Dex woke up cold and reached over to pick up a couple sticks and stir the fire back to life. When the tip of one of the sticks caught from a coal, hie held the other one over the flame until it caught too, them laid them together so that they'd both burn. Once they were burning brightly, the heat warmed hies front. After a bit hie turned hies back to the fire to warm hies wings.

As hie turned to face the cliff, hies eyes flashed wide. Dex turned violently, pushing up, hies wings exploding from hies back, arching up to lift himrself to safety. Syrdian, roused by Dex's violent motion and the boom of hies wing extension also startled awake, wings lifting, then curling suddenly back down in reaction to pain from the sudden movement. Dex and Syrdian unconsciously shuffled together, staring at the cliffside where glowing red lines had appeared. "*What* is that?" Syrdian asked.

"I don't know!" Dex whispered.

"I've never seen anything like it before! Do you think those glowing lines are on the face of the cliff every morning?"

Dex turned to look behind himr with hies fore eyes, for a moment thinking the sun might be rising back there and shining through some kind of gaps in the trees to create the lines. But no, just as hie'd seen with hies back eyes, behind himr was still the darkness to the west where the sun had set. The sun would be coming up in front of himr to the east, on the other side of the cliff and the mountain. There weren't any fires burning behind them that might cast such an eerie glow either.

Dex turned back to look at the cliff itself. Could there be something in the cliff itself that glowed? There were a few faint bluish spots in the wall of the Yetany tribe's cave that glowed for a while after sunset. Not as brightly as this though! Perhaps it was the spirit of an ancestor?

Syrdian said, "Dex! At the bottom... the red lines look like a dalin, seen from the side!"

Dex's wings rose involuntarily and made a soft downbeat as hie looked at the lower lines. *It* does *look like a dalin!* Genex, Dex's drunken parent, had been famed for scratching representations of animals into the limestone of the cave walls. Dex took some pride in the awe that visitors from other tribes still evidenced when they first saw the images. Dex had occasionally tried scratching some images in the dirt himrself. But Genex's or Dex's scratched drawings... though more complex, weren't as cleanly representative as the elegantly simple glowing lines on the cliff face in front of himr. And Genex hadn't ever drawn a dalin, only animals.

Neither had Dex.

Dex and Syrdian both jumped a little in a startle reflex when another dalin appeared next to the first one. Both of the drawn dalins appeared to be looking up at the cliff. *The cliff!* Dex suddenly realized the lines in front of the dalins looked the way the cliff would appear, if seen from the side. The lines went up about six body lengths as compared to the drawn dalins, then showed the relatively flat area at the top of the cliff. Oh! And the lines *behind* the dalins in the drawing were trees! Dex looked around... like the trees surrounding Syrdian and himr. "Is that a drawing of you and me at the bottom of the cliff?" hie whispered in an awed tone.

Syrdian's wings rose a little as hie stared. "It is?"

"*I'm* asking you?"

Syrdian's head tilted one way then the other as hie stared. "I think you might be right!"

The drawing changed again, startling Dex and Syrdian into lifting their wings a bit. This time one of the dalins was represented climbing the cliff side, hands and feet on it as if its claws were sunk in. The drawing changed to one showing the dalin back on the ground, rubble at hies feet, with a defect in the cliff where the dalin's claws would have been.

After a pause, the drawing shifted again. This time it

showed one of the dalins flying near the top of the cliff with a rope... no, a vine, dangling below it. Dex drew hies head up and back. This was amazing!

The picture shifted. The upper dalin was tying the vine around the base of a tree while the other end dangled to the bottom of the cliff where the lower dalin held it. When the drawing shifted again the dalin was flying to the top of the cliff with a second dangling vine.

A final drawing appeared. This time the lower dalin appeared to be walking up the cliff. Hie had hies hands on the vine that was tied to the tree at the top of the cliff. The second vine looked to be tied around hies waist. The dalin at the top of the cliff was leaning back, pulling on that second vine.

Dex stared in wonder. It was as if the drawings were telling himr and Syrdian how to get up the cliff! Hie stepped closer to the cliff to look more closely. Would there be more to see up close?

Suddenly part of the drawing disappeared, then the entire drawing disappeared! Syrdian cried out.

Dex stepped back, hoping that the drawing would reappear, maybe it had been frightened by hies approach. Hie also turned to see what'd frightened Syrdian. Syrdian, eyes wide, was staring at Dex. "What?"

"How are you doing that?"

"I'm not doing anything!"

"You are! The red glowing lines are on your back not the cliff!"

"What! That can't be!"

"They did!"

Dex stretched hies neck up and over to examine hies own back, "There aren't any lines on me!"

"There were. They appeared on your back when

they disappeared on the cliff. They looked like part of the picture from the cliff, just smaller. You *can't* tell me you aren't making them!"

Dex felt hies wings ripple in... excitement? Dread? Hie walked back around to where Syrdian had crouched by the fire. Hie put another stick on the fire and looked back at the dark cliff face. The sky over the top of the mountain had lightened, but everything not lit by their fire still remained black and indistinct. Syrdian touched hies leg. Dex looked down, Syrdian pointed at the cliff face. The glowing lines were back; showing the dalin flying over the cliff face trailing a vine again. After a moment, it changed and the dalin was tying the vine to a tree. Then flying back up with another vine. Then the lower dalin was climbing the cliff by pulling on the vine tied to the tree while the upper dalin pulled on the vine tied to the lower dalin's waist.

Dex looked at Syrdian. The glowing lines showed the flying dalin with the vine. They went on through all the images again. Dex crouched next to Syrdian, "I think the lines are trying to tell us how to get up the cliff," hie whispered.

Syrdian nodded though hie said nothing.

Dex lay down, saying, "Maybe we'll try it when it's light."

Syrdian said, "I'm hungry," but Syrdian crouched down next to Dex. They stared at the glowing lines as they repeated their pictures over and over on the face of the cliff.

~~~

When the glow in the clouds over the mountain had had brightened enough to see easily, Syrdian got up and said, "I'll try to get us some food."
~~~

Dex said, “Shall I come with you?”

In a low voice Syrdian said, “No, you get the vines shown in the pictures.” Hie walked down off the ridge and into the forest, carrying a pointed staff and Dex’s flyer swatter.

Dex shrugged hies wings and walked out into the forest looking for a vine. He found an area with thousands of them, but hie didn’t know how hie’d get one as long as those in the pictures. Dex cut one near its roots and pulled on it. It pulled loose from little rootlets and guided himr over to a tree that it ascended. Hie pulled harder and harder to get it to come loose, but when it was about a body’s length above himr it would no longer come loose from the tree. This tree had quite a few vines going up it and those other vines had entangled with the one Dex had. Now Dex was actually trying to pull several vines loose, all at the same time. Hie leaned hard on it, it was strong enough to support hies weight as hie’d seen in the diagram, but looked like it was pulling the bark off the tree. If hie climbed up and cut more of it loose, how would hie get back down?

Dex tried a couple of other vines without success. One pulled loose to about three body lengths because it was young and new and mostly on top of the other vines but then it broke. Young, new and smaller didn’t look like a good choice since it wouldn’t be strong enough to bear Syrdian’s weight. Dex looked for one that ran along the ground so hie could bend down and cut it loose, but they all promptly went up trees. Dex climbed a tree, clinging to several vines instead of the bark while trying to cut a single vine loose. Hie had to beat hies wings to help climb while trying to cut the vine loose. It was exhausting and, before hie had the six body lengths of vine hie needed, the vine became small and weak. Hie pulled it loose and fluttered back to the ground.

Dex scratched the base of hies right hind wing and looked around. Hie wondered, *why do the red lines want us to use vines instead of rope?* After some thought hie decided that even if the lines wanted them to use vines, that rope should work for the same purpose. Hie walked back to their little clearing and was about to take off when Syrdian came into view climbing up onto the ridge. Hie had a swimmer! And it looked big enough to feed both of them. Dex was amused to realize that hie hadn't thought *Syrdian* had a chance of getting them food. "Syrdian! How'd you get the swimmer?"

Syrdian shrugged hies wings, "I like catching swimmers. I saved a little of the flyer from last night for bait."

"Really? How do you catch fish with bait?"

"I use this little bone spike I made, tied to a fiberlin string." Syrdian pulled out a length of fiberlin with a sharp bony point aimed back along the string. "You put the bait over it to hold the point against the string and dangle it near the swimmer in the water. When the swimmer swallows the bait, you tug on the fiberlin and the little sharp end pops out to the side and catches in the swimmer's stomach. Then you pull the swimmer out of the water with the fiberlin."

Dex admired the swimmer a little more, glad the morning wouldn't be as hungry as hie'd expected. "I'm going to fly up to the cave and get some rope. I can't find any vines like the red lines showed in their pictures. Well, at least, I can't get pieces of vine that are long enough to reach the top of the cliff."

Syrdian frowned, "Maybe we're supposed to tie several short pieces of vine together to have ones that're long enough?"

"Do you really think it matters if we use vine instead of rope?"

Syrdian shrugged hies wings, "I've never had advice from the spirits before. But Bultaken always wants the tribe to do things *exactly* as hie saw them in hies spirit dreams."

Dex raised hies head in surprise, "Do you think those were spirit dreams we had last night?"

Syrdian shrugged. "It's like we're our own tribe now. And both of us are having the spirit dreams."

Dex said, "I've never heard of two dalins having the same dream. I saw glowing red lines on the cliff face, showing a dalin climbing a cliff using vines." Hie tilted hies head, "Did you see the same thing?"

Syrdian dipped hies head yes.

Dex waved hies head uncertainly a moment, then said, "OK, I'll get some pieces of vine to tie together, but I'm worried they won't be strong enough."

~~~

By the time Dex returned with several lengths of vine, Syrdian had finished cooking the swimmer. Hie'd also collected and chopped up a few small tubers from near the campsite. They ate with gusto, the crunch of the little tubers going well with the soft flesh of the swimmer. Syrdian had even thought to fill a skin with water when hie was down at the stream so they could have something to drink.

They laid out two pieces of vine end to end. Dex said, "How do we tie them together?"
~~~

Syrdian's head went up and back, "*I* don't know! You're the leatherworker."

Dex tilted hies head, "Vines aren't exactly like leather, you know," he said quietly, picking up the two ends and wrapping them into the first throw of a knot. The vines were stiff and the second throw didn't form a good knot. Hie looked at the knot a moment then said, "Pull on that end."

Syrdian picked up the vine on the other side of the knot and began pulling. The knot cinched down, but the vine started cracking and splintering as hie pulled hard. Eventually the vine pulled into something that resembled a knot, but had corners and splinters rather than the smooth roundedness Dex was used to.

Syrdian looked at the knot curiously, "Do you think it'll be strong enough?"

Dex waved hies head in negation. "I don't think you should trust your life to it."

"How can we make it stronger?"

"Add a rope?"

"Do you think that would be OK with the spirits?"

"I don't know, but it'd make me feel better."

"Me too," Syrdian whispered.

***

Deltain sighed as the rest of the tribe launched themselves into the air for the second day of the migration. Wings sagging, hie turned back and looked to the north from whence they'd come. Hie knew in hies hearts there was no chance Dex'd appear in the distance, flying Deltain's way. Yet hie could hope... With aching hearts, hie slowly turned to lift into the air toward the south.

***

Wilson Daster was on "voyeur" duty, as he thought of it, watching the teecees on Saturday afternoon. Once Manuel'd finished his drawings the rest of the group had broken up and taken off to enjoy the weekend because the teecees themselves were boringly asleep. The rotational period of TC3 was surprisingly similar to Earth's at 23 hours and 43 minutes. Currently, sunrise at the TC3 camp would've come at about 10:35, but because the teecees lived on the western slope of a huge mountain Tau Ceti didn't actually crest it until about noon and it didn't go down until nearly midnight. Wilson had been watching in the late morning when the teecees first woke in the dark and saw the laser tracing out Manuel's drawings on the cliff face. Although Goldy'd put the rocket down on its side, by luck he'd laid it over a bump that held the laser window slightly above the ground. The window was facing a little bit downward, but Allan twisted it with a gentle shot from the rotational attitude jets. They shot compressed air, but the hiss they'd presumably made hadn't seemed to disturb the teecees.

Wilson had a moment of panic when Goldy stepped in between the rocket and the cliff and into the beam of the laser. He'd barked at his AI to shut the laser down because he wasn't sure whether the beam might be strong enough to burn the Teecee. Allan, Ell's AI, had confirmed the power was low enough it shouldn't cause harm, but Wilson had left it off until Goldy was well out of the way. The teecees had appeared to be somewhat panicked and Wilson considered leaving the laser show off, but eventually he resumed displaying the series of pictures.

The teecees had apparently gone back to sleep, but when their campsite was fairly well lit by sunlight diffused through the clouds, they'd gotten up and gone their separate ways. They left the rocket lying there, so Wilson had no idea what they were doing. When the teecees returned Goldy was empty handed but Silver had a fish! Well, when Wilson was able to see it clearly, he could see that it was quite different than Earth fish. Brown in color, it must be slippery because Silver held it with her claws slightly extended to provide a grip. Torpedo shaped, the head drooped a little as if it had a muscular but boneless short neck like the teecees, the burrower, and the flyers. The body appeared to be less flexible than Earth fish and instead of a tail with fins, it looked like it had the standard plan of four hind limbs, two of which were much enlarged, flattened and looked like they performed the function of a tail in an Earth fish.

As Silver cleaned the fishlike animal, Wilson sent a message to Wheat, letting him know another "dissection" was underway. Wilson watched interestedly as the fish was suspended over the fire and occasionally wondered where Goldy'd gone. When Goldy returned with several short lengths of vine, Wilson wondered why he hadn't brought back a longer one. She? Wilson realized he'd subconsciously decided Goldy was the male and Silver the female part of a mated couple. He shrugged, thinking to himself that it didn't matter much what he thought their sexes were, at present the important question was—why not a full length vine?

Having an "aha" moment, while the teecees were eating the swimmer Wilson scanned back through the images of the hike the day before. Though there were lots of vines, they were all tangled together and going up trees. *It might be impossible to untangle a really long one like the one they'd had the laser draw.*

Back to the present, Wilson saw Goldy tying two vines together but the knot didn't look very strong to him. *Maybe if they bound the knot with a smaller vine?*

Goldy flew away.

Silver didn't do much while Goldy was gone. At one point she came over and examined the rocket, giving Wilson a close up view of her head. Then Goldy reappeared and picked up several of the short vines, taking off with them and flying back up into the air. Wilson wondered what was happening.

After a bit, a vine was lowered down the face of the cliff. It appeared at the edge of the field of view of the camera and looked odd, as if it were double stranded? Narrowing his eyes and leaning forward, Wilson said, "Allan, zoom me in on that vine at the right edge of the picture." As the digital zoom took him in, he saw there was something else, a black second strand, accompanying the vine. Something else flashed into view, then was gone. "Zoom out." A second vine seemed to be hanging just at the edge of view. Wilson could only see leaves, not the actual main vine or whether it also had a second strand of black. He wondered whether they were in fact taking direction from the laser drawings the team had sent them, or whether this was something they'd planned to do anyway.

Silver appeared in the frame and went to the cliff

where the vines hung. First she picked up the black strand and wrapped it around her waist, tying it off. Wilson had Allan zoom in again, *It looks like rope!* Silver picked up the vine and wrapped it around her waist, also tying a loose knot in it. Then she picked up the other vine, pulling it into view. It also had a black rope. She pulled on it firmly, as if testing its strength. Or the strength of the rope anyway. Wilson noticed that the vine didn't really come tight. Even though Silver had both in her hands, all the weight seemed to be on the rope. He tilted his head wondering, *Why are they using a vine, if they have a perfectly good rope? Could they be trying to follow our instructions to the letter, even when they make no sense, but backing them up with something that does?*

Silver looked up the cliff face and tested her weight on the rope again. The rope around her waist pulled taught. Her wings fluttered a moment, then she climbed out of view, leaving Wilson to wonder what was happening.

***

Just when Wilson was wondering if he should have the rocket right itself and fly up the cliff to look for the teecees, there was a flash of wings and Goldy landed at the campsite. He moved around the camp, picking up a few items and attaching them to his harness. Finally, he approached the rocket, picked it up and reattached it to his chest. Wilson's point of view flew back into the air and circled out over the forest, climbing hard. Silver came into view beside a small tree at the top of the cliff, working on the vines she'd climbed. Goldy landed beside her and picked up the vine. In a moment it became evident that the black strand was indeed a rope and Silver'd been untying the vines from it. Once it was separated, they coiled the two ropes and each took one as they began hiking up the slope again. The area near the top of the cliff was relatively clear, perhaps because it wouldn't support large trees, but in a few minutes they were back in some low density forest.

***

Norris took over from Wilson as the teecee's broke out of the trees and approached a large limestone formation. It wasn't an endless cliff like they'd encountered before, there was forest to either side of it. It was pretty massive though and it had a large dark shadow on it Wilson thought might be a cave.

The AI was stabilizing the video image, but it didn't have great detail because of the slight blurring of each image caused by the motion of Goldy walking. Norris had to wait until they got pretty close before he confirmed it actually was a huge cave. It had a big ledge out in front of it. Once Goldy and Silver entered the cavern, they went to a recess and unloaded the two ropes in an area that had a lot of other supplies. More ropes, wooden shafts, chunks of rock Norris thought might be flint, baskets, pottery and a lot of other objects Norris didn't recognize were all stacked in the chamber. Goldy leaned the rocket up against a large stack of what Norris thought must be firewood. This became certain when Silver took several pieces of the wood to a blackened area and began starting a fire with them.

The position of the rocket let Norris see much of the cave, though he suspected it went far back into the mountain darkness beyond where he could see. Perhaps he was only seeing the entrance? He wondered if the teecees mostly lived out near the front where there would be plenty of light.

While he surveyed the space and watched the teecees walking back and forth in it, he became more and more astonished at the size of the cave. It was enormous! It seemed much bigger than he would've thought would be reasonable for two beings like Goldy and Silver to live in, yet the way they moved about in it bespoke familiarity. Just the quantity of supplies stacked near the rocket seemed like the stores of a community, not a couple. Yet if this was the living space of a community, where were the people? *Or where were the teecees, to be more accurate? Were they all out hunting, or farming, or something like that, and they'd all return just before sunset? Had something happened to the community, leaving Goldy and Silver as the only survivors and Silver injured?*

Goldy flew off out of the cave. Silver propped a large flat rock up on edge next to the fire and backed away from the fire to begin preparing a dead flyer it'd been carrying. After Silver skinned the flyer and skewered pieces of it on a stick, it propped the stick over the fire, then went back into the storage area. It came back out with a paddle shaped stick, a large urn and a small pot. It poured something powdery out of the urn into the little pot, then dribbled some water into the pot from the water skin it carried. Using the stick, it stirred the little pot, then took the urn back into the storage area. That done, Silver turned the spit over the fire and went to stand in the shade near the lip of the cave, staring out over the valley below with wings slightly spread. Norris got the distinct impression that Silver felt overheated.

After a bit Silver went back to the fire and, wings folded behind it as if to keep the heat off them, flipped the big flat rock on its back with the hot side up. Silver poured a pasty whitish material out of the pot onto the hot rock, spreading it with the paddle shaped stick. Silver again went to stand, wings partially spread, in the shade near the lip of the cave.

~~~

After a while Goldy returned with no indication of where it'd gone. The teecees ate the flyer and what appeared to be flat cakes baked from the paste Silver put on the hot rock. They spent the remaining time until sunset looking through the storage area, bringing stuff out and making a pile. Then putting some things back. Norris had the impression they were arguing about what to put on the pile at several points.

If only he could hear!

***

Kant Fladwami walked into his meeting with President Flood. Several of the President's other advisers were already there. The President turned, "Kant, I've got a lot of people riding my ass about this new run of bad weather! Is there any basis for their claims that we need to reduce CO_2 emissions even further?"

Fladwami shrugged, "I'm your science adviser, but
~~~

global warming isn't one of my own areas of expertise. Nonetheless, I've been talking to some people I trust who *are* experts. They tell me we should certainly be concerned. Since they found all that frackable cheap natural gas here in the States there's been less reason to move to non-CO_2 producing energy sources because gas has gotten so cheap. Governmental pressure on manufacturers and power plants to reduce output has helped, but hasn't kept up with the increased usage of the cheap energy. When you burn a lot of gas, you're going to create a lot of CO_2 and there's a limit to how much of it you can sequester. Donsaii's little ports that let cars get electrical power directly from the power company should help. Not only are large power plants more efficient, cars that burn hydrocarbons don't sequester *any* of the CO_2 they make and the power companies do. As we move away from fuel-burning cars we'll do better."

"How much better?"

Fladwami shrugged, "Not a whole lot, but better than nothing. Direct power through ports will also let us move away from batteries in the electric cars. The manufacture of those batteries is hydrocarbon intensive."

The President sighed, "I still kind of think it's all a load of crap, but I'm dealing with a lot of hand wringers, both here and abroad. They *all* want us to do better." He looked up at the ceiling a moment, then sighed again, "I hate bowing to pressure." He bowed his head, "Nonetheless, I'd like to be able to tell them we're going to do something substantive. Any ideas?"

"We could start taxing hydrocarbon burning cars to push them off the streets. We could increase the tax on the power plants for unsequestered CO_2 production to push them to do better. We could push farmers to do better with methane reclamation from manure. Decreasing the methane released would really help; it's a far worse greenhouse gas than CO_2."

The Secretary of Defense leaned forward, "I've got one, odd, piece of advice I follow. It might apply..."

"What?"

"When you've got a problem you can't solve," he said, "'try calling Donsaii.' Came to mind just now, since you guys were already taking her name in vain."

The Secretary of Agriculture barked a laugh. "Come on guys, the girl's pretty and smart and her ports are pretty neat tech, but she isn't going to have a solution to global warming! What do you think she's gonna do, install a port in each cow and vent their flatus into space?"

Several people in the room looked at each other, then a laugh broke out. "You might be onto something there Harvey," Fladwami said, "though we'd have to run numbers. But it might not be a good idea to vent stuff out into space where we can't get it back if we need it someday. CO_2 has a lot of O_2 in it, you know."

Flood sighed, "Kant, ask Donsaii if she's got any ideas," he said, "Teller told me that he wished he'd talked to her more. Now, on to the rest of our agenda..."

Chapter Seven

At the Tuesday morning "team Teecee" meeting, as Ell was calling it, Wheat and Norris attended remotely. Ell said, "Any new developments with Goldy and Silver?"

"Nope, since they packed up and left the big cave Sunday morning they've just been climbing the big mountain. They're carrying a lot of supplies and look pretty tired. You know Norris had the idea that Silver was hot during his Saturday night observation. I graphed out the temperatures recorded since the rocket landed. They *have* been higher in the past few days than when the rocket first set down."

Wheat broke in, "I surveyed the teecees behavior when the temps are up late in the day and they do tend to stand in the shade and lift their wings as if they might be pumping blood through them and using them to radiate away their heat."

Roger said, "I've looked over the orbit. Not only is this the time of the year that the southern hemisphere tilts toward Tau Ceti, but it's also closer to the star this time of year. I think they're going into a pretty hot summer. I'll bet they're climbing the mountain to get out of the heat."

"Maybe the rest of their group or tribe is already up there?"

Wheat said, "I'm worried because it doesn't look like they're getting much to eat while they're on the move.

They've been eating those cakes they cook from the powder they picked up at the cave, but my impression is they aren't happy about it."

Emma leaned forward to eye Manuel, "Maybe our resident artist could draw them some diagrams of a bow and arrow to help them hunt on the move?"

Wheat shook his head, "Bow and arrow is actually pretty sophisticated tech. You need springy wood for the bow and straight shafts for the arrows." He wiggled his eyebrows, "And feathers for guidance, remember there don't seem to be any birds on TC3."

"Maybe they could use stiff leaves?"

"Getting that across in a drawing could be pretty difficult. Remember their literal use of vines instead of their own ropes when we helped them climb? If we drew a leaf that was poorly suited, they might use it anyway. Anyway, even after you've built your bow and arrow, learning to shoot accurately is no trivial task. They already know how to make snares. What I can't figure out is why they don't set snares out at night. There ought to be a pretty good chance of catching some nocturnal animals. Goldy put two out the first afternoon in that clearing and caught one of the burrowers during the night."

"Those two depended on springy saplings and there aren't many of them in the shade of the forest. The one clearing they overnighted in recently didn't seem to have any saplings in it. It was probably cleared by a recent burn."

Wheat said, "Well we could draw them some snares that don't depend on sprung saplings."

Manuel said, "Help me pick out some snare pictures off the internet, ones you think would work on TC3. I'll redraw them for the laser."

Wilson said, "It may be a while before we have a nice place like a cliff wall to project your pictures though."

Emma leaned forward and raised an eyebrow, looking around, "*I've* got some news..."

As the pause extended, Ell narrowed her eyes "Are you trying to make us drag it out of you?"

Emma drew back putting up her hands, "No! No. Me um tell you right now Bosslady!" She wrinkled her nose and grinned, "Well, I'll let you listen." Odd sounds issued from the room's sound system, squeaks, swishes, thumps. Seeing the furrowed brows around her Emma pointed at the screens showing Silver walking up the mountain in front of Goldy and the rocket's cameras. Suddenly they recognized the synchronization of soft padding sounds with Silver's stride. A flittering sound was one of the small flyers going by.

"You got the laser acoustic pickup going!"

"Yup." Emma sat back and grinned.

"Way to go!" They all sat back to listen to the sounds of the world they'd been watching silently for a while.

Roger frowned, "Do all the sounds seem a little high pitched to you guys? I mean, even the sound of their footfalls sound high." he turned to Emma, "Could you have an error in the algorithm?"

"Nope."

"Are you sure?"

"Want to bet a dinner on it?"

Roger narrowed his eyes, "Okaay."

Emma grinned at him. "It's the increased air density. It raises the pitch and tamber of the sounds." She leaned back and looked up at the ceiling, "I think I'd like to eat at... La Mez."

Roger laughed, glancing momentarily at Ell, then back at Emma, "OK, you're on. I'll take you and Ell to dinner tonight."

Ell saw a brief disappointment flash over Emma's face, but winked at her, saying, "Hmmm, are you sure La Mez is expensive enough for us, Emma?"

Emma grinned back, "I think so," she arched an eyebrow at Roger, "as long as he doesn't call my skills into question again."

Roger laughed and leaned back, holding his palms up, "I surrender, I surrender. I have nothing but admiration for your ability to coax sound out of a rocket not intended for it."

A loud squeal of sound issued from the speakers. On the screen Silver turned to look at Goldy and more distant squeaky sound ensued. Daster tilted his head, "Is that them speaking?"

"I'm pretty sure it is," Emma said, "though they don't open their mouths to do it."

"Wait, how do they make those sounds then?"

Wheat said, "There's no rule that says they have to bring air in through the same orifice they bring food in through. That's the way *we* do it, but I think they pull air in through that dark spot at the base of their necks."

"But... that spot's furry!"

"Filters out dust?"

Roger laughed, "OK, but then how do they clean the filter?"

"If you watch them, they use those prehensile necks to reach their heads down to the base of their neck pretty frequently. I think they may be grooming their air intake."

"So, you think they're speaking out of that hole at the base of their necks?

"No. I think that's the air intake, I'm pretty sure they exhaust their air out of that opening on their lower chest. They pull air in, pass it through their lungs, and send it out the lower opening. More efficient oxygen exchange than pulling it in and out of the same windpipe like we do. Our using the same passage results in some dead air that never delivers oxygen. They'd be able to make sound better using the outgoing air at that lower vent than at the intake."

Emma said, "Hah! I've been noticing they speak, or whatever you want to call it, continuously. I mean, without stopping to take a breath." She tilted her head, "Perhaps I should say," she got a devilish look on her face, "They 'squeak' continuously. I wondered how they could possibly do that, but if they're constantly pumping air through..."

Ell sighed, "We need another expert, this time to help us translate."

***

Roger found Emma and Ell at Emma's workstation. "Hey, I thought I was buying you ladies dinner tonight?"

They turned and smiled. Ell nudged Emma, "And here I thought he'd forgotten his debts."

Emma grinned up at Roger, "I'm the one he owes."

As they walked out to the parking lot Roger said, "That really was pretty cool, Emma, working out how to use the laser as an acoustic pickup."

"Almost as cool," she grinned, "as figuring out that the sounds are different because of the increased air density?"

Roger sniffed aristocratically and pretended to

ignore her, “Let’s all go in my car, yours can follow along.”

As they were getting in Ell said, “Whoops, I’m getting a call. You guys go on ahead and I’ll meet you there.”

“We can wait.”

“No, you go on ahead. Hopefully I’ll be right over, but this *could* be quite a while.” As she pulled her head back far enough that only Emma could see, Ell winked at her.

~~~

Emma got a little lump in her throat, but turned to Roger, “Hey, I’ve been meaning to say, I thought that was pretty sharp how you figured out that the weather’s going to be getting hotter there on TC3.”

Looking warmed by the praise, Roger nonetheless said, “Well it didn’t really come together for me until Wheat pointed out that he thought they were trying to cool themselves.”

“Still, that was a good pickup. Also, I haven’t gotten to thank you for taking me home from the hospital. Maybe *I* owe *you* dinner?”

“Naw, shucks Ma’am. ‘twern’t nuthin’. I’m pretty amazed at you though, shot one night, back at work the next!”

“Arrgh, ‘twere only a flesh wound,” Emma grinned at him.

~~~

After they’d been at the table in La Mez for about ten minutes, Ell called to say she couldn’t make it after all and told them to have a good time. Though he was disappointed, Roger had a delightful time. When they left, he thought to himself that Emma’d become an amazing friend. Smart, pretty, fun and great to talk to. *If I weren't already in love with Ell,* he thought to himself, *I could really fall for her.*

***

Ell leaned back in her chair at her house, rubbing the bridge of her nose. Recently she'd been trying to understand some of the issues with the accelerating expansion of the Universe that had led to the hypotheses that required "dark energy." But tonight she couldn't seem to concentrate on the math she'd been working on for the past few weeks. She'd tried watching the teecees, but they were just hiking up the mountain. Her thoughts kept coming back to Roger and Emma driving off to La Mez. Rationally she felt happy for them and could tell herself that their relationship was a good thing... Despite all that, she felt an undefined ache. "Allan, put through a call to Phil Zabrisk."

"Ell?"

"Hey, how's my favorite astronaut?"

"Great! I've been up on training missions three times so far. Now that you've made it cheap enough to be realistic, NASA's talking about a mission to the Moon to build a real Moonbase. You may be able to say you know a moonman pretty soon; I'm angling for a spot on the construction crew."

"Hey, once you get the Zabrisk Moon Resort built, you'll have to let me know so I can come visit." Ell found herself hoping that Phil would repeat one of his frequent invitations for her to visit him in Houston.

Instead Phil said, "I will. Hey, you'll be glad to know

that I've finally stopped dreaming that *you'd* fall for me someday. I've started dating one of the lady astronauts. I think you'd like Carol, she doesn't let me get away with anything either."

Distantly, Ell heard herself say, "Sounds like the kind of girl you need. I've got to pity her though. Have you warned her about what she's gotten herself in for?" Surprised that her voice didn't break, she felt tears slowly begin to run down her cheek.

Phil laughed, "No! And don't *you* tell her either. A guy like me's gotta have a few secrets to even have a chance."

Ell laughed too, hoping it sounded normal, despite the frog in her throat.

Phil said, "Hey, I've got to go before Carol finds out I've been talking to the love of my life. Catch you another time?"

"Bye," Ell whispered, then buried her head in her hands, wondering how she could feel so devastated that her two "friendly boys" had finally found, or been found by, girls who *would* promote them to boyfriend status. She should be happy for her friends... not devastated by their good fortune. She contemplated calling her friend Gary from Las Vegas, but decided that, the way things were going, he'd turn out to be engaged or married.

That'd make her even more depressed...

She'd just need to wait until her date with Gordon Saturday. Maybe she could get her love life on, after Velos' show in Raleigh. Ell turned back to the screen with her dark energy calculations. After staring at the screen for another thirty minutes without seeing anything, she got up, went into the bathroom and put on her "Raquel Blandon" disguise.

Walking down the stairs, Ell met Bridget coming up. Bridget said, "Where're you going, this hour of the night?"

Feeling like Bridget could see the desperation oozing out of her, Ell said, "I thought I'd go see how Vic's bar is doing now that the opening buzz has worn off. Wanna go with?"

Bridget smiled brightly, obviously delighted, "Sure, I desperately need some kind of social life, just let me put on my heels."

~~~

Ell had been going to walk through the woods to get the little pickup truck she used when she was in disguise but Bridget offered to take her car instead. In the car Bridget asked, "Why are you going as... 'Raquel' right?"

"People treat me weird when I'm out as 'Ell.' I don't want to be signing autographs. I just want to be an ordinary person tonight."

"Hah! 'Ordinary.' *That's* hard to imagine for you, but it'll be fun. Maybe next time I could dress up as 'Ell' and sign autographs. I'd like to be that person sometime."

Despite her previous funk Ell giggled, "We *should* do that."

~~~

Vic's had a good crowd, though it didn't compare to their opening night with Velos. Bridget and Ell threaded their way up to the bar to get a beer for Bridget and Ell's usual Coke. The band, named "Parker," played bluegrass with a Celtic flavor. The peppy rhythm had them swaying before they even got out into the main club. All the tables were occupied so they stood near the dance floor, just taking it in for a bit, then Bridget said, "Let's get out there and dance!"

Ell frowned, "Where are we going to put our drinks?"

"On the rail here."

When Ell set her drink down she realized a lot of people must leave their drinks on the rail. She wondered how they kept them straight. She bent her straw over and looked carefully at the depth of the Coke so she'd be able to tell if it'd been disturbed. Soon Ell and Bridget were out on the floor freestyling.

After they'd been dancing a little while, an enthusiastic young man stomped his way out onto the floor spinning and thumping his feet. A girl on the other side of the floor turned toward him and started doing the same thing. Ell turned to Bridget, "Is there a name for the dance those two are doing?"

"Clogging."

"Do you know how to do it?"

Bridget shrugged, "Kinda." She started a simple kick, step, kick, step rhythm and Ell quickly accompanied her. Ell turned to watch the young man. After focusing on his feet a moment, she added his "double toes" and "rock steps" to what she was doing, enjoying the challenge of matching him.

Bridget went back to simply dancing freestyle to the music while watching in amazement as Ell quickly added more and more of the steps the young man was performing. She shook her head. With anyone else, she'd have thought that they'd been teasing when they asked what the dance was and then immediately demonstrated that they were an expert at it—but of course she'd seen Ell dance in amazing fashions before. She suspected that picking up clogging simply seemed easy to Donsaii.

A few minutes later Ell was doing everything the young man was doing, essentially following him in the same steps at the same time and occasionally throwing in a flourish of her own. When he turned, she turned. Even though they were across the floor from one another, it looked like they were dancing as partners. She really liked it, the fast pace of the foot movements was great exercise, though she wished it incorporated something for her hands to do. She grinned, the joyful activity had brought her out of her funk. She looked at Bridget and raised her eyebrows. Bridget grinned back at her.

The song drew to an end and Ell headed back over to her drink. Bridget came behind her, "Don't you want to dance another one?"

"Hah! I was *workin'* out there, not just lazy freestylin' like you were. I need a break."

Bridget laughed, "OK," she put her hands up, "I'll admit. I took the easy way out." She looked to Ell's left and raised her eyebrows.

The guy who'd been clogging out on the dance floor was standing next to Ell, obviously waiting to speak, but not wanting to interrupt.

When Ell turned to him, he said, "Hi, I thought I should come meet my dance partner. My name's Shan." Tall and rangy looking, with shaggy blond hair, he held his hand out to shake.

Ell thought, *wow... handsome!*

Ell shook his hand, "Hi, I'm Raquel," she motioned, "this is my friend Bridget."

"Where'd you learn to clog?"

Bridget opened her mouth to say, *she learned here*

tonight! But Ell beat her to answering, saying, "Oh, just here and there, a little bit at a time."

Bridget opened her mouth to protest, but caught a little head shake from Ell and subsided.

"Have you clogged with a partner? I mean other than dancing the same steps with me like you just did?"

Ell shook her head.

"Would you try it with me?"

Ell shrugged, "Sure, but you'll have to teach me how."

The band swung into the venerable "Orange Blossom Special" and Shan held his hand out. Ell took it and they headed out to the floor with a lot of other enthusiastic dancers. Shan took her hands and turned her into a cuddle, which Ell was familiar with from swing dancing. Then they started doing clogging footwork similar to what they'd been doing across the floor from one another. Shan started taking her through some turns. Ell found it different from the swing dancing she'd done in the past because the footwork was much faster but the turns far slower. She really enjoyed it, but realized that, with her poor stamina and the fast pounding of their feet, she'd be exhausted pretty quickly.

~~~

Shan felt excited to be clogging with someone really good at it. She matched his footwork effortlessly. When he threw in a different step from what he'd been doing, he could barely tell her feet lagged his before they were doing the same thing. It was as if she could read his mind and knew what he was about to do with his feet. Or else, as if she were supernaturally fast to correct what she'd been about to do, changing it to what he'd
~~~

already started doing. She followed him effortlessly through turns, no matter how complex. When Orange Blossom finished he tried to get her to stay out on the floor for another dance, but she insisted she needed to rest.

Shan worried, to look at her, the girl was in great shape. He didn't think she could really be very tired. Maybe she just didn't like dancing with him? Usually, because most guys either couldn't dance or were terrible at it, girls kind of flocked around him wanting to dance. So, usually he had his pick. But this Raquel danced so well he could easily imagine she might be bored with him. There was just something about her… he really wanted to get to know her better. He noticed the red wristband indicating that she was too young to drink. "So are you a student or have you joined the workforce?"

"I work out in the triangle and take a couple of classes at UNC."

"I'm a Tar Heel too."

"What are you studying?"

He shrugged diffidently, "Math."

Ell had the impression he took a lot of pride in his major, but didn't want to sound like he was bragging. "Hey, that sounds hard."

He wrinkled his nose, "Some of it's pretty tough. But I like it, so it's mostly fun for me."

"What are you gonna do with a math degree when you're done?"

"There're lots of jobs in statistics and analysis and finance, but I'm hoping to stay in the ivory tower, teaching and trying to do innovative things."

Ell grinned at him, "Sounds cool, you ready to dance

again?"

Shan said, "Sure," turning toward the floor, wondering whether he'd sounded too pompous with his "ivory tower" remark. *Oh well,* he mentally shrugged to himself, *if she doesn't like it, there're a lot more fish in the sea.* His dad often said that to him. But... there was just something about this girl...

~~~

After another fun dance they came back to their usual spot to find Bridget was taking a turn out on the floor, freestyling with a young man. Shan said, "Can I buy you a drink?"

Feeling guilty having a presumably poor student buy her a drink, but reminding herself that this was how the game was played, Ell nodded, "Coke please?" She admired Shan as he headed over to the bar. He looked older than the usual student and quite handsome in a rugged, ropy kind of way. *Could he be a grad student?* She wondered, thinking that he certainly didn't look like the prototypical math nerd.

Bridget came back and introduced "Raquel" to Ryan, the fellow she'd been dancing with. "What happened to Shan?"

"He's at the bar."

"Is not," Shan's voice said over her shoulder, "He's back with the goods." He set a Coke down in front of Ell.

"Thanks!" Ell said taking a sip and then introducing him to Ryan.

"Actually, Ryan's my housemate."

Bridget rolled her eyes, "Don't tell me you guys are out as a team and we've just been picked up by a smooth talker and his wingman?"

Shan put his hands up in surrender, "Now, now. A
~~~

man and his housemate go out in the evening. While he's out enjoying a solo dance, a beautiful young woman starts dancing with him, even though she's all the way across the floor. Merely to be polite he goes to meet the girl he's been dancing with. His friend happens to innocently notice that the clogging girl has a beautiful friend. Completely innocent series of events."

Ell lowered an eyebrow, "Hmmm, sounds entirely too well rehearsed to me. What do you think Bridget?"

Bridget looked back and forth from Shan to Ryan, "I would have characterized it as, 'Two young ladies go out intending to devastate the men of the town. Shortly after demonstrating their astonishing dancing skills they find they've attracted two hapless victims.'"

Shan and Ryan laughed, "A much more accurate depiction. No doubt that's what just went down." Ryan said.

Ell turned to Bridget, "Now that we've got them where we want them, what are we going to do with them?"

"Dance some more?"

~~~

This time when they got out on the floor, Shan asked, "Do you swing dance?"

Ell nodded and he took her hand, pumping gently to establish a slower step rhythm, then beginning to twirl her around the floor. Shan's eyebrows rose. He'd been surprised at how well she'd followed his rapid clogging footwork, but the way she followed him through the rapid turns and twirls of swing dancing astonished him. She followed effortlessly, never getting a cue wrong, never turning the wrong way. Her elegant, graceful form as she spun rapidly back and forth seemed more
~~~

like a ballerina than an amateur dancing for fun.

"So what classes are you taking?" Shan asked when they'd returned to their drinks. He noticed that she was staring at her drink, "Is something wrong?"

"Somebody moved my drink," Ell said, looking around. "Maybe they mixed it up with their own?" She carefully set it down and stuffed the napkin in the top of it so that she wouldn't forget and take a sip.

She didn't tell him how Steve frequently reminded her to be careful of her drinks in public places. This was the first time her precautions had ever recognized a change.

Shan looked at her drink, surprised she'd ruined it with the napkin just because it'd been moved. But maybe she thought someone had taken a sip? "Do you want me to get you another?"

"No thanks... I'm taking classes in astronomy and biology."

"That's a weird pair, what degree are you working toward?"

"I'm... not, actually. Just taking classes because I'm interested." She smiled, "Trying to better myself."

Thinking that she sounded kinda aimless, Shan asked, "Where do you work?"

"Quantum Research."

Shan frowned, "Never heard of them, but that's an interesting name. What do they make?"

"QR's really small, they mostly do research. Tell me more about you. You don't look like the prototypical nerdy mathematician?"

"Oho! I've been stereotyped! Just 'cause a guy likes math, it doesn't mean he can't like sports too, you know?"

Ell lifted her chin in question, "What sport?"

"I like 'em all, B-ball's probably my favorite though."

"Hmmm, I played a little basketball back in High School."

Bridget and Ryan came back off the dance floor, "Hey, you guys look awfully serious!"

Ell said, "I've been learning about Shan. He's a Math major. What do you do Ryan?"

"Student. Biomedical Engineering."

"You going to design the first successful artificial heart?"

"How'd you know?" he grinned.

Ell grinned back, "You're wearin' your heart on your sleeve."

They all had a laugh, but then Bridget finished her beer saying, "Well, some of us have to work in the morning."

Ell turned to Shan, "It was good clogging with you. Thanks for the lesson."

"Can I call you sometime?"

"Sure, I'd like that."

As Ell rode home with Bridget she felt peaceful. Shan seemed nice and it was kind of fun flirting with someone new. Maybe he wouldn't replace Roger or Phil, but perhaps someone would. At least her love life didn't seem as bleak; after all, she'd met someone interesting on her first foray with Bridget.

When she got home, her interest in the dark energy problem had returned. She worked on it until her usual 4AM bedtime while occasionally checking wall screens that showed the teecees huddling together under Goldy's wings as a steady rain dripped down on them through the forest. *Maybe we can show them how to build a shelter,* she thought, surprised that they didn't already know how.

***

Dressed as "Belle," Ell trotted up the stairs of the Smith building on UNC's campus. She'd opened the door when Allan, her AI, said, "You have a call from Dr. Kant Fladwami, the Presidential Science Advisor."

Ell kept walking down the hall to the restroom. "Yes?"

"Hello Ms. Donsaii. I'm calling at the behest of the President to see if you have any ideas for dealing with greenhouse related climate change? I realize this is a little outside your usual area of expertise, but we had a crazy suggestion that we could vent CO_2 into deep space through your ports. I personally think that'd be a bad idea because I don't think we want to lose that carbon and oxygen forever. However, we need some out of the box thinking."

He gave a little laugh, "I wouldn't expect that climate change's something you've been working on, but if you do come up with any ideas?"

"We actually may have something that would have an impact, but you'd have to deal with more of those dreaded economic upheavals."

"Well, we appreciate the slow release of your technologies so far. That's helped significantly with the economic disruptions to this point. Perhaps you'd do the same with whatever you are speaking of? What is it?"

"Oh, sorry we really aren't even sure it'll work yet. Can I get back to you in a week or two?"

"It'd sure help if I could give the President some idea

what you're thinking. Some other method to sequester CO_2 perhaps?"

"No not sequestration. Sorry, I really don't feel comfortable talking about it yet, but I *will* get back to you."

"OK," Fladwami said reluctantly.

Once Allan had disconnected the call, Ell stepped into one of the stalls in the bathroom and began removing "Belle." The padded pants and platinum blond wig went into her nearly empty backpack along with the cheek pads. She pulled out some wet wipes and wiped Belle's thick makeup off. Stepping out of the stall, she stepped up to the mirrors and wiped off a few smudges she'd missed. She put on a baseball cap that covered much of her hair and shaded her eyes. Satisfied, she headed back out into the hall. She saw Steve from her security detail fidgeting in front of a bulletin board. Putting her head down so the bill of her cap shaded her face even more, she headed into the linguistics faculty offices. An internet search had revealed that a Dr. Kira Piscova had written a paper on translation methodologies for unknown languages. It was a review of various methods used by linguists over the centuries when faced with languages that didn't have living translators. Most of the examples pertained to written languages, but it seemed that it had been a long time since anyone had truly encountered a new spoken language.

There really weren't any experts available who'd actually translated a new language.

There were scads of popular fiction stories in which people learned a language by pointing to objects, saying their own word for the object, then waiting for the speaker of the other language to use their own word for the same thing. In the situation confronting team Teecee at present, they couldn't point to anything and say the word. However, if they could somehow substitute their new rocket for the old one, they might be able to. The new rocket would arrive on TC3 next week, but Ell could see no reason why they shouldn't, to some degree, get started on the translation problem now. After all they already had some recordings of the teecees talking.

Because Dr. Piscova's office hours came right after Ell's biology class, it saved her a trip to campus, only requiring her to do the change out of the "Belle" disguise. Keeping the bill of her cap as low as possible Ell looked around and finally came to an office labeled with Piscova's name. To her relief no students were currently in the office. She knocked on the doorframe.

~~~

Piscova looked up from her screen, "Come in." She looked curiously at the slender young woman in the door. "Hi..." The student looked familiar, but Piscova would've sworn she didn't actually have her in one of her classes. "Are you taking a class remotely?" Students who took courses online rarely came in to the office. If they took the class over the net, they tended to do everything over the net. The girl sat down in the chair that faced away from the door and took off her hat. "Oh!" Piscova covered her mouth, wide eyed. "Ms. Donsaii...!"

"Yes Ma'am."

Piscova frowned, "Are you..." *taking a class*, she'd been about to ask but it seemed ridiculous on the face of it. She turned fully in her chair. "How may I help
~~~

you?"

"We need someone to translate a completely unknown language. We're hoping you'd like the challenge... or know someone who would."

Piscova narrowed her eyes. "Are you trying to say that you've found some unknown tribe somewhere? The world has no longer has any places untouched by civilization." Her eyes widened as she thought about what Donsaii was known for, "Wait, did you find an artifact out in space with writing on it?"

Donsaii shrugged, "I can't really tell you more until you've signed a confidentiality agreement."

Piscova frowned, "Wait this is some kind of secret? If I were to work on translation... what would I get out of it? It doesn't sound like I'd even be allowed to publish?"

"Yes Ma'am, you'd be able to publish, we'd just want you to delay for a couple of years. We'd also be happy to pay for consulting."

Piscova's eye's widened. No one had ever offered to pay her for linguistics consulting. "I'd have to check into consulting fees. Can I see the... what did you call it...? 'Confidentiality agreement'?"

~~~

Ell left the building, hat low over her eyes again. One girl, climbing the steps when Ell came out, turned to stare, but otherwise Ell seemed to go unrecognized. Piscova had agreed to check with her department head about any policies regarding consulting and call Ell that afternoon.
~~~

Chapter Eight

Dex saw a red glowing spot underneath the meteorite! Were the spirits who showed himrself and Syrdian how to climb the cliff sending another message? If so, was the message somehow coming out *beneath* the meteorite? Hie leaned hies head down to look closely. The red spot was on the ground beneath the meteorite, not on the meteorite itself though a red glow did light the underside of the meteorite. Hie tried to lean in to see the red spot and determine whether it was another picture, but hie couldn't see it because the meteorite blocked hies view.

Gingerly hie reached out and grasped the meteorite. Could hie move the meteorite without disturbing the glowing lines underneath it? Hie picked the meteorite up just a tiny bit and moved it farther away so hie could see the lines.

The glowing lines moved with the meteorite! It was as if they were hiding under it! Syrdian said, "Dex, what... what's that?!"

Dex shrugged hies wings as hie wondered why the lines would hide. They'd seemed bold enough the first time, appearing over a huge area on the surface of the cliff. Hie lifted the meteorite slowly up away from the glowing spot under it. To hies astonishment, the glowing red area slowly enlarged as hie lifted the meteorite, growing from a small red splotch to a... a drawing... A small drawing, true, but obviously a drawing, similar in color, detail and style to the drawing on the cliff wall, even though this drawing was tiny.

Deciding to move the meteorite completely out of the way, Dex lifted it further, turning to put it aside. Hies wings trembled as the drawing enlarged further, then swung away from himr as Dex turned the meteorite. Hie moved the meteorite back and the drawing came back! Did the drawing *emanate from* his beautiful meteorite?!

Dex had never heard or seen anything like it. The closest hie could come to an analogous event was the casting of shadows on the wall of the cave from the sun or a small fire. Moving an object that was casting a shadow, caused the shadow to move similarly and some dalins were talented at casting shadows with their hands. Shadows that looked like animals, kind of like the glowing drawings. Dex looked momentarily up into the air, thinking that hie might see something up there that might be casting, well, not shadows, but light that made the drawings.

There was nothing up there.

While holding the meteorite still, Dex slowly reached under it and felt the edge of the glowing red drawing with a claw.

Dex dropped the meteorite when a glowing red line appeared *on* hies claw! As the meteorite fell and rolled away from himr, the drawing diminished in size down to a splotch, then shot away towards Dex and disappeared. Dex danced away from it so that the red spot didn't touch himr.

Dex stood staring, wings extended, hearts pounding, breath pouring through himr and whistling out hies vent. Hie heard rustling-thumping sounds that hie distantly recognized came from Syrdian running into the forest. Hie saw a faint red glow on one of the watery clear spots on the meteorite and bent to look at it. Hie picked up a nearby twig and reached gingerly to touch the clear spot with the twig. As hie did the tip of the twig flashed red also!

Dex found himrself a couple of wing beats away, still staring at the meteorite. It appeared as harmless as ever. Walking gingerly back over, hie examined the twig hie'd dropped. It appeared normal. Dex turned to hies own claw which had turned red and studied it. It also appeared unchanged. Picking up the twig again hie put it in front of the clear spot and watched it turn red, then backed it away, seeing it go from one bright spot to a few lines across the twig as hie pulled it away.

Finally, hie reached out and picked up the meteorite, lifting it away and pointing the clear spot back at the ground. Trembling, hie saw the picture zoom in from the side and appear on the ground right below the clear spot. Hie could tell it was showing one of its drawn pictures, but the image was distorted by pebbles, twigs and grass. Gently hie set the meteorite back down and cleared a spot, smoothing the dirt.

Picking up the meteorite, Dex gingerly moved it over the smoothed area. The glowing red lines clearly showed a picture now. What was it? Hie tilted hies head back and forth studying it. It looked like it showed a forked stick, either stuck in the ground, or a cut off sapling. Or was it an entire tree? A string, or maybe a rope, went up through the fork and back down to hold the end of a much larger stick, or maybe a log up off the ground.

The picture changed. What was that? Oh! Hie recognized the western horizon by the outline of Wayvern mountain. The big red spot must be the sun.

Suddenly the sun appeared closer to the horizon, then halfway behind the horizon, then gone and all the lines dimmed. Maybe the pictures were trying to show night time?

The picture of the forked stick with the string reappeared, now with the glowing lines looking dimmer. Hie saw that the other end of the string was tied to a trigger like hie used on hies bent sapling snares. That trigger was attached to a noose suspended over... oh a trail. The next picture appeared, showing an animal on the trail. The animal looked like a burrower. The picture changed so that the animal's head entered the noose of the snare. The next picture showed that the log or heavy stick had fallen, pulling the noose tight around the animal and lifting it into the air.

With a sense of sudden dawning, Dex realized it was simply showing himr how to use a weight instead of a sprung sapling for hies snares. It looked like it might also be telling himr to use them at night on trails?

The pictures had started over. Dex wondered why a weight instead of a sprung sapling? As hie stared at the picture hie realized it showed the boles of trees. *Oh! It's showing snares in the forest! There aren't many saplings in the right places underneath the forest canopy, but there're a lot of dead branches I could use for weights!*

Dex looked around. It was getting dark, but maybe hie could put out one snare? Working quickly, Dex set up a snare powered by a weight along a small game trail. Hie had to finish setting it mostly by feel in the darkness.

When Dex returned to the campsite hie was pleased to see that Syrdian had returned, cleared an area and started a fire. Four tubers they'd dug up earlier in the day were roasting over the fire. The meteor lay quietly where Dex left it, no glowing red to be seen. "Are you OK Dex?" Syrdian asked quietly.

"Yes. Thank you for making dinner."

"You're welcome, though I wish some flyers'd attacked us today. I'm hungry for some meat... Did the glowing red lines attack you?"

"No. This is hard to believe, but the red lines seem to... come out of the meteor. Once I held the meteor correctly, the lines made pictures like they did that night at the cliff. The pictures seemed to be telling me to make a new kind of snare and put it out at night in the forest."

"At night? Aren't the animals sleeping then?"

Dex shrugged hies wings, "Maybe not all of them?"

Syrdian tilted hies head, "Maybe some hunt at night like the taklor."

Dex tilted hies own head as hie considered. The taklor was a hunting flyer, smaller than the talor, that mostly hunted at night. It had large eyes and seemed to track prey mostly by infrared. Watching taklors attack hot rocks thrown out into the night in front of the cave was a popular pastime for young dalin. It irritated the grown dalin who had to send the youth out to get more rocks the next day. "Maybe. But the drawings showed a burrower caught in the trap."

Dex and Syrdian ate the unsatisfying tubers and crouched down to sleep.

~~~

In the night Dex woke to a loud hissing sound. The fire was out, so hie couldn't see much except the infrared glow where it'd been. No! There was a bright
~~~

red glowing spot in the air over where the meteorite had been lying! Wings quivering hie poked the fire with a stick and looked around. Behind himr hie saw a large infrared splotch!

Dex grabbed one of their pointed wooden staves with one hand, two pieces of fire wood in the other and leapt to the other side of the fire.

Syrdian anxiously barked, "What?! What?!"

Dex said, "Come over here!" I think a beast from the forest is approaching that side of the fire."

Syrdian scrambled around to Dex's side but, to Dex's dismay, failed to bring hies pointed staff. Dex gave Syrdian the pieces of firewood, "Try to start the fire back up!"

Syrdian crouched to poke up the fire. Dex peered into the darkness at the large infrared splotch. Suddenly a red glowing dot appeared in the middle of the infrared splotch, then it spread forming horizontal glowing lines covering a large animal, obviously some kind of predator from the shape of its mouthparts. The eyes seemed large. Its head had drawn up and back in reaction to the red lines.

For a moment the animal looked like it would back away into the forest but then it suddenly began to rush forward…

Dex's wings lifted and hie could feel Syrdian's doing the same, though even if both of them could have flown, there wasn't enough free space to fly inside the forest. Hie gripped hies staff with trembling hands and pointed it with a sinking feeling…

Suddenly the lines outlining the predator coalesced down to two brilliant spots centered on its eyes…

With a howling sound the predator turned its head

and tore away into the forest...

The fire rising up from Syrdian's efforts showed Dex his meteorite standing there on its bottom end like it had been when it first landed in the meadow. Hie looked down, its little legs were out. The glowing redness hie'd seen when hie'd first woken was gone now, but hie had no doubt it had come from the same clear spot where the glowing red lines emanated.

Syrdian's arms crept tremblingly around Dex. After a moment, Dex cast an arm back around Syrdian, then folded a wing around himr too. Syrdian whispered, "What just happened?"

Dex said, "I'm not sure. I think the meteorite hissed to warn us of the predator... Then it shone the little flame that makes the red lines into the predator's eyes to drive it away. Maybe? But I'm not *sure* that's what happened."

"When did you put it up on its little legs?"

"I didn't," Dex said with an awed tone.

"Do you think... it put *itself* up on its legs?"

"I think it's very powerful. Who knows what it can and can't do? But if it drove away that predator, I'm glad it seems to be on our side..." After a little pause, he said, " Let's not anger it."

"How do we... not... anger it?"

"I don't know." Dex said quietly.

***

Ell settled back, trembling slightly in reaction. When Allan had first drawn her attention to a large infrared object approaching the teecees, she'd thought surely they'd sense its approach. As it came closer and closer and the teecees kept sleeping, she'd gotten more and more concerned. At first she thought she had no way to sound the alarm, but then she thought of the attitude jets and the hissing noise they made. Using them to right the rocket and set it on its legs had seemed inspired, not only waking the teecees, but positioning the cameras for a better view. Even better when she thought to have Allan paint the approaching animal with the laser. But the better view showed her the size and long pointed teeth of what had to be a very large predator. It looked fully capable of taking on both Goldy and Silver. Despite the low light cameras, she couldn't see the teecees well in the deep dark of the forest, but the way they'd scrambled to her side of the fire didn't give her the feel that they were confident about dealing with such a predator. When it started to rush toward them she'd had Allan turn up the power on the laser and shine it into the predator's eyes.

Only after the predator had bolted back away into the forest did she think that using the laser on high power might've provided the teecees with some food.

Perhaps not too. The laser was powerful enough to ablate tiny bits of rocks for spectroscopy, but it'd take quite a while to burn through water laden flesh down to a vital organ. Especially if you didn't know where the organ in question was located. *And* if the flesh you were trying to burn through was moving.

As the teecees settled back down, crouching by their fire, Ell slowly relaxed.

Eventually she returned to the calculations she'd been doing for Roger's steam engines— he began reading all you want you the ones to be powered by heat from the sun.

***

Syrdian awakened with the brightening light in the morning to find the fire stoked up but Dex gone. Hie stood and looked about without seeing Dex. With hunger pangs gnawing and no prospect of food, Syrdian warily left the camp to go down to the stream they'd been paralleling. Water would quench hies thirst and fill hies stomach temporarily. A little way out of camp hie encountered Dex returning with a full water skin and an odd looking animal with large eyes. Syrdian stared, "What's that?"

"Apparently some kind of forest animal that goes out at night. It crept into the snare the red lines said to build and put out at night. Look, it has big eyes like the taklors. Hope it's tasty."

Syrdian dipped hies head, "As hungry as I am, *anything* would be tasty this morning."

~~~In all you be

As they ate the, tasty as predicted, night animal. Syrdian said, "You were right about climbing the mountain. It isn't as hot up here, but it's getting harder to breathe. The air just pours through me when we're hiking these days."

Dex said, "Maybe we should start looking for some kind of shelter to live in and set up a camp for the summer."

"Do you think we can find a cave?"

Dex shrugged hies wings. "I don't know. They aren't very common, but maybe? Next time we reach a clearing, I could fly around and scout?"
~~~

***

Kira Piscova's AI said "Ms. Donsaii's returning your call."

Piscova said, "I'll take it... Hello, Ms. Donsaii?"

"Yes, Dr. Piscova. Were you able to work out the issues regarding consulting fees and non-disclosure?"

"Um, yes. I can sign the agreement at your convenience and the consulting fee you've offered is quite generous. Thank you."

"Do you have a PGR equipped AI yet?"

"Sorry, no. I don't really keep up with the latest tech. Even though everyone tells me it's the greatest, what I have now works fine for my needs."

"Well, we'd like to outfit you with a high end PGR connected AI. Both to help you with analysis and to make sure none of the data we provide you goes astray. Could you drop by D5R so our tech people could fit you up and install your AI's personality on the new headband?"

"Okaay."

"Then we could talk about exactly what it is that we need your help with?"

"Sure." Piscova signed off, wondering exactly what she'd be doing for them...

***

In Ell's ear, Allan said, "Presidential Science Advisor Fladwami is returning your call."

Ell put up a finger asking Emma to wait a moment, "Put him on... Dr. Fladwami?"

"Yes Ms. Donsaii?'

"I was calling back as you requested regarding CO_2 emissions. We think we might have a partial solution."

"That's great! We're having a conference on the reduction of greenhouse gas emissions next week with a lot of the big players in the transportation and energy industries represented. Do you think you could come to D.C. and make a presentation regarding your ideas at the conference?"

After a pause Ell said, "Sure… I'll probably have Dr. Emmerit make the presentation though. It's mostly his idea."

"You'll be there too though, right?"

"I can be."

"We'd really appreciate it."

Ell disconnected, amused to realize that Fladwami hadn't asked what the tech actually was. For a moment she wondered if she should give him some warning, but eventually she shrugged and turned back to Emma.

***

Piscova looked askance at her new AI headband. Its high end design didn't exactly fit her eclectic image. However, the actual computer they'd given her for the AI to reside in shocked her. It wasn't high end, it was *very* high end. She couldn't figure out why she would need such an astonishing AI for translation, but she wouldn't look a gift horse in the mouth. The young man who'd been fitting her said, "Is it OK?"

Kira shook herself, "Sure, what next?"

"I'm to take you to see Ell."

Surprised by his casual reference to Ms. Donsaii by her first name, Piscova said, "OK."

~~~

When they arrived in a conference room Donsaii looked up saying, “Oh, Hi Dr. Piscova. Come in!”

“Thank you.” She raised an eyebrow, “Do I finally get to find out what this is about?”

“Yes Ma’am. First I’d like to introduce you to the team you’re joining.” She was introduced to an astronomer from UNC and a biologist from NC State as well as some employees of “Quantum Research,” apparently a subsidiary of D5R. “As to what this is about, currently we’re observing some intelligent aliens on the third planet of the star Tau Ceti. We can hear them communicating acoustically, but we aren’t having much luck understanding the sounds.”

Piscova laughed, “Sure you are.” She looked around at them. “No, really, what’s this about?” She leaned back, expecting the others to be disappointed that she hadn’t fallen for their little joke. Instead, they all stared at her seriously.

“Allan,” Donsaii said, “brighten the display so we can see the teecees.”

The screens on the wall of the conference room brightened up and Kira saw some very strange beings there. The images looked like low light photography, devoid of color information. The creatures looked somewhat like perched birds, wings up top, large clawed feet under, bizarre tiny heads turned back over one wing, and, front limbs that looked like a cross between birds’ feet and human hands. Her eyes narrowed, they didn’t seem to be breathing.

Donsaii then said, “Now please play a recording of the teecees communication with one another.”

The screen jumped to a daylight picture of the
~~~

creatures next to a fire on which they were roasting something on a stick. Noise issued from the speakers, consisting of high pitched tweedling. Piscova stared for a moment then looked around at the group, "I'm not sure if this is some kind of joke, but these supposed aliens aren't breathing. If you aren't breathing, it's pretty hard to stay alive, much less speak."

Wheat, the biologist from NC State said, "That's a quick pick up." He grinned, "Actually, the first time I saw video from TC3, I thought it was a trailer from a new movie, so I know how you feel. However, I've watched a number of, well we *call* them dissections, although they're just the teecees 'cleaning' their catch prior to cooking it. But, anyway, I think I've come to understand how their respiratory system works."

Glancing at Piscova again, he then looked around at the others, "This is new to the rest of the group too." Addressing the group he said. "At first I was puzzled about the mechanics of their respiratory process. We pull air into our lungs with our diaphragms. The diaphragm is essentially a large muscular sheet that pulls downward, sucking air into the chest cavity and lungs. When it does so, it pushes the contents of the abdomen downward, thus when you take a deep breath, your stomach moves outward. But the teecees seem to have ribs around their entire body cavity so their abdomen can't expand to accept a displacement of volume from their chest." He looked around to be sure everyone seemed to be tracking what he'd said. "I've told you that I thought they pull air in through that hole at the base of the neck and exhaust it through the vent on the lower chest. And, as Dr. Piscova notes, the way they talk makes it seem like that airflow is pretty continuous. From one of the dissections yesterday, I now believe that they have two lungs, like we do, but with a diaphragm *between* them, rather than below both lungs like ours is. Instead of pushing the abdominal contents down like our diaphragm does, theirs pulls air into the left lung while squeezing the right lung and pulls air into the right lung while squeezing the left lung. Thus airflow into the intake and out the vent is almost continuous. Something akin to vocal cords in the vent makes the continuous sound of their speech." He looked around again, "I think it's very elegant and efficient."

Kira looked around at the group. They all appeared to be taking this completely seriously. Stifling a hysterical laugh, she turned back to look at the screens where the "teecees" were gesticulating. She closed her eyes briefly, but when she opened them everything had stayed the same. "Really?" she asked.

They all nodded solemnly.

***

Dex and Syrdian broke out of the forest into an enormous meadow. It sloped down on one side to the stream they'd been paralleling as they hiked to higher and higher altitudes. Like the meadow they'd started their climb from, it had some large rocks protruding from the upper end. "This looks like a good place to hunt." Syrdian said, then hies wings sagged remembering that hie couldn't hunt a meadow since hie couldn't fly. Hie lifted hies wing to look at the sutured lacerations. "Dex, I think the wounds in my wing *are* healing. Do you think I could try flying?"

Dex looked at Syrdian with some surprise. *Why*

would hie think I'd know? Hie stepped over closer and peered at the wounds, then gently tugged on them. The sutures were a little loose and the wound edges did seem to be stuck to one another by themselves now. "Does it hurt when I pull on the wound?" Hie tugged again.

"It aches a little."

Dex tilted hies head, "I think you should wait until it doesn't hurt, you don't want to rip them open again."

To Dex's surprise, Syrdian dipped hies head in acquiescence, "OK."

"I think I should look for a place for us to live near here. A permanent camp for the summer, I mean. Could you see if you can catch a swimmer from the stream? I'm starving."

"Great idea!" Syrdian said with enthusiasm because hie desperately wanted to contribute and so far catching swimmers had been the one thing hie was better at than Dex.

Dex beat into the air, surprised at how much harder flying had gotten as they climbed the mountain. No wonder the tribe preferred to fly a long distance to the south rather than a short distance up the mountain for the summer. Spending the summer flying in this thin air was going to be… very trying.

~~~

Wistfully, Syrdian watched Dex fly away. Syrdian felt melancholy, both for hies lost ability to fly—even though hie could see that flying was a struggle at this altitude—but also for Dex. Dex, whom Syrdian had never given a second thought to in days gone by. Dex, who daily seemed to surprise Syrdian with new capabilities.
~~~

Syrdian found himrself admiring Dex. Not only for hies ability to adapt to a situation which would have led to Syrdian's death if Dex hadn't been there, but also because Dex was a handsome dalin. Why hadn't Syrdian ever noticed this before...? Was it only because his tribal rank had been low?! Syrdian turned to the stream, happy to note it had several large pools visible along the side of the meadow.

~~~

Dex flew a large circle around the enormous clearing, hoping hie might see a cave of some sort. The only rocks hie saw were the ones in the clearing and the ones bordering the stream. Hie thought about making another, even larger circle, but with his breath whistling through himr, hie decided to stop and look more carefully at the rock outcropping in the meadow first. Hie circled it as hie came in to land. As hie looked at it hie got the impression that one huge rock had rolled down from one of the rocky areas that could be seen higher on the mountain. It had then broken into two huge cracked rocks that'd settled into the dirt of the meadow. The larger split separating them was a little wider than Dex's wingspan. Dex walked around the rocks hoping for an unseen recess that could act as a cave, but found nothing like that. Maybe they could build a roof over the big split and make their own cave? Hie turned to walk down to the stream, hoping that Syrdian had caught a swimmer for dinner.

Approaching the stream, hie saw Syrdian sitting on a large rock overhanging a pool with a fiberlin string in hies hand. "Any luck?"

Syrdian's head turned to put fore eyes on Dex. Hie whispered, "Yes, but speak quietly and I may get
~~~

another. Dex curiously walked out onto the rock, but Syrdian hissed, “Don’t show yourself over the edge, it’ll spook the swimmer.”

Dex stopped, watching curiously. The fiberlin held loosely in Syrdian’s hand started to move, the kinks in it from being wound on the stick slowly pulled straight. Suddenly Syrdian straightened from hies crouch, raising an arm over hies head and jerking the fiberlin straight. A moderately large swimmer flew up out of the water and Syrdian kept rapidly pulling it up, hand over hand with the fiberlin. It landed on the rock to flop around. Syrdian pinned it with a foot, then reached down with hies knife to stab the brain at the base of the neck.

“Way to go!” Dex exclaimed, admiring the large swimmer. “That’ll make a good dinner!”

Syrdian smiled happily at Dex. “Did you find us a cave?”

“No. But maybe we could build a shelter amongst those big rocks up in the meadow.”

Syrdian let hies wings sag sadly, waving hies head in disappointment, “I guess I just have to do everything,” hie sighed.

Dex’s head rose indignantly up and back. *After all I’ve done!* Then hie realized that Syrdian’s wings were quivering with laughter.

Syrdian said, “Behind you.”

Dex’s back eyes picked up the large shadowed area before hie turned hies fore eyes to see the shallow cave cut back under the rocky bank hie’d just walked down. Grinning, hie turned and beat a wingful of air at Syrdian. “Way to go *again*. Dinner *and* a place to stay. A good day’s work I’d say.”

Syrdian stretched, “Ah yes, and now I’m all tired out. Perhaps you’d fetch some firewood while I rest up?”

Dex laughed and sent another wingful of air Syrdian's way. "OK." With a lot of effort hie beat back into the air and flew to the verge to look for deadfall.

~~~

When Dex returned to the cave by the stream, Syrdian had broken down the swimmer Dex'd seen himr catch, as well as two smaller ones that hie'd apparently caught before Dex had arrived. Dex looked around. "Looks like I should get some green sticks to cook with. Anything else?"

"More firewood."

***

Dr. Fladwami felt quite proud of the conference he'd arranged at President Flood's direction. The companies he'd invited had presented a number of strategies they were proposing to use to further diminish greenhouse gas creation or to increase removal of the gasses from the atmosphere.

One thing that had surprised him was how many of the new strategies presented depended to some extent on the new ports created by Donsaii's company D5R. This included many plans for the capture of methane, to burn it for energy instead of allowing its release. One company actually did believe that each cow could be fitted with ports to catch the flatus and belches that contained so much methane. Fladwami's eyebrows had risen at this proposal. He seriously doubted cattle would tolerate the devices they'd proposed, but he wasn't sure. The transportation industries all had plans to deliver electricity to motors in cars, trucks, boats,
~~~

ships, airplanes and helicopters via wires passed through ports. Of course that only passed the CO_2 problem to the power companies. Admittedly, big power companies were much more efficient and produced less CO_2 than a hydrocarbon burning motor in each vehicle did, but there'd still be a lot of CO_2 production going on.

However, ports were even going to figure into carbon sequestration projects. Weighted ports dropped into deep-sea formations could inject CO_2 into basalt where CO_2 hydrates would sink, keeping them from escaping.

The exception to ports figuring into the plans were the solar, wind and water powered projects. Solar, wind and water power were nice, but expensive and still couldn't provide a large enough percentage of the energy that we use, so Fladwami didn't feel very enthusiastic about them. The administration would support them because of politics, not because they believed they'd significantly reduce greenhouse gas emissions.

Fladwami was looking forward to the next talk though. It was to be given by Donsaii's associate Emmerit. Fladwami wondered whether they were going to run with his suggestion to export CO_2 to space somehow. If so, he hoped that they had a plan to store it somehow. Then if needed someday, the carbon and oxygen might somehow be retrieved.

Emmerit and the young girl assisting him had wheeled a small table to the front of the room and put it up on the podium before this session. It had some coiled piping on each side of what looked like some kind of pump hooked up to an electric motor. Fladwami wondered what the device could show that couldn't be more easily demonstrated with a few slides.

The previous speaker left the podium and the moderator introduced Emmerit. As he approached, he pushed the table up beside the podium where everyone in the small auditorium could see it, then turned to the microphone. "We appreciate the invitation to present our own contribution to the modification of the energy-CO_2 axis. Since this is the last talk of the session you should all be able to come up and examine this... apparatus after I'm done speaking. It's a fairly simple and pretty crude proof of concept device. We are certain significant improvements can be made by qualified engineers. Essentially on your left you see a tubing coil. What you can't see is that inside that coil is an interior coil of tubing that's connected via small ports to a black tube we've placed in a near solar orbit. There, the high incidence of solar radiation will maintain the temperature of a black body at about 343 degrees Centigrade. That's about 650 degrees Fahrenheit for those of you more comfortable with that system. A heat transfer fluid can be circulated through the solar tube then back through the tube here." He turned a switch, "I'm initiating pumping now. The outer tube here is filled with water. The water's being converted to steam by the heat from the transfer fluid and..." he pointed to the pump/motor, "the steam's beginning to turn this small steam turbine. It, in turn is spinning this generator."

Fladwami sat up straighter, realizing that he'd had it backwards. He could see it beginning to spin. It wasn't a motor to turn a pump. It was a generator being turned by a turbine!

Emmerit continued. "Thus, this device's generating

electricity from solar energy without producing any CO_2. Additionally, rather than exhausting the spent steam out where it would heat our planet, the steam's then circulating into this tubing over here on your right. This second tubing has a tube inside of it through which a low temperature heat transfer fluid's being pumped. This second fluid goes through a finned pipe out in deep space beyond most of the asteroids. We've chosen that orbit because a black body there receives enough solar radiation to maintain a temperature of about minus 100 Centigrade. That's warm enough that our low temperature heat transfer fluid doesn't freeze even if we aren't pumping fluid through the pipe. But it's still cold enough to quickly re-condense the steam into water to be recirculated back to the engine."

Emmerit looked back up at the audience. "This little demonstration model is pretty inefficient, but still generates about five kilowatts. Ideally it should be able to produce nearly ten times that." He shrugged, "It needs a good engineer to optimize it, especially the fluid flows. However, even poorly optimized, it's producing five kilowatts without producing *any* CO_2 or heat.

"I'm sure you recognize that electrical generation is only one possible use. The shaft from the steam engine could be used to drive wheels or otherwise power machines directly.

"Also, of course, heat transfer could be used directly to heat or cool homes and buildings…" Emmerit stopped speaking as the initially stunned audience broke into pandemonium. Some people were cheering. Some were angrily protesting something they could see would break their companies and destroy their livelihoods. Many were rushing the exits, presumably to call their corporate headquarters.

Fladwami stood uncertainly. After a day and a half of presentations on tiny incremental improvements in the way we use fossil fuels to generate power and energy with slightly diminished productions of greenhouse gasses... Donsaii's group was going to produce power, heating and cooling, without using fossil fuels *at all*. Not only weren't they going to produce greenhouse gasses doing it, but they were going to do it without producing excess heat! He walked down toward the front, wanting to speak to Emmerit. For a moment he wondered where Donsaii was, she'd promised him she'd be here.

Damn! The girl who'd been helping Emmerit wheel things in and set them up *was* Donsaii! She'd been wearing a baseball cap, but now he could see a fringe of her reddish blond hair sticking out from under it. He should've recognized her! She just looked so dammed young! A crowd had gathered around Emmerit, apparently they were also too excited to recognize Donsaii. He walked over to where she amusedly watched Emmerit doing his best to handle the excited crowd of people. "Hello, Ms. Donsaii. I'm Kant Fladwami, thank you for coming. I'm reminded of my predecessor Chip Horton's admonition that I should try to stay abreast of what you are doing *at all times*. I cannot believe that, after his warning, I still failed to ask you what you were going to present to us today."

"Well, in retrospect it seems like a pretty obvious extension of the use of port technology. But like a lot of good ideas, it only seems obvious now that Dr. Emmerit realized it could be done. He's licensing the technology to ET Resources and they plan to place the heat transfer tubes into near solar and deep space orbits and then sell the “heat” or the “cold” to users here on Earth.”

Fladwami shook his head. “You realize that you made most of the other talks at this conference irrelevant?”

“Oh, no sir. It’s going to take a long time to roll this tech out. We’ll need those things in the meantime.”

Fladwami’s eyes narrowed, “Why would it take quite a while? It seems to use ports, which you have well worked out, and heat transfer fluids which are an established technology. The steam turbine technology is very mature once you’ve created the steam, and pumping the hot or cold fluid through air conditioning coils shouldn’t take much engineering.”

“Ah…” she got a wistful look. “Because it’s going to *destroy* the petroleum industry and I think we should let them down easy. Just like the other new technologies resulting from ports, I think it’s got to be done a little at a time. I’m hoping President Flood’s administration will provide us with an extension on the patent, like President Teller’s people did for ports themselves—so our investors’ll be willing to release it slowly?”

Fladwami tilted his head. “Damn, you’re right. I should have considered the economic implications of just turning this stuff loose myself. I’ll talk to the president.”

She tilted her head as well, “You might want to also do a press release on the low tempo rollout to slow the run on petroleum stocks?”

Fladwami’s eyes widened, “Crap! There are reporters and bloggers here who’ve probably already put this on the net! I’d better call the President *now*.” As he turned and started trotting out of the auditorium he called back over a shoulder, “Sorry to leave you so suddenly!"

Chapter Nine

Dex wearily flew back to camp. Hie'd unsuccessfully stooped on several burrowers. At this altitude, beating back into the air after a miss felt exhausting, though hie kept telling himrself it couldn't really be that bad. The snares hie'd put out hadn't produced, and hie couldn't imagine why. Hie'd caught several animals at those locations a while back, but after a while they just stopped catching anything. Hie'd even gone out into the forest with hies "flyer swatter" but the little flyers that attacked didn't seem to live this high on the mountain. Swatting flyers that weren't attacking never seemed to work, they easily avoided himr. *Maybe Syrdian caught some swimmers?* As hie coasted in over the meadow hie saw that a family of zornits had taken up residence in the meadow. Zornits were larger cousins of the zornic they'd encountered in the forest. Omnivorous, but leaning toward eating mostly meadow vegetation, nonetheless, they could be bad news. Too big to kill, dangerous to attack and territorial to a fault, they were likely to drive away some of the smaller prey.

Dex landed just above the cave and looked back at the zornits. Hies wings drooped. Hie looked down at the camp. An empty handed Syrdian looked back up at himr. "No luck?"

Syrdian shook hies head. "I've caught all the swimmers in the nearby parts of the stream. Maybe I could teach you how to catch them and you could fly farther up than I can hike?"

Dex dipped hies head yes. "Some zornits've moved into the meadow. I think we should try to chase them away."

Syrdian's wings drooped also, "I'm not sure we could. Maybe we need to move to a new area? Then you could put your snares on new paths? I could try a fresh section of stream?"

Dex's head rose. Put the snares on different paths? What a great idea, maybe I've just caught all the animals that use the paths I've got the snares on. "I'm going to go move some snares."

"OK, I found a big nodule of flint. Do you know anything about making blades?"

Dex shrugged, "Not much."

"I'm going to try making a knife. I've re-flaked mine a couple of times and they're getting small."

"Good luck," Dex said, turning back out to the meadow and hies traps. Syrdian looked thinner. Dex found himrself liking Syrdian more and more, no longer a distant infatuation, but now what hie thought of as true love. To hies horror, just as hie fell in love, Syrdian seemed to be wasting away because Dex couldn't provide enough food to keep himr healthy up here on the mountain.

Just before hie took off, Dex noticed that hies meteor was standing erect on the top of the bank above their cave. For a moment hie wondered why Syrdian had put it there, but then hie shrugged and took off to move hies snares.

***

Wall Street Journal—The Presidential Conference on

Global Warning was stunned today by an announcement from D5R, the technology startup responsible for the ports that saved the space station and deflected Comet Hearth-Daster. As if the ports themselves weren't going to result in enough changes to our world, D5R revealed plans to provide really cheap solar power.

Oil stocks have plummeted…

Ell walked into the Five Eighteen West restaurant in Raleigh and looked around for Gordon but didn't see him. As she approached the hostess stand the woman's eyes widened. "Good evening Ms. Donsaii. How may we help you?"

"I'm meeting a Gordon Speight. Is he here yet?"

"Oh my, yes!" She grinned, "Having him here's caused quite the uproar. Having you here at the same time is really going to…" She ran down.

Ell thought the girl would go cross-eyed pondering it. "Can you take me to him?"

"Oh! Yes, sorry. This way please."

They went up the stairs and around a corner. Ell looked around as they entered the room. She didn't see a table with only one person at it? Then she tracked the direction the hostess was heading and realized that Gordon was sitting at a table for four that had *girls* seated in each of the other three seats!"

The hostess approached Gordon and said, "Mr. Speight, Ms. Donsaii says she's here to meet you?"

"Yes, yes!" Gordon bounded to his feet. "Ell, how are you?" He looked down at the girls at his table, "Ladies, it's been nice meeting you. I need some time to myself now, OK?"

With moues of disappointment the young ladies

slowly got up and moved away, one of them giving Gordon a desperate looking peck on the cheek before she departed. Another said "We love you!"

They didn't go too far. It turned out they had a table nearby. Gordon said, "Man, nowadays Velos fans seem to be everywhere! I guess you'd know what dealing with fans is like though, huh?"

Ell shrugged and sat, reflecting that in her experience women seemed to be much more aggressive in their pursuit of famous people than men were. She'd certainly never had three men approach her in a restaurant and sit down with her. "Are they going to the concert tonight?"

He grinned, "Yeah, and pretty pumped to have run into me at dinner."

He glanced at them so Ell did too. All three were still looking his way. As Ell watched, one of them blew Gordon a kiss. Ell said, "They're pretty assertive. Do you run into a lot of girls that're... so aggressive?"

Gordon shrugged, "More and more."

Their waiter arrived and interrupted their conversation with questions about their dinner. After he departed Gordon turned the talk to Ell and what was happening in her life. The dinner was excellent and they enjoyed themselves, but the three girls came back over during dessert to ask Gordon for autographs. Ell was torn when he acquiesced, both disappointed because he interrupted his time with her to sign them, and proud that he hadn't been rude like Olympic sprinter Michael Fentis had been to Ell years ago.

~~~

At the auditorium Ell entered with Gordon through the "artist's entrance," surprised at the way people
~~~

kowtowed to him. Gordon introduced her to his business manager and a sound man that he'd had train with Vic. Then there were some other musicians that Velos had hired to "round out" their sound. Ell and Gordon didn't really have any more time to talk as Velos prepped itself for the show.

~~~

Ell put on her ball cap and went out into the audience to take in the show. She stood in the shadows, tapping a foot, enthralled by the music and happy that the few people that recognized her moved on without making a big deal of it. Velos sounded good, though not as good as the recordings they'd made at Vic's. Those'd been climbing the charts.

The crowd went crazy when Velos played their hits.

Gordon'd been fun at dinner, and she kept rationalizing the girls at his table. He needed to be good to his fans after all. As an entertainer, fans were his lifeblood. But Ell felt put off by the whole thing. She wasn't sure she was ready to come in second to his fans.

If her relationship with Gordon developed further, could she take it?

She wondered if these issues afflicted the relationships of many famous people. Since getting into music Gordon'd pretty much ignored Ell's alter ego, his old friend "Belle." He'd returned the money "Belle's aunt" had loaned him to jump start his career. As she thought about it, she realized she felt terribly uncomfortable with the way he seemed fascinated with the famous "Ell," but uninterested in the more ordinary "Belle."

On the other hand, was it fair to be hurt because he
~~~

wasn't as interested in the version of herself that she had purposely made less attractive? Her head swam with the ramifications.

Over the break Ell went back to Gordon's dressing room. When she pushed the door open she found the dressing room packed with fans carrying VIP passes. Ell's eyes narrowed, all but one of the "fans" were attractive young girls. The three girls from dinner were among the crowd gathered around Gordon. As she watched one of them threw her arms around him, crushing her body against his and kissing him on the lips! He broke the kiss after a moment, looked around the dressing room, saw Ell and disentangled himself. "Ell!" he called, "Come have some of the goodies!" He waved at a large table set with hors d'oeuvres.

Reluctantly Ell entered the room and made her way to the table. Gordon chattered brightly with the girls gathered around him while Ell filled a little plate. She stepped closer to Gordon who put his arm out, "Stancil!" he called to Velos' manager, "Get a picture of me with Ell." He put an arm over her shoulders, saying, "Are you going to dance during the second set?"

Ell swallowed, smiled for the picture, then shook her head.

"Aw, come on. It'll make you even more famous."

Ell grinned at him, "I'm already more famous than I want to be."

Gordon's eyebrows rose, "You can never be too famous! Stancil, get me a picture with all my fans here!"

Ell slipped out from under Gordon's arm as the rest of the girls crowded in for the picture.

As she squeezed out the door, a last glance showed her another of the girls from dinner plastered to

Gordon's side.

Tears trickled down Ell's cheeks during the ride back home. Recognizing that many men would be intimidated by her success, she'd been thinking of Gordon as someone so successful that he wouldn't be affected that way.

He'd seemed like someone she could love but… not any more. Would she ever find someone? Someone not just chasing her for her fame or money? Someone undaunted by her fame? Someone who loved Ell for Ell?

***

Dex woke hungry. Hie and Syrdian had collected and eaten a few edible plants the night before, but plants alone wouldn't sustain them. Hie climbed up the bank to where the meteor stood. Again hie wondered why Syrdian'd put it up there.

Hie liked the thought of it up there, watching over them at night.

Hie looked out over the clearing, the zornits were nearby, grazing. Hie looked at them speculatively. Even a little one would feed Syrdian and himself for hands of days. But dalins usually hunted large animals by dropping onto them with knives. Zornits were awfully big for that method. Dex'd never heard of anyone hunting zornits by any means except driving them over cliffs. That was difficult because zornits were wary of a precipice and cliffs tall enough to kill one weren't common. Trying to attack a zornit with a knife could get you killed. A zornit's dorsal limbs were somewhat dangerous, the zornits used them to drive away small flyers, but even if you braved the dorsal limbs and landed on a zornit's back it would promptly roll. This forced you to lift off or be crushed.

Dex didn't think the steep bank at the edge of the stream would hurt a zornit, even if hie did manage to drive them over it somehow.

Dex shrugged hies wings and flew out to check the snares hie'd set the night before.

~~~

Syrdian looked up at the sound of Dex returning. His wing beats sounded... happier, more alive. Sure enough when hie coasted down over the bank and dropped in beside the cave hie had hies hands full of small game. They would eat well this morning at least. Syrdian excitedly cast arms and wings around Dex, "Thank you! I've been *so* hungry!"

Dex, very happy to have Syrdian's arms around himr, said, "Me too! Let's hope the snares keep working this well."

"Did you do something different?"

"Yes, you inspired me when you said you thought you'd caught all the swimmers in this small stream. I realized that the snares might have caught all the animals that used the paths I had them on and I should move them to different paths. Thank you."

"Thank *you*," Syrdian said, taking Dex's catch.

***

Ell sat down at their weekly TC3 meeting. Everyone else had already arrived though their three professors were all attending remotely. "Sorry I'm late. Who's got something interesting to tell us?"
~~~

Emma said, “Our new rocket’ll arrive tonight. We flew the old one up to the bank above the Teecee’s cave while they were gone yesterday and they didn’t seem to be upset by it. I’m hoping to fly the new one down to the bank and the old one out of there while they’re gone hunting and fishing tomorrow. The new one looks very much like the old one except it’s about a half inch bigger around and three inches longer so we’re hoping they’ll just think it grew a little. Once we’ve made the swap, Professor Norris can fly the old one out to survey the planet the way he’s been wanting.”

Wheat interjected, “Promise me you’ll fly it south first to confirm whether or not there are teecees down there that could’ve migrated from Goldy’s cave area.”

Norris smiled, “Yeah, yeah, we’ll check out a few of your silly biological questions before we move on to the important stuff like the planet itself.”

Wheat said, “And we need more specimens tested for DNA. One sample could have been contaminated by some DNA from Earth in the chamber.”

Emma and Manuel protested, “We cleaned that…”

Wheat put a hand up, “Yes, yes, I’m sure you did, but we can’t publish without repeating the test.”

Ell said, “I hope you’re not planning to publish right away.”

“No, no,” he waved dismissively, “but, someday…

“Also,” he continued, “I’ve got to say I’m worried about Goldy and Silver. I don’t think they’re getting enough to eat. I’m pretty sure they have no experience with living in that area with its higher altitude and different flora and fauna. I suspect that normally they get most of their food by hunting from the air. We’ve seen Goldy stoop on burrowers a few times. But Silver can't fly at all and Goldy isn't flying a lot. When the rocket's in position to see Goldy fly, it looks like getting into the air's a bit of a struggle. They've been fishing in the stream and did well for a while, but I think they may have overfished that little stream because Silver hasn't been bringing in much lately."

"Is there anything we could do to help?"

"Should we be interfering in the natural course of events on another planet?" Several of the group looked at Emma when she asked this and shrugged, but no one entered into a debate on the question.

Manuel said, "We could teach them how to make an Ojibwa bird snare with a few drawings."

"What's that?"

Manuel said, "It's a pretty simple little trap to catch birds. I've already made drawings." He scrolled through them on the screen. "I don't see why that snare wouldn't catch flyers on TC3 as easily as it does birds on Earth."

Norris said, "Good idea. Another thing that's been bugging me is their staves. They have those pointed staves they've been carrying and holding like they're spears, but I've never seen them use them."

"When that big animal looked like it might attack, they held them point out as if they hoped to defend themselves with the staves."

Roger frowned, "I wouldn't think they would make very good weapons. It's hard to imagine getting a relatively blunt wooden point to penetrate much, even if they've heat treated them."

"Agreed," Norris said, "but they have flint knives. Why haven't they hafted some flint points onto those shafts?"

Emma said, “During my watch last night, Silver broke a big lump of rock I think might’ve been flint into some smaller chunks and seemed to be flaking them as if trying to make some more knives.”

Wilson said, “I’ve looked into this a little. Flint’s usually found in limestone and here on Earth limestone is typically the remnants of coral and other marine organisms. So, on another planet, with different life forms, there may not be coral. Therefore, maybe no limestone, and possibly no flint?”

The group looked at Wheat. He shrugged, “Look around. It’s a different planet, but the life is DNA based. There are tree analogues, grass analogues, bird analogues and fish analogues. I’ll bet when we get to the sea we’ll find coral analogues, or *something* that builds underwater structures out of carbonates anyway. Most caves here on Earth occur in limestone and you’ll notice we’ve encountered some caves.

Manuel tilted his head, “So, do you think if I drew them pictures of a hafted spear, they might be able to take down one of those large grazers in the meadow?”

Wheat shrugged, “Seems like it would be a lot safer for them than it was for our ancestors. Goldy can just fly over a grazer and plunge a spear into it. He, excuse me, *it* doesn’t have to worry about being run down by an angry bull that survives the attack. If *his* attack fails, he just flies on by.”

Manuel said, “Looks like I’ve got some more drawings to make.”

Ell looked over at Kira Piscova. “Any luck with translation Dr. Piscova?”

Kira tossed her hands up gently, “This is *very* difficult. All the languages we use here have breaks to define separations between words, but my impression is that the only breaks in the sounds they make may signify what to us would be sentences. They seem to emit several frequencies at the same time, as if they have several different sets of vocal cords, or vocal cord analogues. Right now I'm testing the theory that pitch shifts act kind of like letters in our words and that they use a separate high or low tone as a modifier of the word. That high end AI you've lent me is helping a lot. I've identified a few sound clips that I think I know the meaning of, at least when spoken by Goldy. This is Silver's name," a tweedle played over the speakers, "and this is 'fire,'" another tweedle, "and this is 'fish,'" a third tweedle played. Of course I'm not even sure if I'm right about those particular sounds." She sighed, "I've got a *long* way to go. Would you allow me to speak to them through the speaker on the new rocket?"

Ell smiled, "Sure. As soon as you're confident we won't be saying something offensive."

***

Dex flew up to the bank above the cave and retrieved hies meteorite, bringing it back down to the front of the cave. It felt great to have a full stomach. Hie set the meteorite on its legs just inside the opening of the cave, then crouched comfortably to ponder it. Hie wondered if it would ever give himr more instructions. *If only I could ask it questions!*

Suddenly a hissing sound came from it and it moved!

Dex had leapt back a wingbeat. Focusing back on the meteorite he saw that, with the hiss, it'd turned part way around. Dex saw a red spot appear and when hie turned to look at the wall of the cave hie saw a drawing of a dalin cutting a point onto one end of a pole. The dalin pounded it into the ground with a rock. It cut a point into the top end and bored a transverse hole through it below the top. Next the dalin took a smaller stick and trimmed it so the base of it fit into the hole in the pole. A noose was made from fiberlin with a knot tied in the string above the knot. The string went through the hole in the pole and then the stick was fitted in to jam the string with the knot just above the hole. The tail of the string was tied around the heavy rock that'd been used to pound the stick into the ground. A noose from the top end of the string was draped over the horizontal stick. The dalin left.

Dex tilted hies head back and forth, trying to understand. Then the pictures showed a flyer landing to perch on the horizontal stick. When it landed, the stick fell out of its hole and the rock fell. The weight of the rock pulled the noose shut around the flyer's legs. The dalin reappeared, taking away the trapped flyer.

The pictures started over. Dex studied them carefully through several repetitions. Syrdian came back from relieving himrself and watched the drawings also. Dex began boring a hole through the back end of one of hies staves.

Syrdian said, "Do you think the drawings are saying that we can catch flyers with a flyer snare made like the drawings show?"

Dex tried to fit a perching stick into the hole hie'd bored. "That's what I think. Do you?"

Syrdian shrugged, "I guess. Can I help?"

"We're running low on fiberlin string. Do you know how to make it?"

"Yes, I'll have to go to see if I can find some fiberlin vine tomorrow."

"Can you unravel some string off a piece of the rope we brought up from the cave?"

"Sure how long?"

"A little more than the span of your arms."

Syrdian gazed fondly at Dex for a few moments, then turned to look for their rope.

***

Washington D.C.—President Flood announced today that his administration, like President Teller's before his, had negotiated several strategies to release D5R's new solar technology gradually and broadly. This strategy is hoped to stabilize the instability recently plaguing the energy sector, especially the petroleum markets...

~~~

Ell's AI spoke in her ear, "Raquel Blandon has a call from Shannon Kinrais."

"Who?"

"The Shan you met at Vic's bar 23 days ago."

Ell felt a flash of excitement, she'd about given up on him. "Oh, OK. Put him on... Hi Shan, long time."

"Hi Raquel. I find I keep thinking about my best clogging partner."

"It was fun... I'd like to dance with you again sometime."

"Well... Do you remember that I like to play basketball?"

"Yeah?"

"I belong to an intramural team and a couple of our guys can't play tonight. I remembered that you said you
~~~

played in high school? Could you fill in? We're desperate."

"What!" Ell laughed, "First of all, I'm broken hearted to find you aren't calling me to go dancing again. Then, even worse, I learn that you're only calling me to fill in on your basketball team and that *only* because you're 'desperate?!'"

"Crap! I didn't put that very well, did I?"

"No! Are you always this clumsy talking to girls?"

"Probably." He laughed at himself, "Do you think that's why I don't have a girlfriend?"

Ell giggled. "Ya think? Yeah. I'd cut you some slack anyway, except I'm afraid I don't have the stamina to play full court without subs."

"Oh, this is half court, three on three."

"When?"

"Six PM. You bail us out so we don't have to forfeit and I'll buy you dinner after."

"OK, but you owe me a night out clogging too."

Shan laughed, "You're a tough negotiator... but you've got a deal."

***

Shan scanned the gym again. If Raquel didn't get here soon they'd have to forfeit. He breathed a sigh of relief; he'd seen her walking around the periphery of the courts. Behind him Ryan said, "Who'd you get to fill in for Jim and Roger?"

"Raquel," Shan murmured staring at the girl approaching. Wearing old sweats that somehow looked... good. Something about the way she walked... Slender, pretty, but... graceful.

"Who!?" Ryan broke in, "A girl!? Why not just forfeit and get it over with? Oh God, it's that clogging girl you had the hots for isn't it?!"

Shan turned, "No one else could play! Just think of it as two on three, they won't let us play without a third player you know?"

Ryan turned away in disgust, "This'll be a total humiliation."

"Even if we lose, we'll still get some practice."

Ryan barked a laugh, "No, the guys we're playing, they *won* the league last year." He waved at four guys walking their way, all dressed in black, the shortest one was at least six foot one, "It'll be an embarrassment."

Raquel stepped up. "What'll be an embarrassment?"

Shan turned to her, "Hi Raquel, apparently we're playing last year's champs and Ryan thinks we're gonna get a beat down. You remember Ryan from Vic's?"

"Sure," Raquel put her hand out to shake. Ryan took it sullenly.

The four guys approached, one stepping forward, saying, "We're team Destruct. Are you the Integs?"

Shan nodded, "Yup."

"Where're the rest of your players?"

"One's sick, one's out of town. Raquel here's subbing."

He rolled his eyes, "Oh, come on! Tell you what, take the loss and one of us'll play on your team, that way we can at least have some fun games."

Shan looked stubborn, "We'll play one game with *our* team. If you guys put a bad hurt on us, *then* we'll take the loss and you can loan us a player."

He shrugged, "Your funeral." He pointed around his team, "Steve, Rick, Larry," he pointed a thumb at himself, "Rand."

Shan said, "I'm Shan, this is Ryan and Raquel."

"OK. We've got five minutes to warm up."

"Right." Shan tossed the ball he'd been holding against his hip to Ryan who dribbled it out onto the court and tossed up a rim clanger.

Shan nervously watched Raquel catch the ball that'd bounced directly to her. She dribbled it a couple of times, as if getting the feel for it, then she bent her knees gracefully and launched a shot with nice form… but it was an air-ball, so short it didn't even touch the rim. His heart sank. He glanced back at her, expecting her to be wincing.

She grinned at him, "Haven't played for years."

His heart sank further. Shan jogged to retrieve the ball as it bounced off the court. He tossed it to Ryan who put it in. Raquel retrieved it and tossed it to Shan, but her pass was low. Why *did I think this would be a good idea? Not even a good idea, why did I think it'd be an* acceptable *idea?* He launched a shot which banked almost in, but bounced off the rim, up and out. Raquel caught this one too, dribbled it a couple of beats and passed it out to Ryan. *There's one good pass*, he thought. Ryan dropped that basket too and Shan developed a little hope. Sometimes Ryan could get really hot. If that happened today, maybe the game wouldn't be too embarrassing.

Raquel rebounded and tossed the ball to him. This time it hit him right in the hands, pretty hard. His eyebrows rose and he took the shot.

To his dismay it bounded high up off the rim. He hadn't made a single shot so far! To his surprise Raquel appeared under the ball and rebounded it again. This time she put it back up. It fell through, nothing but net…

One of the league refs showed up and said, "Let's get this game going."

Shan and Ryan pulled off their sweats and after a moment's pause Raquel shrugged and did the same. Shan's breath caught a moment when she pulled off the pants. *Holy shit! Look at those legs!* Then she pulled off the sweat top. As it came up, it pulled her snug little tank top up briefly to reveal her abs. He blinked, *the girl's ripped!* He thought of how well she danced, *She's gotta be pretty athletic. Maybe we won't be* too *embarrassed?*

Team Destruct won the toss and brought the ball in to Rick. Raquel was supposed to be guarding him, since he was the shortest guy on the other team. He tossed it, uncontested, to Larry back at the foul line and Larry brought it back toward the basket with Ryan defending him. Ryan pressed him hard enough that Larry picked up his dribble, but then he passed it hard to Rick who pivoted and sank a jump shot over Raquel's head.

Shan brought it in to Ryan, who dribbled it back to the foul line and brought it back up court. Though Raquel was very loosely guarded by Rick, Ryan made a pass back to Shan who had Rand all over him. For a moment Shan thought he'd lost the ball, but he managed to keep it and put up a wide shot. Rick rebounded the miss and tossed it back to Larry near the foul line.

In short order the Integs found themselves behind 14 to 4, Ryan having put in a couple of baskets. Ryan called a time out.

"Shan feed it to me, I'm making baskets and you're cold as ice."

Shan shrugged; it was true, "OK."

Raquel grinned, not looking fazed at all by the debacle the game had turned into. "What do you want me to do?"

Ryan shrugged, "Bring the ball in, try to get some rebounds."

She grinned again, looking as if she were having a great time. "OK."

My God, Shan thought in humiliation, *she could at least have the decency to look embarrassed.* Then he thought, *Though, we haven't really given her a chance. We're playing pretty much like she isn't out there.*

Raquel took the ball over to the baseline to bring it in. Shan was dismayed to see Rick step up to the line, arms out. It looked like he intended to make it impossible for her to even get it onto the court. Shan was torn between being angry they were going to make it so hard on her, and embarrassed that they could. To his amazement, as Ryan stepped down near the baseline, trying to give her a target, Shan saw her wink at Rick, then the ball suddenly rocketed past Rick's hip, not to the nearby Ryan, but to Shan. A long pass that should have been in danger of interception... except it was hard, fast, and right to Shan's hand on the far side from Rand. *Did she get lucky? Or did she just do that on purpose?*

Shan took it across the foul line and dribbled back up court with Rand pressing him hard. He fired a bounce pass to Ryan who put it up... but it bounded off the rim and towards Rick. Shan's heart sank but then to his astonishment Raquel darted in front of Rick and slapped wildly at the ball. Frantic as her slap had been, the ball bounced directly to Ryan. This time his shot went in.

Rick stepped over the baseline to bring the ball in

and Raquel stepped in front of him. She didn't have her hands up! Ryan shouted, "Get your hands…" He stopped because Rick had made his inbounds pass from up high where Raquel's hands couldn't reach. But one of her hands *did* wildly touch it, deflecting the pass. Only a little bit, but instead of going to Larry it went right to Ryan.

Ryan fired it back to Shan and Shan dribbled it back up court. Ryan broke free of Larry, and Shan fed the ball to him. Ryan rushed the shot and it bounced erratically off the rim. However unpredictable that bounce off the rim might have been, the gods smiled on them because it fell right where Raquel'd been going. She glanced at Ryan, but Larry had him well covered at the moment and Rick was blocking the expected pass as well. Shan had the fleeting impression that she shrugged before she stutter-stepped to the right and put the ball up herself!

Perfect arc, right in the hole…

Games were to 21 and they lost that first one 21-18. Yes it was a loss, but it wasn't an embarrassment. They declined to take the loss of the match and one of Destruct's players, opting instead to continue playing for themselves.

They just got luckier and luckier! Raquel didn't make any "steals," just accidental deflections. But the gods smiled and the deflected passes always seemed to bounce into his or Ryan's hands. She didn't seem to put much effort into her passes, but they moved fast and arrived hard… and *exactly* to their recipient's hands. Well, that wasn't strictly true, to catch them he or Ryan usually had to step a little, but that step always took them away from their defender. She'd only shot twice the first game, but she'd drilled both of them.

Nothing about her play seemed to be... remarkable. Except there were no errors. And her unintentional plays... like when she managed to deflect one of team Destruct's passes, or somehow was right under a rebound were *so* lucky. Not only were they deflected enough to miss their intended recipient, but also didn't dribble out of bounds, instead they went to Shan or Ryan. As they were taking their break, Ryan turned grudgingly to Raquel and said, "Nice passes. This time *you* go back to the foul line and bring the ball up. Feed Shan *or* me."

Raquel shook her head and grinned. "Nah, I'll get all tired and sweaty if I have to run up and down that much. I'll just stay down here near the basket, unless I have to chase one of them on defense."

Ryan narrowed his eyes and looked like he would protest, but then shrugged his shoulders and turned back to the court.

They won the next game... and the one after that. They led most of the time. It seemed like the Team Destruct player that was on Raquel made a lot of mistakes. Shan wondered if they were just flustered to be playing a girl. Or by her willowy good looks? Or...?

In any case, they fumbled their dribbles—perhaps because Raquel got a touch on the ball? They let her deflect their passes, perhaps too confident that she couldn't?

~~~

When they'd won the third game for the best two out of three and the overall win, Ryan slammed into Shan with a bear hug, lifting him off the ground. "Man, we were on *fire!* Way to go!" He turned to Raquel, "You
~~~

play a decent game little lady, thanks for helping us out." He jogged away, calling back, "Gotta go!"

~~~

Shan honored his commitment, taking Raquel out to Five Guys for burgers afterward. As they sat down he said, "Hey, you're pretty good with the b-ball."

She shrugged, "I'm pretty quick is all. Caught those guys by surprise and they didn't seem to be able to adapt to it."

"I'll say... Hey, I looked up your company, it's Quantum Research?"

She nodded.

"It's a spin-off of D5R isn't it?"

She nodded again.

"Have you met Donsaii?" he asked eagerly.

"Well, I've seen her around."

"Oh man, I'd so love to meet her. I study the math she came up with to describe quantum effects and her 5th dimension and it's so... fascinating! You've gotta promise to invite me to your next work party."

Raquel narrowed her eyes, "She doesn't like people bugging her."

"Aw hell, she doesn't even need to talk to me. I'd just like to be able to brag that I shook her hand. Or maybe that I'd knelt down and worshipped the ground she'd walked on?"

After their burgers and fries, they walked to an ice cream shop where to Shan's amazement, he had a small cone and Raquel sucked down a large milkshake.

~~~

Back home, after working on his math a while, Shan found himself musing about how the games had gone.

After a while he skimmed through his AI's video of the games. She didn't take a lot of shots, nor make every shot, but his skin prickled when he realized that she missed every time if they were leading and made every shot when they were trailing... He frowned... *what a weird coincidence.*

Finally he turned back to Donsaii's beautiful equations.

Chapter Ten

Dex landed and Syrdian felt relief to see that hie had a couple of small burrowers. Syrdian'd only caught one flyer with the pole snares that day. When they'd first started putting snares up in the meadow they'd caught quite a few flyers each day. But it seemed that the flyers had gotten wary. Syrdian moved the snares every day, but had begun to think hie needed to move them to another meadow.

They were eating better than they had been, but still went somewhat hungry most days. Dex worked tirelessly putting out snares and hunting small animals from the air. Syrdian found himrself admiring Dex and wishing hie had the confidence to tell Dex how hie felt. But hies chest hurt when hie tried to talk about things like that. Despite Syrdian's higher status in the Yetany tribe, it felt to Syrdian that, in their little tribe of two, *Dex* held all the rank—and if so, that Syrdian should be respectful and wait for Dex's notice.

~~~

As Dex helped break down their catch and prepare them to be roasted hie glanced covertly at Syrdian. They'd been eating better, but Syrdian still looked thin. Hie mused to himrself over how hies love for Syrdian at a distance last winter had proven false when hie'd come face to face with the real Syrdian after the talor's attack. That Syrdian had seemed shallow, pathetic and not at all the kind of dalin that Dex would have wanted
~~~

to spend hies life with.

But after Dex had agreed to try to help Syrdian live through the summer despite hies torn wing, Syrdian had changed. Instead of hies initial incompetence and arrogant attitude, Syrdian had assiduously done whatever hie could to help and carefully learned how to do anything and everything Dex had been willing to teach him.

When it turned out that the flyer snares needed to be checked frequently to keep flying predators from taking their prey, Syrdian had volunteered for the job in order to allow Dex time to do the things that required flight. These musings led himr to wonder... "How's your wing feel now, Syrdian?"

"It doesn't hurt anymore. I'm worried because some of your little threads have gotten loose. Do you think they need to be replaced?" Syrdian sounded apprehensive over the prospect.

"I don't know, let me see." Syrdian raised the wing and Dex bent hies head near. The sutures were more than loose. On the surface hie could see and Syrdian could not, many of them were broken. The skin of the wing around them was discolored. Dex plucked at them with a claw, "Does this hurt?"

"It's sore."

Dex grasped the tissue to either side and tugged in a direction to pull the wound open. Nothing separated. "Does that hurt?"

"No."

Dex pulled the wing up to look at the underside. The threads were loose and had actually pulled out in a couple of places leaving pieces of thread dangling. Hie tugged on a loose loop with a claw and the thread pulled right out of the wing. "I think you're healed. I'm going to try taking the stitches out." Hie pulled another one loose.

"But, what if... what if the wound comes open again? I don't want you to have you put them in again. I don't think I could take the pain."

"They're loose. They aren't doing anything anymore."

"What if the suture spirits are...? I don't know... doing something even though the sutures are loose."

"Spirits? These are just stitches, like I make to hold leather together."

"But if you take the threads out of leather, it comes apart!"

"Leather doesn't heal. I think your wing's healed."

"They aren't doing any harm. Please leave them in?" As if begging, Syrdian dipped hies head in submission.

Taken aback, Dex wondered why Syrdian would dip submission, hie was so much higher ranking than Dex. "OK, I think you should try beating your wings some to see if you think it's strong enough to fly."

Syrdian's head went way up and back. "Really?!"

Dex shrugged hies wings, "Have to try it sometime."

"Let's get these burrowers roasting first."

~~~

Once their catch was roasting, Syrdian said, "Shall I try it now?"

Dex shrugged, "Sure."

Syrdian stepped out and away from the cave so hies wing beats wouldn't disturb their fire. Hies wings lifted and beat a few tentative strokes. Dex asked, "Did it hurt?"

Syrdian shrugged hies wings, "It feels funny and a little sore."
~~~

"Let me look." Dex stepped up close and looked at the wing top and bottom. "It doesn't look like it's coming apart. Try a few harder beats."

Syrdian stepped back and beat hard enough to scoot hies feet along the ground. "It still doesn't hurt. Do you think I can fly again?"

Surprised to be asked, Dex said, "I think you should see how it feels in the morning. If it's still good, try flying then."

Syrdian said, "OK." Respectfully.

Dex stared.

~~~

They moved back to the cave area and Dex picked up hies meteorite from where it stood in front of the cave. Hie crouched studying it, turning it, reaching around it with hies hand. At one point hie tied it back to hies chest harness, walked around a little, then undid it and set it back down, backing away to study it more.

Syrdian, having turned the spits over the fire said, "What are you doing with your meteorite?"

"Have you noticed it's bigger than when it first landed?"

Syrdian raised hies head in surprise, "It is?"

"Yes. Not a lot bigger, but it's a little longer and a little bigger around too."

"Has it been getting bigger all along, just so gradually we never noticed?"

"No, it seemed to get bigger all of a sudden several hands of days ago. I don't think it's gotten any bigger since then."

Syrdian came around and studied it, "I can't tell."

"I'm not sure I would either if I hadn't carried it all that time. My hand doesn't reach around it as far, and if
~~~

it were on my harness again, it'd be more in the way than it was back when I first got it. It also has this little patch of holes in it that didn't used to be there."

"Well I wish it would tell us more ways to get food. I'm so tired of being hungry all the time."

"Hey maybe if you can fly, you can go up and down stream to get more swimmers?"

"Or over to the next stream. I've been hoping I could fly soon. It'd really help. Do you think I could fly down far enough to get to some of the lakes and big rivers we normally catch swimmers in?"

"Maybe, but it'll be hot."

"Ugh."

"Well, maybe you could stand the heat briefly?" Dex looked off into the distance and then shrugged, "But then, when you were feeling the worst because of the heat, you'd have to fly a long way up into thin air getting back here. You'd better be sure you're flying really well before you try it. Even then you should just go partway down there to see what it's like before you go all the way."

"Yeah, I'm not sure I want to try it. Last spring I flew almost down to the sea, but it was hot and exhausting. I can see why we go south for the summer."

~~~

While they were eating, Syrdian saw a faint red dot appear on the side of the meteorite. Wordlessly hie pointed.

Dex stood up excitedly, stepping to the meteorite. The red dot brightened and lines appeared on the wall of the cave. At first the lines seemed to show a straight stick, pole or shaft. Then the picture focused in on the end of the pole. The end of the pole developed a slot in
~~~

it.

Next the pictures showed something that looked very much like a flint knife without its handle. Then it showed something that looked like a flint knife except it looked like it'd been flaked so that it had sharp edges on both sides.

The pictures went away for a moment, then reappeared, this time with the knife next to the shaft. Then with the haft of the knife in the slot in the shaft. Then with fiberlin wrapping around the shaft and haft; and finally with it tied off to produce a knife with an extremely long handle.

Hie stared. A handle that long would make the knife too clumsy to use. Why would anyone do *that*?

Then his eyes widened. The picture showed a weapon! A weapon which would be much more devastating than the fire hardened points on their shafts and would have a much longer reach than a knife. Why hadn't hie thought of this himrself?

Now the pictures showed the double edged flint at the tip of the shaft. Such a device would provide much better protection than the fire hardened points on their shafts! Fire hardened points were helpful for fending off attackers and large predators, but a flint tipped shaft wouldn't just fend off, it could penetrate and injure an attacker.

Syrdian's eyes widened when the images showed a dalin flying with the flint tipped shaft in a hand and a small zornit beneath it. Then the zornit got bigger. The zornit got bigger yet. *Wait, maybe the dalin's supposed to be flying closer and closer and that's why the zornit seems to be getting bigger?* Then suddenly the dalin appeared to be plunging the shaft into the zornit. Then the zornit had the shaft sticking out of its side as the dalin got smaller—or flew past it?

Next the zornit appeared, laying on its side with the shaft sticking out of it and the dalin on the ground next to it, cutting it up. Dex felt so excited hies wings were quivering! "Do you see it Syrdian?"

"Is it saying you could kill a zornit from the air with a long handled knife?"

"Yes, yes! I think so! Let's give the knife a name. We could call it a 'spear.' Where's that flint you found?"

~~~

Dex took hies remaining shaft with a fire hardened point and cut a deep slot in the blunt end of it. Then hie flaked a double edged knife from Syrdian's flint. It wasn't a great knife, but it fit the slot he'd made in the shaft. With fiberlin hie bound the split in the shaft shut around the blade hie'd made. Hie flaked a couple more blades hie could haft onto shafts the next day.

As soon as hie had good light and could find some nice straight shafts.

~~~

In the morning, Dex and Syrdian climbed eagerly up to the meadow after a meager breakfast of the remnants of their meal from the night before. Dex inspected the wounds in Syrdian's wings again in the better light of day; finding the wounds looked much like little wing rips that'd healed, just bigger. There were slightly thicker ridges where the tears had been, but even when hie picked at them with a claw, or pulled on them with hies fingers, no openings appeared.

Syrdian said it didn't hurt. "Shall I try flying?"

"I guess. I think you should try a short distance first."

Syrdian spread hies wings and tried a few tentative

beats, then re-inspected hies wounds. Finally, hie beat hard enough to lift off and fly about five body lengths.

Dex beat over to look at Syrdian's wing again. Syrdian said, "Oh! That little flight was... so much harder than I expected! Do you think my wing's not working right?"

"No, it really is a lot harder to fly high up here on the mountain. And your wings are weak because you haven't been using them." Dex looked around; there weren't any zornits in the big meadow this morning. "I'm going to look for more shafts for the other flint points."

Syrdian dipped hies head, "I'll set up a few flyer traps, then I think I'll try upstream a ways for swimmers." Hie didn't say it but hie hoped that hies wings would help climb areas of the stream that were a struggle; even if hie didn't actually *fly* up the mountain.

~~~

"Syrdian! You got some swimmers!"

"Yeah," Syrdian lifted hies string of three, "I went a little farther up the stream than before. It's easier to climb, now that my wings are helping. Did you have any luck?"

"A couple of burrowers."

"Good! Enough to eat for a change!"

They fell to breaking down their catch for roasting.

Syrdian asked, "Are the zornits back?"

Dex shrugged hies wings disappointedly, "No."

***

At their Teecee group meeting Kira Piscova said,
~~~

"I've worked out what I believe is a vocabulary of about a thousand words for the teecees. You've said I can try to talk to them when I'm sure I won't offend them. I don't think it's possible to be sure they won't be offended. I can't even be reasonably sure of a lot of these words until I see how they react to them."

Norris said, "You can make those tweedling sounds?"

"No, but my AI can. It just plays back copies of the words that the teecees said. What I'd hope to do is to speak the English words we have likely translations for, then the AI'd play the corresponding Teecee tweedle it has recorded for that word."

"And when they speak to us your AI would do the reverse?"

"Yes, although their sentence structure is different than ours. So far I haven't tried to have the AI rearrange them into our usual structure."

Ell looked up at the screen where video from the previous evening's take was playing. It showed late afternoon on TC3. Silver could be seen approaching the Teecee's camp, carrying some fish. "Could you let us listen to a translation of what they're saying in the section of video playing there?"

Piscova shrugged, "You won't be very impressed." She spoke to her AI and the audio from the ongoing video on the screens came on with a series of tweedling sounds.

A moment later the translation came on with a mechanical AI voice saying, "Fish... Silver... have."

"Yes... stream... wings... earlier... up."

"Two... small animals."

"Eat."

"Grazers?"

"No."

Piscova said, "As you can see, so far mostly we have nouns. Figuring out verbs and other parts of speech is going to be much more difficult."

"What do you think guys?" Ell said looking around at the group, both present and remote. "Should we try to say a few words to them?"

A chorus of affirmatives came back at her. Emma said, "This'll be pretty historic. You don't think we need an ambassador or something here?"

"We landed without the government's approval." Ell shrugged. "I don't think we've done any harm, a track record not shared by many of the governments in the past. Though," she tilted her head, "I'd hope that our modern government would do better than the ones did in the past. The teecees'd be pretty hard to exploit anyway due to distance. At least I don't *think* they can be exploited... Though I can't be sure yet." She sighed, "My personal preference would be to keep this secret a while longer with the thought that, if we thought that somehow they *could* be exploited, we could keep them a secret forever." She raised an eyebrow, "Or *try* to keep them secret anyway." She looked around and was pleased to see nodding that seemed to indicate the group agreed.

~~~

Back in her office Ell found that Emma had followed her there. "Hey, Em' what's up?"

"Roger took me out to dinner last night."

Ell threw her arms around Emma, happy for her, but once again finding her own heart was sinking. "Good for you!" She whispered in Emma's ear, afraid her voice'd
~~~

break if she said it out loud.

Emma hugged her tight, then leaned back seeing Ell's glistening eyes, "You're upset!"

"Yeah." She choked out, "Silly me. My friendly boy's growing up and moving on. Even though I'm pushing him out of the nest, it still hurts."

Emma's eyes brightened, "I could push him back your way, he was yours first."

"No, no. You love him a lot more than I ever did. I don't know what's wrong with me. I'm happy for you guys. Really! Very happy, but still somehow, sad as well."

"Well, he's torn up about it too. Worried that he did wrong, taking me out without talking to you about it first."

"OK, I'll try to say something positive to him about it."

"Thanks!" Emma said, giving Ell another hug.

After Emma left, Ell sank into her chair moping. Allan said, "Raquel has a call from Shan Kinrais."

Ell's heart leapt a little. She wasn't even sure whether Shan was "friendly boy" material yet. But with all her other semi romantic interests defunct, she felt happy to hear from him. "Put him on... Hi Shan, how's the B-ball going?"

He laughed, "OK, though I kinda miss havin' you playin' on our team."

"Well anytime you need me to bail you out again, just let me know."

"Hah! Ryan still thinks our win was entirely due to his bein' on fire that day."

"He *was* on fire!" Ell said, suddenly worried she hadn't been subtle enough with her abilities that day.

"He was. But he doesn't give enough credit to the teammate who fed him all those fine passes."

"We did make some nice passes didn't we?"

Shan thought back to the several times now that he'd watched the video from those games. He'd come to realize her passes weren't just "nice" they were *excellent*, often pulling Ryan away from his defender and positioning him perfectly to cut for his shot. Maybe it'd all been luck, but he had a feeling it hadn't been. "Well, enough basketball talk. Velos's going to be playing at Vic's, the bar where we met. How'd you like to go out for dinner and dancing? I've got tickets."

For a moment Ell panicked at the thought that Shan knew he was talking to Ell Donsaii, a known Velos fan. "Uh sure, that'd be fun. Can we clog to Velos' music?"

"Hah, you can clog to anything if you want to. But you do remember I can dance other styles?"

"When is it?" Ell asked, though she knew very well.

"Saturday night, two weeks. Donsaii likes Velos so you have to promise me that if she shows up you'll introduce me."

"Uh sure… " Ell said, amused to find herself irritated at being asked to introduce him to herself. *My life's entirely too confusing,* she thought.

***

Dex climbed up the bank to the meadow. When hies head got high enough to see out into the big meadow hie stopped and called back down, urgently but not loudly, "Syrdian! The zornits are back!" Hie scrambled excitedly back down to the cave.

"Where?"

"In the meadow!"

"I figured that! What part of the meadow?"

"Oh. Near the bottom end, about half way to the other side."

Syrdian turned and picked up Dex's two best spears. "Good! You can fly in over the trees so they won't see you until the last moment."

Dex's head rose, "Do you think the zornits will be afraid of dalin?"

"They're probably afraid of talors. If they see a flyer coming their way they may start to run."

"I could still catch them!"

"Not if they run into the trees."

Dex shrugged hies wings. "OK, you're right. I'll circle out and come at them just over the tops of the trees."

"I'll be right behind you."

Dex stopped and stared at Syrdian. Syrdian had picked up two more flint tipped spears. Dex didn't want Syrdian to get hurt, but felt uncomfortable saying it. "Are you sure you're ready for that kind of flying?"

Syrdian shrugged hies wings. "No, but I'll only attack if you've wounded a zornit and we need to finish it off. I've been flying pretty far the past hand of days, you know. I haven't just been flying with you."

"OK. But I've been practicing sticking spears into that mound from the air. It isn't as easy as you might think."

Syrdian grinned and beat a wingful of air at Dex. "I've practiced too. Days when you were gone for a long time."

Dex beat a wingful back at himr, grinning. "OK, let's try it then!" Hie turned and beat into the air over the stream, coasting down the mountain then up into the air over a recently burned section of the forest. Like other dark areas on the ground it usually had a nice updraft. Hies back eyes showed Syrdian back-low-left from himr.

They circled a few times, gaining altitude, then turned out, swinging over the forest and back "up-mountain" toward the big meadow. From this altitude hie could see the zornits peacefully grazing near the low end of the meadow. At the left end of the little herd, hie saw a smaller one and hie marked its location just over a slightly taller tree.

Dex dove, dropping out of sight of the zornits and gaining speed…

Hie shot out over the tree line.

There was hies small zornit.

With a flick of hind wings Dex stooped on it…

It obviously saw himr with its back eyes. It hunched a little and then began running, turning to the right in the direction of the rest of the herd.

The entire herd began running and turning hard right. They were turning into the trees!

Dex dropped hies right wing, turning hard with the zornit. At the angle hie was diving hies speed rocketed up. Hie dropped hies right wing further to turn with it and drew back the spear…

Then hie flared wings to avoid crashing into the panicked zornit…

With all hies strength Dex slammed the spear into the zornit just ahead of its right high shoulder. Heart lung and brain were all there in that forepart of the body…

The spear sunk deep as Dex flashed over, wheeling up and turning right to see what had happened…

Syrdian flared over the zornit…

With mighty thrust, Syrdian's spear sank into the

zornit as well, they both beat wing to follow the zornit as it continued to run, now directly toward the forest. Was it going to get away? With two spears deep in its forequarter?!

It stumbled!

It stumbled again!

Its front legs collapsed and it crashed into the grass just short of the verge.

Dex dropped to the ground beside the zornit, amazed, yet wondering if it could really be true. Had they really killed a zornit?!

Syrdian dropped beside himr with an ululation of joy. Dex turned to himr and opened hies arms. Syrdian threw arms and wings around Dex and Dex did the same to Syrdian. They hopped up and down, wings involuntarily luffing with each leap.

Dex's hearts filled with ecstasy—to be holding Syrdian on such a joyous occasion was the best he'd ever felt.

~~~

Syrdian thrilled at the feel of the solid musculature underneath Dex's soft fur. Admiration for Dex, beautiful, handsome Dex. Dex the inventive. If only Dex could love himr...

~~~

Dex, clasping Syrdian to himrself, cursed hies own low status that meant Syrdian could never be hies...

Syrdian's neck touched hies...

Tentatively Dex curved hies neck slightly around Syrdian's.

With joy hie felt Syrdian's neck wrapping around hies own. Tighter and tighter their necks wrapped, squeezing, a feeling Dex had never experienced, but which felt so *right*, so wonderful...

They rose straighter and straighter, more and more of their bodies coming into contact.

Dex felt hies wings ripple in pleasure around Syrdian as their bodies came together.

Waves of ecstasy rolled over himr—was *this* what mating felt like?

Without thinking that it might happen. Without expecting that Syrdian might consider himr a suitable mate. Without discussing it. Without parental permission. Without the pseudo-mating that young dalin often engaged in.

Dex and Syrdian were mated—and Dex's hearts sang.

A niggling doubt surfaced. Had hie somehow forced Syrdian into this? Taken advantage of Syrdian's dependence on himr? Coerced Syrdian into a mating far below hies station? Slowly they disengaged and Dex drew hies head back to look into Syrdian's eyes.

Dex's hearts lifted. Syrdian smiled and joyfully lifted wings! "Are you OK?" Dex whispered.

"Oh, yes. Yes! I've been hoping... wondering why you haven't... uh..."

"I never dreamed that you might accept me, my status is... is so low..."

Syrdian laughed, "Dex! You just killed a zornit from the air! Your status should be... *exalted*!" Syrdian paused, then in a whisper said, "In my eyes your status is higher than anyone I've ever known. You killed a talor and repaired my wing! No one else's *ever* done these things! You stayed with me when Qes declared me dyatso." Syrdian whispered in a juddery voice, "You rescued me. You... worked out how to stay alive here in the summer and how to live high on the mountain."

Dex's head drooped, "But my parent Genex... hie brought disgrace on Deltain and myself."

"Oh Dex! Your status only depends on your parents when you're a child. That childhood status follows you into young adulthood, but then your status depends more and more on what you do yourself! I should know—my parents *constantly* remind me that the high status I get from them will... vanish ... if I don't contribute as an adult. But, Dex, even if your status did remain low, I, I... *love* you. I want to be your mate no matter what. I'm just glad you're willing to be my mate, even with my injured wing..." Syrdian's head went up and back in alarm, "*Do* you want to be my mate?"

"Oh yes!" Dex stepped forward, wrapping hies arms and wings around Syrdian again.

They stood rocking slightly back and forth, clasped in each other's embrace and joyfully rubbing their necks against one another's until Syrdian ruefully said, "We'd better get to work before our zornit decays, rots, molders and disappears."

With a laugh Dex slowly released Syrdian.

~~~

The zornit was heavy! At first they tried to pull the entire thing across the meadow to their cave. Eventually they cut it into front and back halves, dragging them one at a time. When they returned for the back half they found small scavengers already at it. Dex scratched a shoulder, "Maybe we should leave it to them. We can't possibly eat it all."

Syrdian said, "We can dry some of it like you did the talor's meat that first night. I *don't* want to be hungry again. Besides the stomach is in this half and Bultaken's
~~~

big water skin was made from the stomach of a zornit."

"Really?" Dex said, surprised because dalins so seldom hunted zornits. "How did hie get it?"

"The tribe stampeded a small herd over a cliff with fire brands."

"Do you know how to prepare the stomach?"

Syrdian shrugged hies wings, "I think so."

They each grabbed a hind limb and started dragging. "You're right, I should harvest the skin too," Dex said with some anticipation. "Its skin's much thicker than the small animals we catch in our snares. It'll be good to have some heavy leather."

~~~

Dex and Syrdian spent the entire rest of the day and much of the next harvesting the bounty of the zornit. Dex rubbed some fat into the zornit's skin and then rolled it up with a mash of molloe leaves to soften it into leather that wouldn't harden. They cut the meat up into strips and suspended them by the fire to dry. They washed out the intestine and stuffed fat into it. Syrdian removed the stomach, washed it and turned it inside out, suspending it with a tea of molloe leaves inside it.

Scavenging dlaks trotted intermittently around their cave, but the fire kept them at a distance.

After nightfall the meteorite sent red lines onto the cave wall again. This time the drawings showed the leg bones of the zornit. They were cut obliquely through the midshaft, leaving points on what had been the shaft of the bones. Then the hollow ends were jammed onto spear shafts. Dex realized they'd make longer, sturdier spear points than the hafted flints. Perhaps not as sharp as the flint, but not as fragile either. Hie'd broken a flint point attacking the zornit, so hie set to making a bone
~~~

point to replace it.

Having plenty to eat and many projects to work on gave the newly mated pair an immense feeling of satisfaction and bliss.

As they relaxed after mating once again, necks still wound loosely around one another, Syrdian asked, “Do you think we’ll have a child?”

Dex shrugged hies wings and whispered, “If we *are* so blessed, I hope hie has your silver wings.”

***

Shan looked around inside Vic’s, wondering if Raquel was already there. He didn’t see her anywhere, but the place was packed. He wandered over to the bar and ordered a Carolina wheat beer. He remembered that Raquel drank Coke and considered ordering one for her, but didn’t want to seem presumptive. He picked up the beer the bartender had set in front of him and had his AI send the man its price plus a tip. The bartender glanced up at his HUD and gave him a pleasant nod.

Shan turned around and found Raquel standing right behind him, arms crossed, one eyebrow lifted. “Hey.”

“Hey yourself, where’s my Coke?”

“Um, I didn’t know...”

“Some kind of date you are!”

“Uhhh.”

She broke into a grin. “Just bustin’ your chops a little.”

Shan raised an eyebrow, “I don’t know if you’re old enough for Coke young lady. I’m thinkin’ a Sprite might be more your speed.”

"Oh, now you're really cruisin' for that bruisin'."

The guitar licks introducing Velos' first set floated over the club and Shan said "Saved by the band?"

~~~

Once they'd obtained a Coke for Raquel, they headed out into the big room to enjoy the music. As expected, Vic's was packed and they had to leave their drinks on a rail to go out and dance. The floor was too crowded to do much in the way of dancing beyond pleasantly swaying to the music.

When the first slow, wistful arpeggios of "Lost" began to play, Shan stepped close and gently put his arms around Ell's waist. Ell realized that, despite watching others dancing like this she hadn't actually slow danced with anyone herself since she'd done it with Phil Zabrisk years ago. She actually had to glance at some of the other slow dancers in order to remember to put her arms up and around Shan's neck. His muscular shoulders felt solid under her forearms. *Nice...* she thought.

After a moment she leaned gently against him and then lightly rested her head on his shoulder. It felt like... things were good in her world that night.

~~~

Shan looked down into Raquel's light brown hair, thinking that there was just... something wonderful about having his arms around her. Soft, yet firm, every movement somehow perfect, even on something as simple as a slow dance. Somehow, they swayed in perfect synchronization. Her fingers gently rubbed the back of his neck.

~~~
~~~

The evening passed pleasantly. None of the active dancing Ell loved but, the music she loved was playing. Shan seemed to enjoy it as much as she did. Swaying to the music with Shan felt like all she needed in the world that night.

She felt truly happy for the first time in quite a while.

The show wound down and they walked out to the street, Ell getting a little chill as they turned onto the street where the incident with Sam had started. Shan said quietly, "Feel like some dessert?"

"Sure!"

~~~

Shan's car dropped them off on Franklin Street, near the old Carolina Coffee Shop. It'd recently become famous for late night desserts. Shan looked on in amazement as Raquel inhaled a large slice of pecan pie a la mode. "Hey, what do you do out at Quantum Research anyway?"

She looked up at him questioningly, "I work on one of the research teams."

"Very cool, what are they studying?"

She tilted her head considering, "Some of it's secret, but one of the things I do is help design some of their rockets."

Shan tried not to let his surprise show. She wasn't even twenty-one yet, how would she be involved in rocket design? She couldn't have an engineering degree at her age. Maybe she just helped draw them up using CAD software? "That's very cool." He arched an eyebrow, "And I suppose you can't tell me any cool things they're discovering out there, huh?"

She grinned, "Nope."

He leaned forward, "Do you see Donsaii very often?"
~~~

"Pretty much every day." She narrowed her eyes, "Are you just fluffing me up to get to her?"

He looked embarrassed, but leaned forward and put his hand on hers. "No. Raquel, I… think you're awesome. You're a wonderful dancer and," he grinned, "a great basketball player.

"But," he resumed, "math's my passion. I don't think I've told you, but I've been working on my PhD, and for my 'problem' I'm trying to extrapolate from Donsaii's math that explains that extra fifth dimension. Using her math I keep getting predictions of some weird effects on light and gravitation over great distances. Astrophysics isn't my strong suit so it's been really frustrating trying to figure out what I'm doing wrong. I keep thinking that if I could just bounce some of my issues and ideas off her…"

Ell felt a prickling sensation in her scalp. *Could this affect the dark energy calculations I've been working on?* Outwardly she grinned at Shan and leaned back, "I don't know… still sounds like you might be dating me to get to Donsaii… *Are* you that devious?"

Shan leaned back, "You're right. I shouldn't try to use you to help me make contact. I like doing things with you and that part of my life should be separate from my studies. Forget I ever asked." He winked, "Sure you don't need another slice of pie?"

She raised her eyebrows, "That'd be wonderful! For a cobbler, I might forward Donsaii an email about your theory?"

His eyebrows elevated in turn, "I was kidding about the pie!"

"I'm not!" she grinned.

Shan watched in astonishment as she ate a large blackberry cobbler. Again a la mode, scraping the dish when she'd finished. When he told his AI to pay the bill it turned out that she'd already paid it. "Hey!" he began.

She put her hands up, "I've got a job; you don't. You got the tickets to the show, the least I can do is get the dessert!" She looked a little embarrassed, "Especially since I ate most of it."

"Thanks!" he put an arm around her, "I had a great time." As they walked out to the street he said, "Hopefully we can do this again sometime?"

She looked almost shy as she quietly said, "I'd like that; it was fun."

Her little truck pulled up to the curb out front, but she turned to him there on the sidewalk. He tentatively put a hand on her hip and she turned willingly into his arms, putting hers around his neck and pulling him down for a kiss. A looong kiss that left his heart beating faster. She slowly pulled away. "Send me that e-mail," she winked, "and I'll get it to the right place."

For a moment Shan felt confused, *What e-mail?* Then he remembered that she'd said she'd forward an email about his math questions to Donsaii. As her truck faded into the distance he gently touched his lips. Wonderingly, he thought to himself that he really liked this girl. Then he shrugged, pretty, great dancer, plays B-ball, fun to talk to. *What's not to like?*

Chapter Eleven

Deltain stood at the edge of the escarpment and looked morosely out over the valley. The Yetany tribe camped on top of this bluff every summer because it provided a relatively flat area for their shelters, and the prevailing winds blew up the escarpment providing an updraft for an easy launch to flight. The valley below and the plains behind both had pretty good hunting. There were molloe trees in the area that provided Deltain with materials to tan hies leather. Deltain had always liked this part of the year in the past. The living was easy this year too, but hie felt desolate.

Hie occasionally heard dalins speaking of Dex, but not with the love Deltain felt. Instead, hie could tell from the glances they sent hies way that some thought Dex might be to blame for the loss of Syrdian. The blame they were putting on Dex had been causing Deltain to lose more status as evidenced by the increased difficulty hie'd been having making good trades for hies leatherwork. Hies wings involuntarily twitched with anger at the way they'd decided Dex was guilty when there wasn't any evidence hie was anything but another victim!

Deltain had stopped Qes once to ask himr again if hie was sure hie hadn't seen Dex on that fateful day when Dex and Syrdian disappeared and Qes returned late. Qes had drawn himrself up and stared haughtily at Deltain. "I barely knew who your child was Deltain. I certainly didn't keep track of hies comings and goings."

Deltain had been lonely before this summer. Hies status had been destroyed by hies mate Genex and by the way hie'd stood by Genex through hies addiction. Most other dalins would've left someone who abused fermented tubers. After Genex's death, Deltain's status had been elevated again by hies skill at leatherwork, nonetheless, it was still low enough that hie found it hard to socialize with the dalins tat the others thought of as hies equals.

Hie looked back over the camp. Sometimes hie thought hie hated all dalins and their constant preoccupation with status! Other times hie recognized hies own inner contradictions. After all, if hie was unwilling to socialize with those dalins currently judged to be similar in status to himrself, but that hie considered to be below hies own rank, how could hie condemn the higher status dalins for not socializing with himr?

Sometimes hie felt betrayed by Dex who'd triggered Deltain's further ostracization by disappearing on the same day as the beautiful Syrdian.

Most of the time though, hie thought wistfully of Dex. Dex was hies only living child, and Deltain had expected great things from himr. Deltain'd long felt wonder at how quickly Dex learned new methods, and how frequently hie thought of an even better way to do something Deltain taught himr. Deltain had been expecting hies own status to rise with Dex's as Dex became an adult and began to contribute to the tribe. Especially if he'd contributed as much as Deltain had thought hie might.

In Deltain's dreams, Genex's problems were forgotten and Deltain's pride in Dex rose to become...

limitless...

Now all those dreams were in ruins.

Much of the summer had passed and, despite Deltain's fervent prayers, Dex had never arrived at the summer camp. Deltain had all but resigned himrself to the reality of Dex's death. Hie frequently thought of leaving the Yetany to join another tribe. Of course, in a new tribe, hie'd start with the lowest possible rank, but Deltain felt confident that hies status would rapidly rise. Nonetheless Deltain had resolved to stay with the Yetany until after the migration back north. Hie had to see for *himrself* that Dex hadn't somehow survived the summer and by some miracle returned to the cave. Even if Deltain only found hies remains, at least knowing that Dex was truly gone would settle Deltain's mind for hies departure from the tribe.

Eventually Deltain turned and trudged back to hies lonely shelter.

Despite the normal tendency for dalin to live in groups of two to five, Deltain shared his shelter with no one.

***

Syrdian looked up lovingly as Dex flared to land beside himr where hie stood beside the pond outside their cave. "Look," hie said, pointing into the pond, "a swimmer showed up this morning."

Dex leaned over to look, "Where...? Oh, wait, I see it now... Are you going to catch it?"

"No. Right now we're not hungry. I'm going to leave himr for a day when we are."

Dex shrugged hies wings, "Good idea."

Syrdian stood and stretched, “It’s getting cooler.”

Dex dipped hies head in affirmation.

“I’m thinking we could move a little lower on the mountain. It’d be easier to fly and there’d be more food.”

Dex turned and looked back at their cave. “What’ll we do with...” hie waved a wingtip at all the supplies they had accumulated. Leather, spears, flint blades and a buried cache of dried meat. Far more than they could carry in this thin air.

Syrdian turned to look too. Things had been going very well since that first successful zornit hunt. There’d been plenty to eat and because they were in the “growing age” near the end of youth, they’d both grown quite a bit. Dex’d had to make both of them new leather harnesses to fit their increased sizes and had used their new zornit skin. Elegant and carefully worked, they were beautiful harnesses. Syrdian was fiercely proud of hies. Without having to hunt all the time they’d had time to practice their new “making” skills. Syrdian had found a trove of flint up the stream where hie’d found the first nodule and, having a lot of material to practice with, had become an expert at flaking spear heads from it. Hie shrugged, “Maybe we could make several trips?”

Dex’s wings sagged, “I guess. It’ll be a lot of hard work but...”

“But having all this stuff will help us establish much higher status when the rest of the tribe comes back.”

Dex brightened visibly, “You think so?”

“Oh, yeah. No one else our age has ever arrived into adulthood as a mated couple with so many wonderful things to contribute to the tribe.”

"Do you think they'll accept our mating? It wasn't approved by the council."

"Hah! Just let them try to object! We could just take our stuff and leave. Then join a tribe that appreciates us."

Dex's head went up and back in startlement, "Really? You think we can push them like that?"

"Dex, you have no idea how important these things are, do you?"

"But, once they see how to do them, they won't need us!"

Syrdian lowered hies head and beat a small wingful of air at Dex, "We don't show up with a *spear*. We show up with a *zornit*! If they want to learn how to hunt zornit, they'll have to accept us. We don't tell them about your *sutures*, we just tell them that you made an enormous rent in my wing heal and show them the scar. If they want someone in the tribe who can heal wings, they'll *have* to accept us!"

***

Allan, Ell's AI said, "The email you've been waiting for, the one from Shan Kinrais to Raquel, has arrived."

Ell leaned back in her chair, surprised it'd finally come. He'd said he'd send it several weeks ago. Since then they'd been out to a movie and he'd invited her to a party put on by his roommate Ryan. She'd had a great time at both and had definitely promoted Shan to "friendly boy" status in her mind. She admired his disheveled good looks, his lean muscular physique, and the fact that he was a guy who liked to dance. Mostly though, she found she simply loved talking to him. He was knowledgeable but never “showed off” his intelligence. He liked talking about the same topics she did and yet led her to talk about things she knew little about. She found herself studying to understand those topics better once she’d gotten home. She’d found herself hoping against hope that he actually did understand her math. She found herself desperately wanting a friend she could talk math with. Someone who actually understood it rather than just admiring what it could do. Someone she could admire in return and think of as a real boyfriend.

Now she found herself dreading the opening of this e-mail. What if it turned out that he didn’t have a clue? *This is ridiculous,* she told herself, *just because he didn’t understand my math wouldn’t mean I couldn’t love him. I’m sure in most marriages the two members of the couple don’t have similar degrees of understanding of all the same topics. One’s strength compliments the other’s weakness and vice versa.*

In her heart though, she knew she’d be terribly disappointed. If he’d never even tried to understand her math, it’d be OK, but to know he’d tried and failed...

With a trembling sigh she said, “Put it up on the big screen.”

The message popped up on her wall, “Raquel, thank you for agreeing to forward this to Ms. Donsaii. I hope I don’t embarrass myself, and you. It’s taken me a couple of weeks just to get this edited into something I’m fairly confident of, so I’m hoping she doesn’t just laugh when she sees it. Wish me luck (and please strip off this message to you before you forward it.)”

Ell closed her eyes. The lack of confidence shown by the message was breaking her heart. With a sinking feeling she scrolled down to the message he'd written to her as "Ms. Donsaii..."

~~~

It was five O'clock in the morning when Ell finally forced herself to turn off her screens and try to get some sleep, head still spinning with the ramifications of what Shan had found buried in her math...

Her thoughts had flip-flopped around... from wondering how she could have missed it... to wondering if Shan was laughing at her for overlooking it, to thinking he must be a genius to have seen it.

Genius, she'd finally concluded.

***

Manuel looked up as Ell walked into the team teecee meeting, "Hey Bosslady, you look exhausted. You OK?"

Ell smiled tiredly, "Yeah, I got some good news last night. It kept me up all night."

"*Good* news kept you up?"

"Hard to explain. How are the teecees doing?"

"Still sleeping. But you know how they spent the day yesterday flying up and down the mountain carrying a few things at a time?"

Ell nodded.

"I thought maybe we could send them a drawing of a travois?" An image popped up on the big screen showing one of Manuel's elegantly simple drawings, this time showing two poles dragging behind a teecee with a load of materials stacked between them.
~~~

***

Dex laughed and set down the handles of the travois, "We may have finally put too much on this thing! Let's take those flint nodules back off." Once they had done that, hie picked up the handles and trundled the travois down the game path a ways. Setting them down hie turned back to Syrdian. Hie threw hies arms around himr. "This'll be easy, especially since we're going downhill! Let's make another one for you."

They were able to load almost everything they wanted to take down the mountain onto the two travois and stood looking at the things that remained. Dex asked, "What should we do with this stuff?"

Syrdian said, "I think we should leave it here for..." Hies voice got juddery with emotion, "For the next dalin that can't fly the migration, injured or old. We can climb up here with them and show them how to survive," hie finished in an emotional whisper.

Dex felt hies own chest constricting and simply dipped hies head yes.

They neatly stacked the leftovers and started down the mountain.

***

Allan, Ell's AI, said, "A large animal's approaching Goldy and Silver."

Ell looked over from the screen of equations she had been studying. The screens showed the teecees indistinctly in infrared. They were asleep and over them Ell could see a large infrared object, getting bigger as it approached.

"Use Piscova's translation program to send the following. 'Goldy, Silver, a predator comes.'"

***

Dex woke upon hearing Syrdian say, "Dex."

Then to his utter astonishment hie heard hies own voice say, "Syrdian."

Then Syrdian said, "Predator."

Hies own voice said "Arrives."

Hie bolted upright and saw Syrdian leaping to hies feet as well. A large animal *was* visible by infrared! Dex bent to grasp hies spears. The animal began to charge toward Syrdian! Dex leapt forward.

***

Ell said, "Target the predator's eyes with the laser. High power!" However, Goldy leapt forward and came between the rocket and the predator. "Move the rocket to the left!"

Ell's point of view lifted slightly and slid to the left, but by the time it got a good view, the predator's head was no longer in view. The entire animal was skidding towards Goldy's feet with two spear shafts protruding from the base of its neck. Goldy and Silver were dancing back, each still holding their second spear.

She leaned back in her chair, Piscova was going to be pissed that she hadn't been around when her translation program was first used.

***

Hearts pounding and breath pouring through him, Dex looked around, "Syrdian, how did you know it was coming?"

"Because you woke me up."

"But you called my name," Dex said, looking around.

"You called *my* name."

They turned to stare at one another. Syrdian whispered, "I heard me too, but *I* never said anything... I thought the voices came from the direction of the meteorite."

They both turned to stare at the spot where Dex had set the meteorite the night before. It wasn't there!

Looking around, they saw it standing down to their left, apparently unharmed. "Did you move it?" Dex asked quietly.

Syrdian waved hies head "no."

Dex walked slowly over to the meteorite and picked it up. Speaking in Syrdian's voice it said, "Hello, Dex."

As Dex's skin crawled and he wondered how Syrdian had made hies voice come from the meteorite hie heard Syrdian say over hies shoulder, "It sounds like me!!" The astonishment in Syrdian's voice told him that Syrdian'd had nothing to do with the voice coming from the meteorite.

Saying some words with Dex's voice and some with Syrdian's the meteorite slowly said with odd gaps between the words, "Sometimes, Dex, Syrdian, I, help."

To Dex's great dismay, the meteorite said nothing further, despite their numerous questions.

***

Shan's AI chimed, indicating a new e-mail. He glanced up at his HUD and stopped in his tracks when he saw "Ell Donsaii" on the header. Heart beating faster, he had her message brought up.

Dear Mr. Kinrais,

I would like to congratulate you on your elegant work and for recognizing that your manipulations of these mathematical conventions have significant implications for the discipline of Astrophysics.

May I suggest we submit the attached paper for publication?

Ell Donsaii

Goose bumps prickling his skin, Shan sagged against the wall. He'd been on his way to a meeting with his advisor, but he just had to look!

When the paper opened on his HUD, the first thing Shan noticed was that the authors were "Shannon Kinrais and Ell Donsaii." *He was first author!* He looked up to the title, "Some calculations regarding the effects of a 5th dimension on gravitation and redshift over great distances: A possible explanation for the galactic rotation and expanding universe problems that does not require dark matter or energy."

Shan called his advisor, "Dr. Rhoades, I've just had a major insight. Can I put off our meeting until next week?"

"Kinrais," his advisor sighed, "I hope this insight results in some progress. I'm really thinking you're going to have to give up working on Donsaii's bizarre math. It's hard to imagine how you're ever going to find something in those equations that twenty other grad students aren't already writing theses on."

"Yes sir, I'll know by tomorrow if I've really got something or not."

"OK. Same time next Wednesday. If this insight turns out to be nothing, expect to talk to me about choosing another problem."

"Yes sir."

Shan practically ran back to his cubicle where he sat and opened the paper on one of his screens. As he read what Donsaii'd written he began running tests and confirmatory calculations using some of the Math Department's computing resources.

My God! He'd just sent this to Raquel last night as a series of questions about the bizarre results he got when he extrapolated her math out into intergalactic distances. This afternoon Donsaii presents him with a completely thought out, beautifully written paper concluding that his "bizarre results" actually explained the increasing redshift of the light from distant galaxies that'd previously been attributed to ever increasing acceleration of the expansion of the Universe! An explanation that didn't require that they invoke any mysterious "dark energy." A difference in the effects of gravity over interstellar distances explained the surprising rotation of galaxies without invoking "dark matter" to provide additional invisible mass. Not being all that familiar with the physics part of the paper he had to keep looking up data on the acceleration of the Universe's expansion and on galactic rotation to confirm that his results did actually correlate.

Suddenly he noticed he was hungry and checked the

time, he'd missed lunch and it was nearly dinnertime! His HUD was displaying a reminder for his dinner with Raquel, damn!

~~~

Shan trotted down the sidewalk and up to the doors of IP3. When he pulled the door open he could see Raquel leaning back, elbows on the counter, tapping her foot and watching the door. "Hey, I'm so sorry, I lost track of time and..."

She crossed her arms and raised an eyebrow, "Yes...?"

"Um, I'm sorry?"

"Pray tell, just *what* was so important that you lost all track of time and forgot about *me*?"

"Uh, Donsaii responded to my email and..."

The eyebrow went back up, but her eyes twinkled, "Are you *really* telling me that you stood me up to read an email from another girl?"

Shan grinned and waved a hand dismissively, "Not another girl. Pssh! A famous scientist. I never really noticed she was a woman, at least not till you just now pointed it out."

"Yeah, yeah sure." She grinned at him, "Are we gonna order, or stand around talking about your other women all night?"

Shan ordered a Stromboli and Raquel four slices of pizza and a salad, once again amazing him by the sheer volume of food she intended to consume. They got their drinks, grabbed a table and sat to wait for their order to be called up.

They talked about some of the pictures of Shan's favorite Tar Heel players up on the walls of the pizzeria while they waited. When their order was called Shan
~~~

went up to get it while Raquel got silverware and napkins.

After they sat Raquel asked "So, did Donsaii explain whatever was going on with your equations?"

Shan raised an eyebrow at her over his Coke, "Are you sure you want to talk about my other woman?"

"No," she snorted, "I'm talking about that scientist that you never even noticed was a girl."

"Oh, that one. Yeah she explained my issues alright. She explained them and incorporated them in a paper she wants to submit for publication. She thinks they explain some of the issues that've resulted in the dark energy and dark matter hypotheses."

"Really? That sounds pretty cool. You going to let her put your stuff in a paper?"

"Oh yeah! She's putting my name on the paper. I'll be proud just to have my name on the same document as hers."

"Hey!" Raquel grinned at him, "Remember you're out on a date with *me*. Don't go putting other women up on pedestals when we're together!"

Shan tilted his head, "Come on. You've got to admit that that particular woman deserves to be on a pedestal?"

Raquel paused momentarily, slice of pizza in front of her mouth, then her eyes crinkled, she mysteriously said, "I plead the fifth." She stuffed in a big bite, her eyes sparkling as she chewed.

As they left for their movie, Shan looked over at her slender form and thought wonderingly about how much she ate around him. He started to worry she might be bulimic.

At the movie he put an arm around her shoulders

and she snuggled in under it. It felt so good he left his arm there *long* after it started to cramp up and go to sleep...

***

Deltain packed the last of the goods hie'd made during the summer into a crevice in the escarpment. Hie packed in the poles that supported hies shelter and folded up the leather cover that went over the poles, putting it on top. Finally hie fit rocks in over all of it.

Strapping the few things hie was taking with himr to hies harness, hie looked out to the north where much of the tribe was already flying back toward their winter home. For a moment hie again considered flying north by east to the winter home of the Olnetch tribe on the eastern slopes of the big mountain. Hie could just start over now. Why fly back to the Yetany's cave?

Finally, admitting once again that hie wouldn't rest until hie returned to the Yetany cave and looked one last time for Dex's remains, hie launched himrself off the escarpment—back toward the huge cave hie'd called home all hies life.

***

The sky'd dimmed when Syrdian called to Dex, "Let's camp at these big rocks."

"But if we pushed on..."

"Dex, we don't need to reach the cave tonight! In fact, I don't think we should take most of this stuff to the cave."

"You don't? But, you said… having so much would help our status!"

Syrdian had turned toward the rocks, "Remember, we don't want them to know about the spears right away. We want to keep our new method of hunting a secret until they've accepted us. We'll agree to teach them and only *then* will we show them the spears."

~~~

The next morning Dex and Syrdian sorted through their bounty. They chose a large crevice in the rock face and packed away most of their dried meat and all but four of their spears. A pile of the harnesses that Dex had made, a stack of cured and tanned skins and a stack of nodules of flint and finished spear heads all went in there too. Then Syrdian carefully fitted rocks into the crevice over it, jumbling the last few so it'd appear more natural. They headed on down the mountain to the cave, arriving about midday.

Syrdian was glad to see they'd arrived before the Yetany tribe's return. Hie'd been fairly confident that hie'd judged the timing of the return migration correctly, but there'd been a niggling doubt. Hie turned to Dex, "They're not here yet! I've got some ideas for how we can prepare for their arrival…"

***

Shan opened the door to the D5R building and stepped inside. He recognized Bridget from the first night he'd danced with Raquel. She was sitting at the reception desk. Making a little wave with his hand, he said, "Hey Bridget. I have an appointment with Ms.
~~~

Donsaii this morning. Can you tell me which way to go?"

Bridget grinned hugely at him and stood, "Shan! *You're* Mr. Kinrais?"

He nodded. "Is there any chance you could take me by to see Raquel while I'm here? I'm a little bit early."

Bridget blinked as if nonplussed, then said, "Uh sorry, Raquel isn't here today." She grinned, "But come on and I'll take you to Ms. Donsaii. I think she's out in the big research room this morning. She won't mind you being early."

~~~

Ell and Emma had their heads together studying a new rocket design on a screen when Emma nudged her arm. "Don't look now, but Bridget's heading this way with a real hunk of man-flesh! Oooo, could *that* be the math whiz you've been waiting for?! Oh my Lord, I didn't think a mathematician's ever looked that good!"

Ell hissed, "Calm yourself girl, you don't want me to have to tell Roger you've been out here salivating over another man do you?"

"Hah! You wait till you see this guy. I have the right to salivate over someone that cute. Surely Roger'd forgive me."

Bridget said, "Ms. Donsaii?"

Ell turned. There was Shan, tousled hair tamed, wearing a jacket and tie. All six feet of handsome good looks that seemed even more impressive today, now that he was turned out and Emma had exclaimed on his looks. She tore her eyes off Shan and focused on Bridget, "Yes?"

"This is Mr. Kinrais, here for his appointment."

"Oh, yes." She stood and extended her hand, "Mr.
~~~

Kinrais, thank you for coming."

Shan felt stunned. Donsaii was about the same height and build as Raquel though she had much lighter skin and her nose wasn't as big. Where Raquel was pretty, Donsaii was beautiful. Still somehow, something about them seemed somewhat alike, especially the graceful way they both moved. *Must be weird to see them together.* "Uh, no problem. It's my honor. Thank you."

Ell guided him to an open conference room. "Those were some amazing insights you had into the 5th dimensional math. I'm very impressed and hope we can work together more in the future. How much longer do you have on your PhD?"

He grinned sheepishly, "Maybe not much longer if I can use some of this material in my thesis?"

"Really?!" She sounded excited, "That'd be fine with me. Shall we talk about it to be sure we agree on what it all means?"

"That'd be great."

They spent about an hour going back and forth through the paper. At one point one of Shan's questions resulted in a period of great excitement in which they tested the effect of one of Donsaii's equations against data on the cosmic background radiation. That data correlated too, leading Donsaii to give him a high five that left Shan's palm stinging.

~~~

Shan left the building, head whirling. He had to present this to his advisor but Donsaii'd already sent the paper to *Science*. He might be able to submit for his PhD pretty soon.

He found he couldn't wait to tell Raquel. His
~~~

thoughts had been frenetic lately. Either focused on Donsaii and her weird wonderful math or on Raquel and her… just plain wonderfulness. Maybe he shouldn't talk to Raquel about Donsaii? He thought Raquel was kidding when she acted jealous about Donsaii, but she couldn't *really* be, could she? It wasn't as if he had any chance with someone like Donsaii. Famous, a genius, incredibly beautiful—Shan Kinrais wouldn't have even had an opportunity to speak to someone like Donsaii except for his lucky insight on her math. He suspected someday he'd be telling his grandkids about the time he'd spent a morning with Ell Donsaii. He had no doubt that this morning would be a highlight of his life when he looked back on it.

Then he remembered Raquel actually worked there in the same building as Donsaii. To her, perhaps Ell Donsaii wasn't a mystical creature.

Even Shan didn't really think of her as legendary and unapproachable anymore. Not after spending the morning with her. Maybe Raquel *could* see her as someone to be jealous of?

Still, Shan desperately wanted to tell Raquel how Donsaii found his math interesting. Perhaps a tiny bit of jealousy would be a stimulus to help Raquel to fall in love with him?

Wonderingly, Shan realized that somehow, without knowing how or when it happened, he loved Raquel. It'd become much more serious than he'd thought, sneaking up on him while he hadn't even been considering it a possibility.

To his AI he said, "Please connect me with Raquel."

A moment later she came on, "Hey big guy, how'd it go with Donsaii?"

"Good, I'd hoped to see you though. Bridget actually

took me around, but she said you weren't in today. Where are you?"

"I got sent away, I guess Donsaii didn't want any competition while she was chatting up my intended boyfriend."

Shan's scalp prickled, *boyfriend?* Could she be as serious about him as he was about her? "Would you like to come over to my place for dinner tonight? Then I can tell you all about it."

"That'd be very nice," Raquel said quietly, "very, very nice."

~~~

Ell leaned back in her chair musing. She realized then just how worried she'd been that Shan would dump Raquel after he met Ell.

She snorted; how weird could she be, to worry because a man liked one version of her better than another? But, she really wanted someone who loved *her*, not the famous "Donsaii." It'd broken her heart when Gordon turned to her famous, dancing version and dropped her alter ego "Belle." Shan calling to ask "Raquel" over for dinner immediately after meeting "Ell" lifted her soul in a way she just hadn't anticipated.

On the other hand, she felt bad about not being honest with someone she cared so much about...

***

Dr. Rhoades heard a gentle rap on his doorframe. Looking up he saw Shan Kinrais. Brilliant, handsome, Shan Kinrais who he feared was going to destroy all his amazing potential while trying to make even a little bit
~~~

of headway on Donsaii's frustrating, incomprehensible math. For a while Rhoades had thought that Kinrais might be one of the few people smart enough to actually do something new with it. But, he didn't want Kinrais destroying his ebullient love of math, just because he couldn't succeed in this one area of math where only the world's most luminous genius had achieved anything so far. How to get Kinrais to give it up without ruining his spirit though, that was the question...

Rhoades smiled at him, "You ready to give up on that bizarre math?"

"Uh, no sir. I'm ready to show you what I've worked out."

"Oh?!" Rhoades said, leaning back in his chair, "Put it up on the big screen." He waved offhandedly at his big wall screen and laced his hands over his stomach.

~~~

Over the next thirty minutes Kinrais astounded Rhoades by demonstrating how he'd found some odd phenomena predicted by Donsaii's math. Then he described how these phenomena explained the increasing redshift of more distant galaxies and the excessive speed of galactic rotation without invoking dark matter or dark energy. Rhoades was a math wizard and could easily follow the odd phenomena that occurred in Donsaii's math when applied to galactic distances. Besides, the computer plotted them out for him.

He turned to Shan, "These are really interesting findings. Of course their importance will be much greater if you're correct about them explaining away dark matter and energy. Having only superficial
~~~

familiarity with the astrophysical phenomena involved I'm not as confident about that part of what you're saying. Have you shown this to any physics experts?"

"Yes sir."

Rhoades tilted his head and narrowed his eyes, "One of your grad student buddies... or someone who really knows their stuff?"

"Ell Donsaii, sir."

Rhoades felt his own eyes widening, "Really?!"

Kinrais nodded.

"And *she* says you've got this right?"

"Yes sir. I only pointed out some odd phenomena that occur at great distances in her math. She's the one who showed me how it explained the red shift and rotation phenomena."

"Oh, so she already knew about this?"

"Uh, no sir. I told her about the distance phenomena I'd observed in her math and she worked out the astrophysical implications over one night."

Rhoades tilted his head back to stare at the ceiling, "Lord *God*, that girl's smart! Well, the two of you should publish this. I'm sure your part in it will get you that PhD you've been chasing."

"Thank you sir. She's already submitting this paper."

Rhoades looked at the screen again and saw a manuscript listing Kinrais as first author. "Amazing! If you're going to be first author on a paper with Donsaii, I should buy you a beer. Hell, the whole department should buy you beers. You up to going out with a few of us?"

"Yes sir. But not tonight though. I've got a date to cook dinner for my girlfriend."

"Hah, I'll bet you burn it!"

Shan grinned lopsidedly, "I probably will."

***

Dex coasted in for a landing on the big shelf in front of the Yetany cave. "Syrdian! I found a small herd of zornits in the meadow just up from the cave!"

Syrdian's head swiveled around, "Great! I've just finished here, let's go get one."

Dex looked around. Wood had been stacked in the fire pit ready to be lit. The big ledge in front of the cave had been swept clean. Hie could see that Syrdian had even stacked and rearranged the supplies in the common storage area. At the north end of the big ledge Syrdian had carefully stacked the supplies they'd brought down to the cave. They were on top of Dex's big zornit hides. There were some of Dex's harnesses, a few nodules of flint, some of the flint knives Syrdian had made, a leather bag of dried meat and, sitting on top of it all, Dex's meteorite, upright on its legs. Hie tilted hies head, "Why is our stuff down at the end there?"

"So it'll be obvious what we're bringing to the tribe if they accept us."

"Oh."

"Are you ready?"

Dex's wings rose, "Sure."

Syrdian grinned at himr. "Don't you think we should take the travois to bring a zornit back on?"

Dex grinned, "If you're so sure we're going to get one, it'd be a good idea, yeah."

"I think it'll bring bad luck to go up there *without* the travois. We don't want the spirits to think we don't expect to have a good hunt."

Soon they were hiking up the mountain pulling their two empty travois. They made a short detour to pick up spears from where they'd hidden them, then took a game trail through a brief stretch of forest into the meadow where Dex had seen the zornits.

Dex's wings sagged in relief when hie saw the zornits were still there. The animals were pretty close to where the game trail came out onto the meadow so they set the travois down and took their spears back down the trail to the open area on the other side of the forested area.

"Ready?" Dex asked. When Syrdian dipped hies head, Dex beat into the air, thinking how nice it was to be flying at a lower altitude again. Once hie had enough altitude, hie checked on Syrdian with hies back-eyes then swept out and back around to drop into the meadow just over the tree line, stooping on the zornits. As usual the zornits scattered before himr. Hie chose one, beating wing after it, then flaring over it to slam hies spear down over its shoulder. The spear hit a rib and bounced off relatively harmlessly. Dex wheeled right, switching the second spear hie'd been carrying to hies right hand. Syrdian, sailed over the zornit, slamming a spear home and wheeling left. Dex finished hies turn and beat hard after the panicked zornit. Catching it again, hie successfully plunged hies second spear into place. It must have hit the brain because the zornit immediately dropped skidding and quivering to the ground.

As per their tradition Dex and Syrdian landed by the zornit, embracing in celebration and dancing up and down. This was their tenth zornit hunt, but only their fourth successful one. Syrdian unwrapped hies neck from Dex's and said, "It's a wonderful omen that we had a fruitful hunt right before the tribe's return."

***

Done up as Raquel, Ell walked up the walk to the little house Shan shared with Ryan. The door opened and Ryan came out. "Hi Ryan. You leaving?"

"Yes," he rolled his eyes, "banished from my own home so my roommate can have his way with you. It's shameful."

"Oh! Don't go on my behalf. I'd be happy to split my dinner with you."

"Hah, no you wouldn't! Shan's told me how much you eat."

Ell blushed.

He leaned close and whispered, "Besides I'm *happy* to go. He's been acting like a lovesick fool. Mooning about '*Raquel* this and *Raquel* that.'" He winked, "I can hardly stand being around him when he's in this state."

Shan appeared in the doorway, an oven mitt on his hand. "Ryan, you promised you'd get out of here without harassing my new girlfriend."

Ryan winked at Ell, then turned to say, "*Your* girlfriend? She's just agreed to go out with me tomorrow night. You'd better hope your cooking's far better than usual or there's no way you're gonna keep her." He headed on down to the sidewalk.

Ell climbed the steps to Shan who put his arms around her. "Don't leave me for that guy. No matter how bad you think my cooking is, his is a lot worse."

"Girlfriend?" she asked.

"You're the one who called me your 'intended

boyfriend,'" he grinned, then drew himself up and put a hand on his chest, "I accept." He looked down at the dish in her hand, "You brought something?" he narrowed his eyes, "In case my lasagna isn't edible?"

"Dessert. I knew you wouldn't have enough for a growing girl like me."

Shan laughed and led her inside.

~~~

To Ell's surprise the lasagna was excellent. She lifted her last forkful at him, "This is amazing. A mathematician clogger, who plays basketball and can *cook*? Who'd have thought?"

"Ah Raquel, Raquel," he shook his head despairingly, "I have depths you haven't plumbed. *Deep* depths."

"Good to hear there's a little mystery left," she said, eyes crinkling. "I'll hope to discover those depths a little at a time, so's to keep me interested."

"Yeah," he grinned ruefully. "I'll have to reveal them one micron at a time so you don't realize just how shallow they are."

"So you were going to tell me what Donsaii thought of the issues you had with her math?"

"She *is* amazing you know?" Then at the appearance of an arched eyebrow he hurried to say, "Though not as amazing as Raquel Blandon, the girl I love."

Ell/Raquel tilted her head, "You *love* me?" she asked huskily.

***

Deltain daydreamed as hie flew near the back end of one of the "V" shaped flights of the Yetany tribe. In
~~~

hies mind hie'd been planning out the locations hie'd check. One last look for evidence of Dex's remains. Hie should be able to check them tomorrow, then head east for his new life with the Olnetch tribe. Hie didn't think hie'd be able to stand it anymore, living with the Yetany at a cave filled with reminders of Dex.

Hie'd never really understood the profundity of hies love for hies child while Dex was still alive. Hies heart ached with the memory of times when hie could and should have told Dex how proud hie was of himr. The beautiful harnesses Dex made. Hies little insights.

They entered a long glide and Deltain realized they were finally coasting down toward the cave. Quite a few flights had already landed and dalin were crowding the big ledge in front of the cave. There were usually a lot of dalin on the ledge right after landing, but this seemed... different. They seemed excited? Or disturbed, or something?

Deltain noticed there was a large fire in the fire pit. Had someone flown ahead to prepare food or something?

As hie coasted in the last bit of the distance hies heart beat faster. Hie saw a distinctive silvery yellow color on a pair of wings. A color that few had and... only Syrdian had such brilliant color. Could Syrdian have survived? Could Dex?! Hies eyes scanned rapidly over the crowd and then settled back on the strapping big golden-brown dalin with the complex harness. Standing next to Syrdian!

Deltain broke hies glide and beat wing to lift himrself up over the crowd, "Dex!" hie cried. "Dex!"

Dex's wings arched and spread wide in response. Hie stepped back, hies spread wings pushing dalin back to clear a space in front of himr and hie waved hies hands for Deltain to land in the opening.

Deltain flared wing to settle in front of Dex. Tall Dex, standing proud, no longer looking cowed like hie had in the past. Standing like one confident in hies own status. Dex strode the two steps to Deltain, throwing arms and wings around himr. Deltain felt overwhelmed, but distantly noticed that suddenly Dex stood significantly taller than Deltain. They wrapped necks around one another, "Parent!" Dex said with a juddery voice.

"Child!" Deltain said in juddery response. "How did you survive the summer?"

"We went up the mountain to where it's cooler."

"We?"

"Syrdian and I." Quietly, he said, "We're mated now."

Deltain's eyes widened, "But Syrdian..." Hie broke off turning to look at Syrdian. Syrdian stood with hies parents, but was looking at Deltain. Syrdian lifted hies wings gently, spreading them. Deltain noticed large slightly rippled marks in Syrdian's right wing with curious little dots along them. Hie'd never noticed those before

Suddenly Bultaken, first among the Yetany, stepped into their little tableau. "Syrdian! You're alive! That's wonderful! We thought that you must have been killed..." Hie stumbled to a stop, staring at Syrdian's wings. Syrdian had lifted them again displaying the funny marks. "What happened to your wing? Where'd you spend the summer?"

Syrdian drew himrself up, "My wing was torn by a talor. Ripped badly, creating *enormous* holes where you see the scars. Qes was there, but he *fled*." Syrdian's tone as hie said "fled" left little doubt about how

Syrdian felt about Qes now. "While Qes flew away, leaving me to the talor, Dex arrived and *killed* it. Then, like hie does hies amazing leatherwork, Dex sewed up my wing."

The crowd had all had their fore eyes on Syrdian. Now, as one, they turned them to stare at Dex.

Syrdian continued with disgust in his tone, "*Qes* left me for dead." Then turning with love in hies eyes, Syrdian said, "But *Dex* stayed with me and kept me alive through a summer when I couldn't fly south."

The crowd near Syrdian had been edging away from himr, a few muttering "dyatso." Syrdian said, "I am *not* dyatso! With Dex's magic sutures holding it, my wing healed and I can fly again." In the space that'd appeared around himr, hie beat briefly into the air to the astonished moans of many of the dalin surrounding himr. Their wings rose involuntarily in amazement.

A commotion appeared in the crowd. Qes pushed through to stare at Syrdian, then stole a glance at hies wing. Qes, who to Deltain's disgust, over the summer had broken up the near-mating of Fantais and Malten by making evident hies wish to mate with Fantais now that Syrdian'd been lost. "Syrdian!" hie cried, stepping forward, arms outstretched.

Deltain felt a quiver run over Dex, but Syrdian blocked Qes' approach with an outstretched arm. "I'm mated to Dex now. Even if I *weren't,* I wouldn't want to be with the dalin who left me when I was injured."

Qes said plaintively, "But you were dyatso!"

"I fly, and I'm not dead!" Syrdian's eyes turned wonderingly to Dex, "Thanks to Dex."

"Is this a zornit?" someone cried from over near the fire pit. Eyes turned that way.

Deltain realized that hie'd been smelling something

wonderful since hie'd landed. Hie turned hies head and stretched hies neck up to look over the dalin behind himr. A very large animal was roasting over a big fire in the pit. Hie wondered briefly if someone had flown in a day early and found a zornit that'd fallen off a cliff or something?

Syrdian said, "Yes, that's a zornit. Dex worked out how to hunt them. We killed it yesterday and began roasting it this morning. It's a gift to welcome you Yetany on your return." Murmurs of awe and interjections of disbelief shot through the crowd.

Deltain turned hies eyes searchingly to Dex, "Really?!"

Dex dipped hies head yes.

"And you repaired hies wing?"

Dex dipped hies head again.

Deltain frowned, "Who taught you to do that?"

Dex grinned, wings quivering with mirth, "You did."

Deltain's head went up and back in disbelief, "I?"

"I did it just like a side to side joint in leather."

"Really?!"

"Really."

Unbelievingly, Bultaken said, "*How* do you claim to hunt zornit?"

Syrdian drew himrself up, "We'll probably teach you. But it'll depend on the rank we're given in the tribe."

Tanif, one of Syrdian's parents, reached out for Syrdian's arm saying, "You still have high rank from us! We can't permit you to mate Dex, hie doesn't have sufficient rank for us to even consider it."

Syrdian dodged Tanif's hand and walked over to Dex. Hie stepped up to the other side of Dex from Deltain and put an arm around himr, "I *told* you, I'm already mated to Dex. You haven't seen the amazing things hie can do—someday hie will be *first* among the Yetany... There's *no* doubt about that.

I am proud to tell you that I carry hies child... and hie mine."

Deltain's head whipped around to stare and hies eyes widened to hear this. For both members of a mated couple to carry child at the same time was a very rare and highly venerated omen... Deltain's wings quivered with the joy hie felt.

Deltain realized that he'd gone from childless and desperately lonely, to the parent of the tribe's most accomplished child... and he had two grandchildren on the way.

Hies hearts sang...

Epilogue

In the morning, Shan woke to the sound of the shower running in the bathroom behind him. He felt indescribably happy and wondered why for a moment, then the events of the past few days washed over him.

Could all this be true? Not a dream? Raquel, the wonderful Raquel, and the sweet joy of the time he'd been spending with her!

His questions about weird extrapolations of Donsaii's math, explained by the amazing Donsaii herself?

The meeting of a lifetime with Ell Donsaii, surely

something he'd remember for the rest of his life!

Realizing that he *loved* Raquel.

Loved her with all his heart.

His advisor accepting his work with Donsaii's math as worthy of his PhD dissertation.

Last night…! Last night had been astonishing in ways he could never have believed before living through it…

He stretched and rolled over to face the bathroom door, ready to enjoy looking at the love of his life again.

After long minutes he was feeling frustrated, but then the door cracked open. He threw his arm up over his face, peering under and thinking, *I'll pretend I'm still asleep as she enters the room.*

The door opened farther and two feet appeared in it, visible beneath his arm.

They were paler and pinker than they should be!

Confused, he slowly lifted his arm, peering under it. Lithe calves and knees, check, but also too lightly colored. Then brunette hair, the right color, but down by her knee?

He wondered, is she bending over?

She didn't move so he raised his arm slowly as if he were stretching in his sleep. A light skinned hand appeared, holding a brunette wig.

Wig?!

Heart suddenly pounding he threw his arm back. Short strawberry blond hair!

There, leaning in the doorframe of his bathroom, holding Raquel's hair and wearing nothing but a towel was Ell Donsaii!

Grinning at him!

"Hi Shan," she said quietly in Raquel's voice…

The End

If you liked reading about the "primitives" in this book you might also like reading the "Bonesetter," series, stories about primitive humans.

Hope you liked the book!

The next in the series is Habitats (an Ell Donsaii story #7).

To find other books by the author try Laury.Dahners.com/stories.html

Author's Afterword

This is a comment on the "science" in this science fiction novel. I've always been partial to science fiction that posed a "what if" question. Not everything in the story has to be scientifically possible, but you suspend your disbelief regarding one or two things that aren't thought to be possible. Then you ask, "what if" something (such as faster than light travel) were possible, how might that change our world? Each of the Ell Donsaii stories asks at least one such question.

"Tau Ceti" continues asking what kinds of cool things we could do with even small wormholes or "ports," but it also asks, "what if" we actually reach another life bearing world out amongst the stars? How might it be different? A common assumption in science fiction is that Earth is the "typical" life bearing world and that the kinds of worlds that might bear life will be similar. For interest there might be some "odd" worlds that are different than Earth in some way. That there might be "heavy" worlds where the beings are massively muscled, or snowy worlds, farther from their suns, but that *they* will be the oddballs.

Here I've tried to consider the question "what if" the "Goldilocks zone" (where worlds are the right temperature for liquid water and presumably life) is farther out because the atmosphere on most worlds is denser and has a stronger greenhouse effect than Earth's? Such a dense atmosphere would mean that more animals would fly, right? Because it would be easier for even *large* animals to fly in dense air. Especially if that atmosphere had a high oxygen content that could support a hotter metabolism capable of driving those wings. One possible theory is that the reason large pterosaurs could fly back in the Triassic and Cretaceous (the biggest birds of today are much smaller than pterosaurs were and yet can barely take off) was because Earth's atmosphere had a higher oxygen content, and that the atmosphere may have been much, much denser back then.

Another interesting question is, "If you were an intelligent flying being who lived a much more three dimensional life than we humans do, wouldn't you have a separate word for many of the different directions in your three dimensional life?" I've tried to give life to this concept by hyphenating a direction such as "back-up-right" thus implying that the teecees might have a separate word for that direction.

I've often wondered if Earth might be at one extreme of the spectrum of life bearing worlds out there. What if Earth is at the big, heavy, thin atmosphered end of the spectrum of living worlds? What if, when we get out there, *we* turn out to be the "heavy worlders" who are heavily muscled and *we're* among the very few intelligent species who *can't* fly?

Bummer.

Acknowledgements

I would like to acknowledge the editing and advice of Gail Gilman, Elene Trull, Kerry McIntyre and Nora Dahners, each of whom significantly improved this story.

CPSIA information can be obtained
at www.ICGtesting.com
Printed in the USA
LVHW080433280622
722253LV00030B/1183

9 781481 826723